NINE MINUTES TILL MIDNIGHT

NASH RUNNING BEAR MYSTERY
BOOK NINE

BAER CHARLTON

Cover design by Roslyn McFarland, Far Lands Publishing

Sketch artist Kelly Eamon

Rogena Mitchell-Jones, Literary Editor
RMJ Manuscript Service, www.rogenamitchell.com

Published by Mordant Media, Portland, Oregon

ISBN: 978-1-949316-48-3 (Print)
ISBN: 978-1-949316-49-0 (eBook)

10 9 8 7 6 5 4 3 2 1

CONTENTS

Powder

1
NINE MINUTES TO MIDNIGHT

EVERYTHING FELT WRONG. Nash's single braid hung long and thick down her back, pulling heavily between her shoulder blades as she looked down. She could see the tiny moccasins beneath the raw edge of the white doeskin dress. The black and red ink lines shone brightly on the white of the soft leather. The moccasins she wore when she was six.

She looked up and out across the desert. Squat thorny brush —*not sage*. Sparse. She could sense the reassuring feel of Powder somewhere close. Behind a bush. *When did she become bashful about peeing in the desert?*

Nash gazed up. The sky was purple. The cloud cover was thickening, but it wasn't angry yet. It would be soon enough. Anger from below. Anger from behind. Why not anger from above and ahead?

She leaned back against the heavy SUV. Frowning, she looked over her shoulder. Nothing. The empty road was just sand. As she turned, she could feel the grinding of the coarse sand under the thin leather of the moccasins. She stared down at the white-tanned dress. It wasn't hers—she never had a leather dress. The moccasins were from when she was six, but the toes of the shoes stuck out past her womanly breasts. She twitched her shoulder. The breasts wobbled. *No bra. No armor. Not even...*

What? She couldn't remember why she was there.

Pulling her braid around to the front, she studied the leather broach. The broach was a coyote sitting in the bowl of a crescent moon. The coyote wasn't howling—just looking, watching. *Maybe it's Powder? But what does the crescent moon mean?* There is no symbol in any tribal markings she had ever seen of a crescent moon, much less a quiet dog or coyote in the moon.

Irritated, she looked around. Where's Powder? What's she doing? The desert felt wrong. Not enough brush—this wasn't her valley. And even the brush was wrong.

"Powder?"

"Who is Powder?" The voice was old and strained through years of sun and wind.

Nash turned at the voice.

"Why are you out of uniform, Lieutenant?"

Her left eye narrowed behind the black wraparound dark glasses. The heavy polarization would explain the purple sky.

"Who are you?"

The man smiled as he raised his arms, spreading his faded, striped caftan. "Abdul Aziz. He who serves the all mighty, Lieutenant Nash Running Bear."

Aziz. The interpreter. They had called him Scissors.

"Scissors?"

The man bent forward in a shallow bow, holding his arms out. "At your service, LT."

Memories flooded back. The man had a sense about which streets or roads not to walk down or drive along. When he walked, his heel marks were exactly in front of his toe marks. Many of her team learned the slight scissor movement of the hip to duplicate the path left. It made the footprints impossible to track and tell how many men had walked the trail. Other than her sergeant—

Esper. The man grew up dodging dog poop and other garbage in East L.A. and walked more in a dance than a stroll.

She studied the salted head of hair over the lines on the face. "You got old."

He chuckled. "LT, I was already a grandfather when I worked for you. You just never cared how old I was. Just that I keep up with you children."

"But how are you here?"

He slowly ground his head from side to side. "I don't know where this is. This is not Kandahar."

Nash stepped a few steps to the bush. She placed her hand around the branch and gently stripped the branch of its leaves by pulling upward. She crushed the leaves in her hands and held them to her nose. Greasewood. Wild desert almond.

"Not Kandahar. But the hills, east of Kabel. But why have you brought me here?"

The man gazed around with his hands on the small of his back. "Bring you? How can I do such a thing? I have no car. I haven't driven for years. And Afghanistan… I left shortly after you did. The mullahs killed my wife and daughter. I didn't know what happened to my granddaughter. I didn't want to think of what kind of hell the Taliban had become. So there was a troop plane leaving, and they were loading Humvees onto a Jolly Green Giant. So I drove one on and stayed."

Nash snorted. "That easy? Of course you did. You always saw how to do things straightforwardly. So what happened?"

"After the long flight, we landed at Tinker Air Base in Oklahoma. They processed me and gave me a job. So I stayed, fell in love, and married."

Nash looked around. The sky was getting angrier. "But how did you find me here?"

"Where is here, LT?"

Her shoulders slumped. "I'm not sure, Scissors. I thought I was in my spirit world. The place where my spirit walks and can talk to other spirits." She tapped her chest with her fingers. "It's like the internet for the part of me who doesn't bleed. It's where I can go for answers sometimes."

His hands came together in front of his crotch. He interlaced his fingers. "Maybe... When we were in a small village in the mountains. You once helped a young girl find her lost goat and returned them to her grandfather."

She bobbed her head with a slight smile that pulled to one side. "We were a few days out of Peshawar. Her name... was something about the bringer or giver of light."

He smiled. "Yes. Her name was Roshina—bringer of light. Her goat was Bibi. The grandfather was the leader of the village."

She smiled. "That was one of the good days. I hope she and Bibi live long lives."

Aziz shrugged. His face was in a soft crinkle of sadness. "The girl? Who knows? But Bibi was food, not milking. You don't milk a boy."

Nash rolled her eyes closed. "Great. Now I'll never get that image out of my head. So why did you bring her up?"

"Can you still find people?"

"Maybe. Where?"

"Oklahoma. I think my wife's granddaughter is missing."

Nash squinted. "You're in Oklahoma?"

The man started a shallow bow, and the image shredded into scratches of mist. The looming storm swirled into the semi-darkness most American cities thought of as night. Nash turned at the poke on her shoulder.

"Your daughter wants out."

Nash rolled over, reaching to bring back the vision. Instead, she only received a soft lick and a cold nose.

Mina rolled over the other way. "Take her for a walk. Whatever the dream was about, you need to figure it out."

Nash groaned. "I'm on it."

She sat, her feet on the floor, and tried to remember the time of year. Standing, she walked to the kitchen, where her phone was charging. She tapped the weather icon. Summer.

Minutes later, she pushed through the large glass front door to the building. Clarence scrambled from the small office. She shook her head and waved him down. "Chill. It's three in the morning. Nobody but the tiny bladder is awake. I think she's still on Barbados time."

He pointed at her boots instead of slippers. "Do you want coffee when you come back?"

"We're only going for a short walk…"

"I'll make a fresh pot."

They walked to the end of the next block. Powder leaned against the small street tree. Three cars drove past. Nash raised one eyebrow as she stared at her phone. "Doesn't anyone sleep?"

The emails were hours old and close to spam. She switched to the phone and scrolled for the general number of Deep Six. She knew any text she sent would appear on every screen in the main computer room.

Is anyone awake at this hour? Nash.

Her phone rang. "Nash."

Ming's voice sounded raw. "Give me something exciting to do."

Nash chuckled. "Uh oh. Are Tree and Felix still in Hawaii?"

"Nah. Felix got some cryptic message from Alex and ran home. Tree figured she was halfway to Australia, so she ran away to check on a couple of projects we oversee down there. Meanwhile, I've been crunching bad code for the last nine days. What's up? Tell me I need to come help you do something exciting like kick ass and take names—or any other secret squirrel stuff."

"Secret Squirrel stuff? You need to stop hanging out with Uncle. Next, you'll be telling me seven ways to cook roadkill."

"That's Chef's job. What has you up at… um… three forty in the morning?"

"Little Bladder for one. But I… had a thought."

The small Chinese woman's voice lowered. "Is that a euphemism for dreams or that spirit thing?"

Nash snapped her fingers at Powder and turned back for their building. "Uncles not the best influence on you. Stick with Jazz."

"You mispronounced Chips. Your secret isn't exactly a secret. So what was the... um... thought?"

"When I was last in the sandbox... In Afghanistan, I had an interpreter attached to my team. His name was Abdul Aziz. Shortly after we came home, he caught a hop and ended up in Oklahoma. The air base was Tinker Field. It's near Oklahoma City. He married an American woman who has a granddaughter."

Nash could hear the clicking of the keyboard. "Anything more on the woman?"

"Sorry. No. If I were to hazard a stab at this, I'd call the base's HR department."

Ming giggled. "The military has HR?"

"I don't know. It's the Air Force. It's kind of like the military, except for the walking around and sleeping in late stuff. I'm just telling you what's in my head at oh-three hundred when I should be snuggled up next to my wife upstairs."

"Got it. I'll get back to you later today."

"You can pass this off to Muna if you hit any DOD road bumps."

"I already copied her all the info. Go back to bed. Hug Mina for me."

"Copy."

Her phone snicked dead as the young man pushed the door open with one hand and held out the large mug with the other. He looked down at Powder. "Yes. I have some treats for you as well."

2

WHY DOES THE SAND TEMPT SO?

Clement Solas held his face toward the sun. The warmth had always comforted his body and soul. At sixty-eight, he considered himself content with his life. He wasn't rich, but he also wasn't poor. Everything in his life he had earned. He worked hard. Greed wasn't on his list... and yet...

As his head turned away from the afternoon sun, he opened his eyes—the three bodies he had not killed. The shot-to-shit, tan, camouflaged jeep looked more like a sieve. Much in his guts told him he needed to keep riding. The horse shifted her weight from the right to the left side. She wanted to keep moving, escaping the smell of the rapidly spoiling bodies.

He wasn't greedy... but the one bag with the shredded zipper yawned open, exposing the volume of money—more money than had passed through his hands in his lifetime.

He looked east toward the distant mesa. Generations before, his ancestors had lived simple lives on the mesa. Now, his hogan was ten times the size that three generations used to pack into on the mesa. He wasn't sure he was happier than they had been on top of the mesa before the white man came.

His eyes drooped in resolve as he caught his breath, leaned

7

forward over the wide pommel, and swung his right leg over the saddle.

"Ch'iidii." *Dammit.*

The moccasins stepped lightly on the coarse sand. No heel marks or toes. It was the same as Clement moving through his life unnoticed. Twenty-seven years as a welder laying pipe from a large barge in the middle of the ocean, and even the barge captains struggled to remember his name. Most settled for referring to him as *that Indian.*

He pulled back the two large duffel bags from the backseat of the topless jeep. The body in the backseat had been holding one bag, with the other beside him. The thick bag of money had slowed down or stopped some bullets, but not the one in his neck and next to his ear.

One bullet had cut the bag away from the zipper, disclosing the money. Others had chewed through the booklets of bills, fluffing the stacks into a tossed salad.

The second bag had a few holes matching the torn inside of the jeep and the holes on the outside of the vehicle. Clement stuck his little finger in one hole. It only fit up to the middle of the nail. Small, but not as small as .223. More like his brother's 30-06. But there was a lot of punching power—more than they ever needed hunting coyote or their annual trek up to Colorado for deer.

He looked at the other two men in the front seats. Both had large automatic pistols, but only the passenger had his hand on his gun, half pulled from the shoulder holster. The driver lay crumpled forward over his hip holster and the steering wheel.

All three wore semi-uniform khaki pants and shirts with no badges or markings. Clement thought about the heavier eyebrows, deep-set eyes, and chiseled noses. These were not Indian, Mexican, or any other Latin American people. The black hair was wavy or curly, but the skin had more of an olive hue than the brown of Latinos.

The black slip-on shoes were the last clue. Those fancy designer shoes you didn't buy at Kroger's in the city. But probably common in the cities bordering the Red Sea.

The cell phone was in a holder, stuck near the front window, and still showed the GPS. But no roads. This one showed locations without any roads or casual witnesses. Someone ambushed the three of them after they parked there to do business.

Clement gently lifted the bags from the jeep and carried them to his patiently waiting horse—the one bag he laid in front of the saddle, with the other behind.

Turning, Clement took out the new phone his daughter had bought him for Christmas. She said she was tired of him having spotty connections with his old flip phone. She never asked him if he wasn't getting service, or if he just ignored her phone calls.

Holding the phone high, he took pictures of the jeep and bodies. They would look like he took them from his horse.

He walked back and took several other photos of the bodies, their faces, and the guns. Maybe someone would ask if he had been there. And if they did, he could show them what he saw.

It was better than going over and over his testimony of the first dead body he had seen when he was fourteen. The white man sheriff either didn't trust the Indian, or he was just being a young kid. Later, Clement learned the desert is no stranger to death or bodies, human or animal.

Standing on the one stirrup, he checked the bags. Both weighed enough to stay where they were. Pepe, his horse, was old enough to just be called E. The pep was long gone. But they knew each other, and Clement didn't have the energy to train another horse.

Swinging his leg over the bag behind the saddle, Clement settled down into the saddle the years had shaped to his butt and legs. The man's single click in his cheek started the horse moving. Water and fresh alfalfa were at the other end of the walk.

Clement adjusted the brim of his hat lower on his forehead as he guided Pepe down the small bank into the usually dry barranca. The water was only eight or ten feet wide, and only the small pools reached depths over an ankle. The brief flow of the early summer's runoff from the high country would only flow for another week or two. Then, rough sand and gravel would be at the bottom of the barranca until the rain started in late fall.

Pepe only splashed a little as she walked up the river. She knew her master wanted her to walk quietly or with the water, to leave no tracks. Her stroll was automatic from the years of hunting or just moving unnoticed through the desert.

Clement's eyes constantly moved. Watching the air and the distant desert, where he knew the roads were. The barranca, being lower than the desert floor, made only the man's shoulders and head visible above the sparse brush. Only someone looking specifically would spot the darker, slow-moving silhouette of the man. The dead bodies hadn't grown cold or stopped bleeding. Someone would be along to investigate the bodies, and probably be looking for the bags of money. Clement could feel in his bones *that* the person wouldn't be a nice person. He clicked his cheek twice.

Pepe splashed more, but the pace would put more miles between them and the shot-to-shit jeep.

3
SO CONFUSED

"No. He was our interpreter in Afghanistan. He's Afghani."

She could hear Uncle scraping something. He grumped. "But he walked in your spirit world."

Nash winced as she laid her boot on the corner of her desk and winced at the scuff mark on her boot. "Not my world. It was the higher deserts of eastern Afghanistan, beyond Kabel. The brush was the thorny shit we hated landing in when we jumped. You'd find stickers days later in your BDUs. Those thorns only come out when you burn your clothes after a couple of months wearing them straight. Bloodstains would fade before you could get those thorns out."

Uncle struck the large wooden spoon on the edge of his cast-iron kettle. "So maybe he drew you over to his spirit walk."

She frowned as she looked across the large office to the redhead guarding the deputy director's office door. "What are you making?"

"I dried juniper berries this last winter. They ferment before they dry, so the alcohol strengthens the berry. Then I infused a gallon of mescal with the juniper needles. Heat it all with deer tallow, bear fat, and sage. When it cools, the medicine rises into the fat on top. It will ease Junior's pain in the scars on his back."

Nash snorted softly. "Juniper rub. Mom made it every year. Powerful medicine. But Thomas needs to get his scrawny white ass back down to the VA and have them cut out some of those nasty scar balls. His back is pulling him apart. And it isn't getting better. So, do you think someone who isn't a shaman can draw someone into their spirit walk? I mean, he seemed more confused about where he was than I was."

"That would be a question for my friend, Red. Drawing someone into your spirit walk is powerful stuff. I only aspire to juniper rubs and roadkill stew."

Nash spotted the deputy director stepping out of his office. The man was looking at her, but talking softly to his secretary, Donna.

Nash took her boot off the desk and sat up. "Roadkill stew sounds good about now."

Uncle's chuckle sounded like some rocks tumbling down a waterfall. "Sounds like your deputy just handed you a moose turd pie. Lots of grass, but nothing appetizing."

"Indian's nose is still working. Talk later." She slipped her phone into her back pocket as she stood. She glanced down at Powder, now standing on all four paws. "Need a potty break?"

The front paws worked on the floor.

"I think we're taking a guest." She looked up at the deputy director as he walked over. "I need to take the little bladder out to service the tree in the atrium. Or is this an office discussion?"

The tall man drew in a breath through his nose and let out a sigh. "Yeah. Air sounds good. Maybe even some coffee and a bagel out front."

Nash pulled the pistol and holster out of her drawer. Shoving the clip onto her belt and leather pants, she squinted with one eye. "You do know that a bagel is the same amount of carbs as four slices of bread?"

Tony shrugged as he waved his hand at Powder. "She can burn off half of it, and you and I can split the other half."

Nash shook her head. "Nope. It's Friday. You're on your own with that plain bread." She turned to the door.

Tony pushed the down button and turned. "What's Friday got to do with anything?"

Nash bounced softly on her toes as she watched the lighted numbers above the elevator door. "On Fridays, Mannie has cranberry orange bagels."

The door opened.

The shade of the small street tree barely covered half of the bench. Courtesy dictated the man sit in the sun. Nash split the difference, sitting half in the sun and half in the shade. She could already see the stains darkening at Tony's armpits. She pulled the bagel apart and held out a piece to Powder. "Uncle wanted to know what moose turd pie you have for me."

Powder closed her mouth over the bread and fingers, then maintained the position half closed until the fingers pulled back. Tony's eyebrows raised.

Nash chuckled. "She doesn't like how I taste. But she might like your fingers."

Tony snorted and held out half of his bagel. Powder sniffed and sat. "What's that mean?"

Nash rumbled. "White man bagel. Try flipping it into the air."

Powder snapped it out of the air. And then dropped it at the deputy director's feet.

Nash laughed. "See. White man's bagel." She turned and tore another piece off her bagel and passed it to her partner. "And the pie?"

Tony chewed on his bite of the bagel as he stared at the half on the ground. "Bank robbery… Well, an armored truck."

"Not my department."

Tony offered Powder the last of his bagel. Powder turned her back toward him and sat down. Rolling his eyes, he stuffed the last piece in his mouth and sipped his coffee. "I think it is."

Tony waited for his heart to slow. "They found the getaway car."

Nash looked down the street. The light turned as three people stepped from the curb to cross. Nine cars waited for the light, as many drove through the intersection. With the heat, nobody was rushing. *Shit.*

She looked back at the deputy director. "And…?"

"Wiped down with accelerant and then lit up."

She sat watching the man sip two and then three sips. There might have been the second sip left in his cup, but she knew he faked the third. "You ran out of coffee two sips ago."

"That's the moose."

Behind her orange aviators, she studied the face of the man she knew, in the office and the field. He didn't shy away from conflict lightly.

"What's the turd?"

"They found it in a tiny town in New Mexico."

"That describes about two hundred and eighty villages in New Mexico."

His head dropped. Five heartbeats later, he raised his head and looked at her. "It's in Yah-Ta-Hey."

"Shit." Her face froze. "It means *like the devil* in Navajo." She looked across the broad avenue.

Tony looked down the avenue at the lack of traffic. "What's it mean in Paiute?"

"Shit."

They sat quietly.

Nash snapped her finger as she pointed at the tree. "Get 'er done. We have office-yelling to do next."

The deputy director opened his mouth. Nash snapped her head around and glared over the top of her dark glasses. Her right thumb and two fingers snapped together. "No. You have nothing more to say. I won't have you ruin this glorious day with more white man bullshit. This was memo shit. It hits a desk in Albuquerque, and some starched white collars draw straws or play rock, paper, scissors. The loser takes the drive. This isn't mine. It's in nation territory—big whoop. Just because I'm the appointed Indian, I don't have to catch every rez problem the LEOs can't seem to manage. I've got a full desk here. Even Muna isn't stupid enough to call me out to San Francisco just because some first people stubbed their toe." She looked at Powder's chin resting on her knee. She leaned forward and kissed the top of the head as she scratched the fuzzy jowls. "At least someone loves me. Come on. Let's find you some jerky."

Tony followed the two females back up the steps and into the building.

Three pigeons fluttered down to the bagel. They would fight over the bagel of empty flavor for an hour. Traffic drove by, and the green lights changed.

Donna looked up as Nash pulled her weapon and stowed it in her drawer. The deputy director continued toward his office.

"Hold my calls."

As Nash walked past, Donna handed her the file. Nash stopped and flipped it open.

Scanning, she pulled back the top sheet and then the second. The frown deepened as she read.

Donna stood and pushed the sheets back into the file. Her perfectly shaped and polished nail pinched the single line at the top. *Requesting agency: Deputy Zapata Yazzie of the Gallup sheriff's department.*

Nash looked up. The word came from deep in her gut. Donna muttered in harmony. "Shit."

Nash dropped it on the deputy director's desk. "Since when can a deputy from a back sand substation call for FBI heat from D.C.?"

"When he knows your name." The deputy dropped into his chair with a sigh. "Look. I get it. It always seems like you catch the strange shit crawling through the sand out on every reservation. But it's not true. There are plenty of other reservations with killings, gambling, and whatever else we investigate. There's a slasher killing up in the Minnetonka area and a shooting in upstate

New York. Florida… oh hell, I don't even want to start with Florida."

Nash sat in one side chair facing the deputy as Powder climbed into the other, circled, and lay down with her back toward the desk. "Once in Florida was enough. Their way of doing the law is more Mickey Mouse than the guy in Orlando. And I know I don't catch everything, but this…?"

Tony picked up the folder. He thumbed to the back page. "Armored car. Stopped at the McDonald's on its way to deliver a pallet to the local bank in Ship Rock. Full-faced gas masks, automatic weapons, and a metal saw. A mother with her children said they cut through the door in less than thirty seconds."

"Eyewitnesses are known to—"

"Staff sergeant with Army Intelligence. Said the guy showed the driver a shape charge and motioned to turn off the truck. They held the guys in the back at gunpoint, but never threatened to kill them. They never spoke. Just loaded all the money into large bags, threw them in a van, and left. They found the torched van the next day."

Nash pointed at the report. "A pallet can be a quarter million in small bills, to a—"

Tony backed up a sheet. "Two and a half million."

"Two large gym bags… to maybe six. That's a lot of cash for out in the middle of nowhere."

"Payroll is my guess. Interview the bank manager."

Nash slowly tipped her head to one side. "Are we going to start a pissing contest about rodeos?"

The deputy director held up both of his hands. "No contest. You've been in a lot more banks than I have. Hell, I don't even go into my own bank. I'm online, or the wife does the banking."

Nash stood and reached for the file. "I'll check with ABQ and see what they can loan me for a four-wheel."

Tony snorted. "They don't make a four-wheel-drive Hellcat?"

She shook her head. "It wouldn't corner for shit."

"Keep me posted as to why they requested you."

Nash stopped and snorted. Grinding her head around, she smirked as she held up the folder. "The deputy, Zapata?"

"Yeah…?"

"His mother only speaks Ute. He speaks English and some Navajo."

"So…?"

"She's buried in Ship Rock. The closer he gets, the louder he hears her voice."

"But she's dead."

Nash winked. "A yup. And this is why we don't tell you white guys all the fun stuff."

He pushed back in his chair. "Do you talk to the dead?"

Her heart thumped slowly as she stared at him. "It's why Oz calls me the bone whisperer."

The deputy director rolled forward and steepled his elbows on his desk. "If Congress doesn't pass the new budget soon, I might have another job for you. But have fun with…?" He frowned with one eye.

"His name is Yazzie, but they call him Zap."

"Isn't Uncle's name Yazzie?"

She snorted as she turned to the door. "Nope. It's Uncle. Just like Sam."

4

SIFTING SAND

Nash pulled off the street into the sand. Stopping, she put the four-by into four-wheel drive. The vehicle surged forward as she eased down on the throttle. "It's got a slight hesitation…"

The beefy sergeant shrugged in the passenger seat. "It's a Ford. We had a Blazer in here a couple of years ago. An agent backed it up in the desert forty miles south of here. Probably died from sand rust. They never sent us another one."

Nash eased the truck to a stop, put it in reverse, and stomped on the throttle. She wound the steering wheel one way and back the other. Sliding to a stop, she shifted into drive and stomped the accelerator again.

The man chuckled. "You must have had Skids Thompson at Quantico."

Nash glanced over as she threw the truck into a drift through the corner. "He retired the year before I had to do field training. But we'd jawed about soft-surface maneuvers in the sandbox. I liked him. He believed agents should be prepared for any situation and be stationed anywhere. He would have liked Adak, Alaska. The corn snow on black ice is a real butt-hole tightener."

"I bet it is. So what do you think?"

She put the Bronco back into two-wheel drive and pulled back onto the street. "I only need it for a few days, so it'll work. But on the highway, I'd rather have my Hellcat."

He pointed north. "I hear they have one up in the Southern Ute neighborhood somewhere. Rumor goes an agent caught a war zone of automatic weapons fire. You might pick it up cheap."

Nash snorted a chuckle. "I was up near Grand Mesa. I don't think even the backseat survived. The woman I was transporting called it a whoop-de-do or something. She likened it to some carnival ride. Made me smile. An experience like that could have traumatized her for life. Civilians don't handle being shot at especially well."

The sergeant chuckled as he looked out the side window. "I had my suspicions it might have been you. Talk hinted ATF and Homeland were also involved."

"Yeah. And DEA. The only alphabets missing were the Marshals and Secret Service. But then, they would have just slowed us down."

The sergeant pointed at the giant garage door. "Where around Ship Rock you headed?"

Nash stopped in front of the motor pool garage. "Town of, is what I heard. The deputy is in Gallup. So I'll see him first. I collaborated with him before, and he likes my driving."

The man rubbed Powder's head one last time and slid out his door. "Well, top it off before you leave. And I'd check the go bags in the back. The agents forget to refill stuff when they use the units. It's not supposed to happen, but check them anyway. If you need anything, it's through the door. If you can't find something, come find me."

"Thanks Stan. I'll check them while the little bladder checks tires."

He gave her a two-finger salute as she eased the Bronco into a parking stall.

Nash looked at Powder. "Let's see what they left in the go bags."

———

THE DEPUTY REREAD THE PASSAGE SLOWLY. HIS MOUTH followed each syllable. It wasn't right, but it said what he needed to say.

The small bell over the door chimed. The clicking of nails on the linoleum floor started his smile. It never grew much beyond a neutral slash across his face, but his face softened as the woman followed the dog through the door.

Zap stood. "Yah hey?"

Nash smiled. "Yah hey, Zap? Why drag me back to the desert you hate? You have more spacemen?"

"I wish, Nash. This one has four roads, and all of them are dead-ends."

Nash pulled up the side chair and sat. She looked down at Powder, looking at her. "You can use the floor for once." She looked up at Zap, pulling another chair out and around his desk. "You spoil her, and she'll forget she's a dog."

"She's the closest I'll ever come to having a dog."

"I thought you lived alone."

He shrugged. "I'm allergic to everything I'd ever want to have in my life. Dogs, cats, horses, goldfish, motorcycles, and a girlfriend. It's my life."

Nash grumped a smile. "How can you be allergic to a goldfish?"

"They require you remember to feed them."

She put her two palms up. "I feel seen." She watched him sit behind his desk. "The four ninety-one runs north through Yah-Ta-Hey. What are the other two roads?"

He nudged his chin up. "Excellent memory. Yes, the four ninety-one runs north and south. The two sixty-four starts at Yah-Ta-Hey and runs west to Window Rock and then all the way to Tuba City in Arizona. It's near the Grand Canyon. Not much between here and there." He shrugged his face. "Not much when you get there, either."

"And the fourth?"

"Basically, some asphalt in the sand. It runs east for a while, then wanders down through the desert, and eventually you're back to the four ninety-one. Nowhere." He stood and waved his finger toward her. "You want some coffee? I just made a fresh pot. It's Navajo, so it might be a little rougher than you're used to. But it's coffee."

Nash harrumphed a snort as she stood. "Define rough? Roadkill Armadillo as opposed to goat steak rough? Or fry bread with splinters for roughage?" She followed him around the corner to the small service kitchen with a plug-in hot plate that looked like it had worked hard since the Korean War. The white enamel had long scorched and turned tan with age.

"Any sugar or milk?" He poured the black liquid into two large earthenware mugs.

"I usually take sucre de dieta, and any kind of white paint is good."

He pushed the squat jar holding packets of fake sugar. Leaning down, he opened a small refrigerator. "My landlady and her daughter have milk goats. They mostly make cheese, but I like the milk I grew up on. I'm allergic to cow's milk."

Nash smirked. "Are you allergic to the meat, as well?"

"Nope." He sipped and then leaned back against the small counter. "Nope. That is my revenge. I have beef once or twice a week. In fact, you can get some from the fine Scottish restaurant up in Ship Rock."

Nash coughed. "Yeah. Mac Dougal's. Read the report. I don't know why it surprised me that they had one. I guess I would have wondered if they didn't. They're like cockroaches. They even had one in Kabel."

"Did you go there?"

"Nah, they warned us it was a favorite place to shoot Americans. I can't imagine they ever served anything that was halal for the locals."

He shrugged as they walked back to the desk. "Who knows? Maybe they had goat burgers. I've heard of stranger things. How did the astronaut work out?"

"It's a dummy from Hollywood. It has a new home, and the San Francisco office has a new resident empty suit to go with the ones on the first floor."

Zap frowned. "First floor?"

"The forensic lab's on the third floor. The first floor is just a regular FBI office filled with high testosterone young bucks who would rather be where the action is, like Los Angeles or Washington." She shook her head slowly. "They rush to get to the big show, and then, too late, they find out things were better where they were."

He nodded his head as he sipped. "The grass is always greener in the next valley."

Nash rocked in agreement as she ran her tongue along the side of her teeth. Is that a splinter? "I'll need to run up to Ship Rock to see where they ambushed the armored truck behind McDonald's. Are you going to be okay with this or are you staying here?"

His face soured, but he nodded. "I'm learning Ute from one of the families who come in for the farmer's market. At worst, I can tell my mother's spirit to be quiet and leave me alone."

Nash smiled behind her mug. "It's a start."

"I figured if I'm going to learn Ute, I need to get better at my own language. I've gone to a few ceremonies—out of uniform. Mostly, I just go and listen. A few people recognize me, but I'm mostly a new old face. But it feels good to be there."

Nash remembered how private the deputy was before. This new openness was good, but she didn't want to have to start singing rain chants or do a drum circle. "Getting back to Yah-Ta-Hey. Want to hazard a guess? We already figured that the east road was a bust."

"I don't know why they would come down to Yah-Ta-Hey, only

to switch cars and drive back north again. But the Family Dollar on two sixty-four has a security camera. It caught a dark car driving past heading west about three in the morning."

Nash cocked her head sideways. "But the stickup was at nine in the morning in Ship Rock. That's only an hour away. When did they torch the getaway car?"

"About three in the morning."

"And they torched the car where?"

"About a quarter mile south of what you might consider the business district for Yah-Ta-Hey. A small dirt road. It wanders around for a mile or so, and then comes back to where it started."

"So where did they stop for"—Nash scrunched her eyes—"about eighteen hours?"

Zap shrugged. "Out east?"

Nash opened her one eye—only a slit. "The road going east. How far does it go before it comes back to the highway?"

"All total? Only a few miles. Maybe someone was going to build a development. But it never happened. I'm not even sure they maintain the road. But I've seen it on a map."

Nash stood and looked around.

"What are you looking for?"

"Bathroom."

He pointed over his head behind him. "Back corner. Past the kitchen."

Nash talked as she walked. "What happened to the armored truck?"

"It's in the impound lot at the main office."

In the silence, Zap studied Powder curled on the small side chair. No part of the seat showed, but she looked comfortable enough to appear to be sleeping. But he knew better. The tactical vest seemed like a second skin to her. All the other K-9s he had seen acted like it was an irritation they had to put up with for a brief time to work. But no treats meant no vest.

"The main office in Albuquerque?" He hadn't heard her flush but realized he had never heard anyone else use the toilet.

"No. Here in Gallup."

Nash flipped her hands in the air and then rubbed them. "You're out of towels."

"It's hanging on the wall above the refrigerator. I usually wash my hands out here in the kitchen. Just in case someone comes in."

Nash nodded with a smirk. "Yeah. Busy office and all. When can we look at the armored truck?"

The deputy looked at the lack of paperwork on his desk. "I guess… um…. Anytime."

Nash looked at her orange dive watch and grimaced. "I don't want to cut into your mini spa day, but how about before it gets dark?"

He hung his head forward and looked at her through his eyebrows. "Are you always this sarcastic, or just when you're around deputies?"

Nash chewed lightly on one corner of her upper lip. "My wife says it's my resting bitch personality. Otherwise, I'm just a timid and demure banshee. Are you always so shocked by life? Or is this a new side of you?"

Zap stood and pulled his pistol out of the top drawer, checked the clip, and holstered it. "I've been taking some of those anger management classes. I'm working on it. Last week, in class, I damn near said a swearword. The teacher has hopes for me. Maybe I'll swear at least two or three words before graduation. What are you driving?"

"I checked out a Bronco from the field office in ABQ. I can drive. Not automatic, but I've taken the class, and it's a four-wheel drive. We can take it up north so you can focus on your mother."

His head snapped at the mention of his mother. But he studied Nash's face for any teasing or sarcasm. Her face was stoic.

She drew a slow breath through her nose. "Just focus on the

language. You've got this. You learning her language must impress her, dead or alive. It means you care. I don't care how hard-nosed she might be—a mother is a mother."

His head dropped as they walked out the north door to the street. "Yeah. Maybe you're right. I hope so."

5

OH, BY THE WAY . . .

THE PATIO at Grandma's Chaha'oh, or shade house, was cooler than inside. There was enough electricity for lights, and the health department required the refrigerator. But nobody liked air-conditioning or the power bills that came with it. Most tourists didn't understand the appeal of a chaha'oh, so they opted for starvation or the golden arches from Illinois. The young, loud kids also preferred the fried potatoes there, which was fine with Clement. It let him enjoy his chili-fried machaca with beans and frybread in peace.

He tore a small piece of bread from the wheel and grabbed a small bite of meat. Stuffing the morsel into his mouth. He chewed contemplatively as he watched the heat rising from the parking lot. The waves distorted the shield on the sheriff's Bronco as the man turned and nosed the truck up to the hitching post. Clement harrumphed at the hitching post. When he arrived, there were two ponies tied to the rail. Well... Indian tied. Most just spun the reins around the post and let it be enough of a sign for the laconic horses to stay. The four tires now replaced the eight hooves.

The door creaked from the ubiquitous sand dust perpetually embedded in the hinges. Nobody cared enough to clean the dirt out —it would just be back the next day and proudly crow its existence by the end of the week. It was the nature of cars, the same as a tourist eating beans and farting. Life.

Clement watched below the open door as the pant leg rose above the boot as the man slid out of the Bronco. Slick black leather. No fancy stitching. Clement smiled softly. Black, no-nonsense boots were the older lieutenant instead of the younger sergeant still trying to prove himself and his college ways. The lieutenant adjusted his cream-colored hat over his tsiiyééł hair bun. The creamy colored wraps on his hair were home-spun goat's hair. His wife probably spun, wove, and braided to tie his hair.

As the deputy stepped into the shaded patio, he removed his cowboy hat and nodded at Clement. His Ya'át'ééh was soft, a little more than Ya'eh.

Clement rolled his body back upright. "Ya'át'ééh, lieutenant. You eating, or just arresting me?"

The lieutenant laid his dark aviators and hat on the table. "Let me get my food. Then we can talk nasty about the other kids." The Navajo and Zuni met at boarding school. Both carried scars from the attempts to drive out the wild animal in the aboriginal boys. Both backs showed signs of having never turned their backs on their heritage. The military had provided them both with a respite from the torture all had suffered, and only some succumbed to it.

Clement watched the waves in the air over the cars as he thought about their years in the school. Whispered conversations spoken in the darkened sleeping room, spoken only in Navajo, Zuni, and Ute. Older students reinforced the learnings of the younger and listened to stories of home. The stories comforted the scared new boys, reminding them they were all equal and shouldn't be forced to change.

Placing the earthenware mug on the table was soft. "You forgot your coffee. I poured you a fresh cup. Maybe someone put cow milk in it. I gave you goat butter instead."

The joke was as old as their friendship from the first day. It went with the scornful insults turned pride-points of being a goat roper and sheep rider. Both had learned how to ride and rope on the smaller animals. As they both found out, sheep aren't easy to ride. They don't buck, but they can peel even the most tenacious boy rider from their back with a single pass through a stickery bush. The late summer Indian rodeos and roundups were only days before the torn-up boys returned to the boarding school for the winter.

The lieutenant nodded at the small pile of meat on Clement's plate. "Looks good."

"It's sweeter than usual. I think grandma snuck some roadkill in there. Maybe armadillo. What did you get?"

"The usual. Coyote and bean." His open hands chopped softly at the burrito. "It keeps me entertained on the long drives when I can't get any radio."

Clement rose on his left butt cheek. The two snickered as if the fifty-five years inserted into their lives never happened. "I thought you were wrangling paper these days. Where are you patrolling?"

The deputy bit the end of the burrito off and chewed. "We're three men down. One had a baby last week. His wife has him cook and clean the house. We're making bets. She's the woman who figures out how to make him breast-feed the baby in the middle of the night."

Clement stuffed another mouthful into his mouth and then sipped some coffee. Chewing slowly, waiting as someone he recognized, but didn't know, waved as they left. He waved back. He watched as they drove off. "And the other two?"

"Both have vacation time."

Clement's face lit up as his head bobbed. "I remember those days. Vacation from work I hated. Trading a hundred and ten degree heat and ninety-eight percent humidity for scorching sun, patching the roof on our hogan."

The lieutenant chuckled. "Or away from the family while fishing down in Mexico?"

They exchanged knowing looks. "We might have caught something if we had ever left the bar."

"Or gone out on a boat."

Clement laughed. "Or even gone to a coast with boats."

The lieutenant wagged his head as he took another bite. He chewed and then pushed the food into his cheek. "Do you ever drink anymore?"

"Hardly worth mentioning, Sam. The wife likes me to make that eggnog stuff at Christmas. I think it has all come out of the same bottle. After a few years, I'll have to break down and quit or buy another bottle. What about you?"

The deputy opened his mouth and paused. He scrunched up his eyes and looked down at the table, then to his left. "There was a party… Someone had a birthday… or a baby. It was a few years ago. I don't even know if I have a bottle at the house or not. I never think about it anymore. By the time I get home, I just want to sit and watch what the wife is watching on the TV and then go to bed."

"So, where do they have you patrolling these days?"

He picked up the last of his burrito, thought, and then dropped it. Picking up the napkin, he wiped his hands and mouth, dropping the white wad on the food. He pushed the plate away from him. His face soured. "Out in the mesas."

Clement sat stoically, waiting. It wasn't like his friend to not finish his food.

Sam reached over and turned his hat an inch. His finger touched the glasses and hesitated. "Some days… I think I'm getting too old for all of this." He looked at the face of his lifelong friend. "You're awfully quiet."

Clement felt his heartbeat. The rhythm beat slow. He had thought long and hard about the desert, the men, the jeep, and what it would take to riddle them with so many bullets. "Ya'át'ééh."

The lieutenant's voice lowered as he leaned in. "You knew… Ya'át'ééh? It's all good? What the hell can be all good about a jeep full of dead bodies? What do you know about the shit show out on the mesa, Clement? It's been three—four days ago. When did you plan to tell me? We go back…"

Clement wiped his hand and mouth with measured, deliberate movements. He placed his napkin on the mostly empty plate and pushed the whole aside. Leaning in, his eyes stayed locked on his old friends as his voice lowered to feral.

"What part did you want to know? How warm were the bodies? Or how the blood was still oozing from the holes in the chests? How I watched the driver's head collapse because his brain had liquefied and run out of the bullet holes? How I stood on the mesa, all alone, and there was nobody to call, or whom I could trust? All I knew was I rode up minutes after they had been shot to shit. What with? I have no idea. But if I were to guess, I'd say one of those mini guns they had there in Vietnam. But then I'd have to imagine the helicopter going with it. Then comes the minimum of three guys to fly and shoot the gun. Where does it stop? Who do I trust with that information? Huh, Sam? Who do I trust? Every bit of peace I thought I had in my world is gone. I go for a pleasant ride in the desert, and the next thing is to see something we never had to experience in the Navy. So tell me. Am I wrong to shut up? What's safe anymore?"

The screen door squealed as they sat with less than a foot separating their faces. Neither looked at the three men leaving. They were both hyperaware of the sound of the two cars starting and driving off.

Sam's shoulders sagged. His voice was barely more than a whisper. "I stopped counting holes when I hit three hundred. I'm sure the ballistics will say they came from a single point of origin. And if there are that many in the jeep and bodies, there are plenty more slugs in the ground around and leading up to them. In the Marines, I saw what a thirty-caliber could do. And how the spray isn't a detailed hit, but spreads everywhere. A helicopter isn't exactly a stable platform for detailed shooting." His eyes wandered over his friend's frozen face. "Did you call it in? They couldn't trace the call. It wasn't from a landline."

Clement drew a slow breath through his nose. "I had to wait until I had a couple of bars. I rode the barranca behind the drum."

Sam eased back to sitting straight. "The call was enough. We don't need an identity. But the location seemed curiously detailed… If you hunt out that a way."

Clement didn't move. "Did you find anything else?"

"Tracks. Two motorcycles. Trail bikes with sand knobbies. From the spray, I'd say larger, like maybe five hundreds. Enduros."

"Just two? How close did they get?"

"One track was a foot from the jeep. Like they were there to verify or find something. The other hung back about ten yards, like they were the backup or protection. Why?"

Clement cleared his throat. "They weren't there to verify. With that much lead flying about, you don't need to send someone to check pulses. You can see dead bodies from a hundred feet away. They were looking for something."

The childhood friend was gone, and the lieutenant sheriff was back as he touched his hat. "What?"

Clement reached his left hand into his back pocket. As his hand returned, it opened, and the folded stack of twenties rolled out semi-flat. The paper band held the hundred bills together as he laid the stack on the table between them.

The lieutenant picked up the contaminated bundle of bank bills. He read the name on the strap holding them. "First National, in Albuquerque." His eyes rose to meet his friends. "How much more?"

"Two large duffle bags. Full. Not seabag size, but bigger than you'd take to a gym to work out. Even if you had a bunch of rackets in them."

"All twenties?"

Clement wagged his head. "Fifties and hundreds. More of the

twenties, though, from what I can see. I didn't dig through the bags much. One was shot open."

"Where are they?"

"I hid them in the desert. I didn't know who I could trust."

The old twitch of the boarding school's conspirator smile pulled at the deputy's cheek. "But you showed up here today. Expecting to find me."

"I do know what you like to eat on Thursdays. What now?"

The deputy pushed the money back at his friend. "Don't spend any. But hold on to this for now. Stick this one in your sock drawer or something."

Clement smirked. "I'll hide it with my peyote and marijuana stash. The wife won't go near them."

His friend rocked. "Yeah, I think that good book of hers has some harsh words about any Indian medicine." He thought for a moment. "Get me one or two of the hundreds and maybe a couple of the fifties. I'll do some checking around. And throw in one of those paper bands. That will help narrow the search."

6

HEAVY ARMOR, TISSUE PAPER
LOCKS

THEY STOOD twenty feet away from the hulking box of steel on wheels. Powder sat patiently next to Nash's boot. A hundred years before, the wooden carved statue in front of a cigar store was more animated than the two standing in the impound yard.

Powder shifted more weight on her right front paw, allowing her to rest her shoulder against Nash's right leg.

Zap dipped his cream-colored hat. His eye studied the profile of the FBI agent from behind his dark glasses. The lack of movement was restful. Having his head empty of his mother's voice, even more so. His voice was barely over a whisper. "Did you want a closer look?"

He wasn't sure if she had spoken or if he had only imagined it. "Did you want to get this over with, or did you want to solve the crime?" It was the tone of the question his mother would have asked.

He turned and walked back into the office.

Two minutes later, he emerged with two cups of coffee. He offered one out. Her hand took it without looking. She sipped quietly. Still no movement closer toward the armored truck.

Zap wasn't sure if she had spoken English or some other language. But it sounded like she had said *Show me boom-boom*.

His eyes followed the dog's determined steps as she circled the truck, never approaching it directly. Her movements were precise and deliberate. Stopping at the driver's door, she rose on her back legs to inspect the handle area without making contact. She then repeated the same pattern at the rear doors, ending a safe distance away from the rear doors, before sitting down and gazing over at Nash.

Nash's smile hardened into a grimace.

"What does that mean?"

Nash glanced at Zap. "It means they didn't use explosives on either door."

"The driver said the robber had shown him an explosive device and motioned for them to cut the engine and hold their hands up."

Nash rocked. "I read that. Let's look at the back door and the locks."

The lock was missing. There was only a hole where the lock should be. Nash gently stuck her finger in the hole and ran it around the metal of the door. She looked over her orange sunglasses at Zap. "I think we're going to find the lock cylinder inside. But the outer ring is somewhere in the parking lot behind the fallen arches."

Zap frowned and looked back at Powder, waiting patiently. "But no explosives?"

Nash wiggled her eyebrows and looked back at Powder. "I asked her to check for boom-boom. This was bang-bang. Or to be more exact, bangity bang. She likes her rhyming words."

"I don't understand. What's the difference between a boom and a bang?"

Nash swung the door open and bent over to look along the floor. She pointed back along the wall behind where the driver would have sat in the cab. Straightening, she turned and leaned against the back bumper. "When you blow something up, it makes an enormous boom, right?" The man nodded. "Who hears the boom?"

Zap scrunched his face as he sensed for a joke. "Everyone?"

"Are you asking me or telling me? Serious questions here. No gotchas."

He paused in thought. "Telling. Everyone can hear it."

Nash nodded. "Have you ever done any construction?"

"Some."

"Ever used a nail-driving gun to drive a spike through a footer into concrete?"

"I've seen them. Never used one, though."

Nash sat on the bumper next to the step. "The old ones you put the .22 Long-rifle shell into them and then hit the gun with a mallet to fire the shell. The charge in the shell drives the spike into the footer and concrete. But with the newer ones, you don't need the hammer. It's more like a rifle, and you lean on it—or lean into it."

"Bangity bang." He looked back at Powder. "And she knew the difference between explosives and gunpowder."

Nash stood. "Right."

"But I don't get it. The driver said the robber showed him an explosive device…"

"So why not just blow it with a wad of Semtex? Simple. Witnesses. Probably a half-dozen people on the other side of a commercial fire door. They would have heard the explosion and come out to investigate. But a twenty-two? They never heard a thing."

"How did you figure the nail gun?"

Nash pointed at the hole in the door. "Stick your finger in here and feel the edges."

Zap ran his finger around the one-inch hole. "What am I feeling?"

"Are there any sharp edges?"

He ran his finger back the other way. "No."

"Right. An explosive would have created a sharp edge by

deforming the metal. But by punching the lock cylinder out with the rifle, the lock is gone, and the door opens. But with a clean hole. More importantly, no witnesses."

"Why not just show the explosive device to the guards in the back and tell them to open the door?"

Nash smiled. "Good question. And when we interview the guards, you get to ask that. I have an idea why, but let's see if I'm right." She pointed at the two objects in the compartment's front. "I wouldn't worry about fingerprints when you pick up the cylinder and the nail. No one touched either of them. And if the nail driving the cylinder out heated the metal enough to cook off any partial fingerprints."

He looked at her for a moment and then climbed into the back of the truck. "How many times have you seen the bullet thing used?"

"Never have."

Zap looked back as he reached for the bent nail. "But you…"

Nash swung her hand and pointed back at Powder. "Nope. She did. If you remember right, I asked her about explosives."

"And she said no."

Nash dipped her head. "She said no to the explosives. But she didn't come back to where we were standing. She stayed here looking at the door."

"So you knew something was up."

Nash rocked her head. "Which is why I felt the lock hole. Now, I guess if you stuck your sidearm's nose against the keyhole, you might shoot the lock out, but you also might blow your hand off." She shrugged. "I don't know how it would go, but I figured the guys doing the robbing had figured it out, and it needed to be simple and muted, but with enough power to blow through the lock."

"And you've used the nail driver…?"

Nash held her hand out for the lock and nail. "A few times in the sandbox. If you wanted something built, you either put in a requisition and waited for a few months or years…"

Zap smirked. "Or did it yourself. What do you think?" He nodded at the lock.

She looked at the cylinder. The nail hole was shallow, but had crushed the keyhole closed. Frowning, she looked at the hardened steel nail made to penetrate hard concrete. She smiled and held up the nail—which should have been the pointed end.

"The nail didn't penetrate the lock and weld it in place because they ground the tip flat. Making it more of a small caliber hammer punch instead of a penetrating nail. The plate armor is heavy and thick… but the standard lock is brass, and only the rings on each side secure it in place. Blow the cylinder out, and the lock becomes useless. The outside ring fell off immediately. The inside probably got swept out with the bags of money."

Nash turned and showed the nail to Powder. The front paws did their little happy dance. Nash smirked at Zap. "She agrees. Let's go find the guards."

"Two live here in Gallup, but one is up in Yah-Ta-Hey."

Nash thought and glanced at her watch. "Lunch on the way and start with the Yah-Ta-Hey." She flinched and reached for her pocket.

Peeking at the screen, she thumbed the green icon. "Yeah, Muna, what's up?"

The sound of city traffic was in the background. "Hey, Nash. Ming just called, wanting to know what we need information on a dead Afghani for. The guy immigrated here and got a green card, but passed away two years ago. He died of lung cancer. Are you in Oklahoma?"

"New Mexico. In the same area where they found your new office buddy. I'd asked her to track down information on my old interpreter in Afghanistan, Abdul Aziz. We're kind of in a meeting about an armored car heist right now. I'll reach out to Ming later. How's drizzle land?"

"It keeps most people off the streets, which leaves the rest of the territory for those who forgot how to drive in the rain. I had an early lunch appointment, and walking back from Chow Fat's, I passed three fender benders. These people would freak out if it snowed."

Nash pictured the San Francisco hills in a few inches of snow. "I'll stay here in the sand and heat." She glanced at her watch and frowned. "Lunch at eleven in the morning? What kind of case…?" Her eyes opened as she turned away from Zap, and her voice quieted. "Or was this personal?"

Muna giggled. "What? I can't hear you. Nash, are you there? Hello? I guess we got cut off."

Nash snickered at the metallic click.

Holstering her phone back in her pocket, she looked at Zap. "Where are we going to lunch, Indian?"

He snorted with a half-smile. "Zuni or Navajo?"

Nash glanced at Powder's steady gaze at the words for food. "Anything above roadkill is fine by us. And even roadkill isn't totally off the table as long as it's done well."

He nodded. "I know just the place. And it's on the way."

———

THE HOUSE OF THE ARMORED TRUCK DRIVER WAS MORE of a remodeled single-wide trailer than a building. The shaded patio proved to be more comfortable than the sunbaked tin can. In the corner, Nash had noted a wooden lounge that looked more like a bedroom than anything inside the trailer. Between the hibachi, chairs, and the bed, Nash guessed the man lived more in the air than between the tin walls.

The driver had grown up in the quiet, tiny community of Naschitti, a small town nestled thirty miles north. In his fifty-four years, he had never ventured beyond the familiar borders, never straying from his roots. The thought of crossing the imaginary state line held no allure for him; it was just another arbitrary boundary, meaning nothing to him. Home was all that mattered for him—the dusty roads and familiar faces of Naschitti were enough to satisfy his wanderlust. Only once had he ventured to the big city of Albuquerque—that afternoon had been enough for Jeb Whitehorn.

Nash slowly drew her glasses off, folded them, and hung the one temple in her white shirt pocket. She leaned more on the arm of the chair than forward. "You said he held up a small bomb. What made you think it was a bomb? Have you had dealings with bombs before?"

He wiped his hand across his days' old stubble. "No ma'am. I've never even seen a stick of dynamite. But I watch them movies and such on the television. Where the terrorist or a bad guy sticks a bomb on the side of a car, and it blows the car to kingdom come."

"Can you describe what he was holding?"

He held his hands like holding a bowl of soup. "It were big, black, with a couple of wires coming out. Kind of like a brick with a deck of cards wired to it, maybe."

Nash nodded at the useless description. "Could you see how it would stick to the door?"

"I think they have magnets or something. That's how they work in the movies. Right?"

Nash looked at Zap's stoic face. And slowly let her eyes wander back to the man in the dirty T-shirt. He hadn't worked since the robbery, and from the look of him and his clothes, it didn't look like he had bathed either. Nash had seen broken men in the sandbox, but this spoke of a fragility that would likely take the man's existence. "Were the men wearing masks of any kind? It didn't seem to be in the report."

The man's cheek twitched—pulling at the eye. He obviously didn't like recalling the day. "Not really. Well, kind of. They were the same some people wore back when they were telling us how we needed to wear doctors' masks. Out here, nobody did. But some did. Crazy times. Glad that's over."

"So, white masks?"

His mouth opened and then stopped—frozen. And then hesitantly closed. "No. No, they wore black masks. Kind of like little gas masks thingies. But without the eye parts."

Nash looked at her phone like it was a notepad. "Now it says here, you described the man as blond." She looked up. "Was that long, whitish blond hair, or short, darker hair?"

Jeb frowned and jiggled his head like he had bitten something sour. "No. I never said blond. They had dark hair. Short. Black, actually. Kind of like a black guy... but not really. More like an Indian, but with curlier hair."

"So they were black?"

"No. Dark, but not black. And not really Mexican or Indian. But not white. Kind of like those guys they show on the news—there in the middle east somewhere. Kind of like that."

"So, Arabs."

"Yeah."

Nash shifted in her chair. "Do you think you could pick them out of a lineup?"

"I only saw their eyes." Nash could see the man was at the edge. "And, well... their hair." His hand jutted out with the palm up.

Nash studied the man for a moment and then tapped her phone. "Right. Got it now." Standing, she slipped her phone into her pocket and nodded at Zap. "I think we're done here. Thank you, Mr. Whitehorn. You've been a big help." She pointed at her card lying on the small table made from a wooden spool for heavy wire. "If you think of anything more, call me."

7

REACH OUT OR BACK

"ALL YOU ASKED WAS to track down your old interpreter. And admit it, you gave me sketchy information."

Nash scratched the side of her face as she looked across the desert. The sun was barely up when her phone pinged a text. Ming wanted to know when she was awake. Nash had sat back down in the chair by the door to her room. Powder was confused, but sat beside her. If breakfast was going to be delayed, she wanted to know why.

"It was all the information I thought I had. Well, it was still unclear, but it was all I had to go on." Nash scratched around Powder's neck and under the lightweight tactical harness. "Yes, your sister Ming says hello, but mommy and her need to talk for a moment." She could sense the screen on her phone as it blossomed into FaceTime. She held the phone so Powder could see.

"Hi, Powder. How's my favorite girl? Are you having fun in the desert with your mommy?"

Powder fluffed with a soft woof. But her feet were dancing with happiness.

The small Asian woman gushed. "I bet you're dancing your

happy dance. I hope you come visit soon so we can spoil you. That's a big hint, Mommy."

Nash chuckled. "No. Really? I would never have guessed. Your spoiling welded five more pounds on my butt last time we came there. Chef needs to cook with lower fat and fewer calories."

Ming laughed. "You misspelled portion control. Someone needs to learn that the business runs on high fat and calories around here. On our light days at the computers, we burn a marathon's worth of calories."

Nash ignored the jab at reality and responsibility. "So, where did he live when he died?"

"Right there in Oklahoma City. He landed at Tinker Air Base and never left. I didn't find any separation from the service date, just his death date. It's like he worked right until lunch and died on his own time. But never clocked out."

Nash nodded as her eyes watched a roadrunner prance across the parking lot. It wasn't moving fast, but then, there wasn't a coyote chasing it, either. "What was he doing for Uncle Sam?"

"The guy I spoke to said something about him being a valuable listener. He also mentioned his work on a C-130J and referred to tube rats. I didn't push it. I figured you might know what he was talking about without talking about it. Like your Secret Squirrel shit."

Nash rolled her eyes at the phone. "Which is exactly what it was —Secret Squirrel shit. Airborne listening station. Probably circling over the Middle East listening to radio chatter."

Ming frowned and sipped on her large Hydro Flask with a backhoe digging from atop a day-of-the-dead skull. "But he was based in Oklahoma…"

Nash waved it off with a side roll of her eyes. "Pfft. With aerial refueling, they can reach their destination in eight hours and stay for two or three days. Catch another load of fuel and be home for Sunday dinner. The world's a lot smaller for military jets than for civilians."

"So they burn a hundred tons of fuel just to go listen to the daily chatter? Why not just tune into Al Jazeera online and stay home?" A white sleeve placed a dish of food in front of her.

Nash laughed. "Bonjour, Chef."

A mop of curly red hair and a glowing smile entered the camera. "Nope. Danny. We're filling in while Chef is away with the boys, battling cyber punks and filling diapers. Good to see you, Nash. You need to get back down to Crystal Cove. They're going to have a giant flat surf contest next month. And we have puppies."

Powder woofed at the word puppies.

Nash laughed. "Keep talking. You have Powder's vote on the puppies. Surfing is too close to SEAL shit. But give Frank my best."

"Will do." His vibrating spread hand was a blur as he slid out of view.

Nash looked at Ming. "I didn't know Danny cooked."

"He doesn't. They're remodeling the kitchen at the Surf Shack, so Cookie is here doing the cooking, and Randy is the consummate server. He knows what we like, and he'll find us and make us eat. So your Scissors was a spook?"

"Appears so. Did it have an age attached to his death?"

Ming looked at another screen. "Um... yeah. Seventy-three. Young."

Nash wagged her head. "Not for the sandbox. They just looked older because of the harsh conditions. But he said he was already a grandfather when he left. And that was, shoot, fifteen years ago."

Ming whistled low. "Young for having grandkids."

"Not if you start when you're only fifteen or sixteen. Send me what you have on him here and his American wife. I'm not that far from Oklahoma. I can at least go pay my respects."

"Sure thing. I'm happy to help. We're in our busy season, so it's just the same old-same old: water depth and mud. At least the Aussies are coming around to rebuilding some of their old storm damage. So we get to impress them with some holographic dog and pony shows about their bays and ports."

Nash smirked. "Go get 'em, tiger. Sick Baby and Chips on them."

She sipped on her coffee as she thought about the barren New Mexico desert and the valley of her spirit world. And then there was the new one with an angry purple storm and sticker brush. It was nothing she had thought about for almost twenty years. Definitely not a place she wanted to go back to.

She glanced at her watch. Early, but she knew the teepee would already be active.

The phone went to voicemail on the first half ring. Uncle was cranky this morning.

The text message pinged.

Junior looking at large buck for freezer.

Nash typed and sent it. *How close?*

The phone rang, and she dropped it on her lap. Picking it up, she glanced at the caller. Uncle.

"First, you don't want to talk to me, but now you do?"

His chuckle was wet and snotty. The croak was deeper than usual. "When the buck is ten feet from the edge of the deck, we didn't want to spook it. All good now. Squatter dropped him with his nine when he looked up at the ding from your text. Keep talking, we'll let Junior figure out what to do with it."

Nash burped a snicker. "Whitetail?"

"Better. Roosevelt Elk. I've never seen one this side of Shasta before, but I'm not complaining. I figure if Tommy doesn't fuck this one up, we should get about four hundred pounds of excellent eating out of it. What's up?"

"How much do you know about the spirit walking and pulling someone into your world?"

"Only what Red taught me. Why?"

Nash scrunched her face. "Red?"

"Oren Redfeather, I think. He was a tiny red baby. Either that or he was just a red chili pepper. He's a powerful shaman. He guided me to come find you when you were in the coma. I guess some of it stuck. You keep pulling me into your spirit world. The roadkill isn't bad, but at least I know how to get back to Bone Creek. I tried to walk out into the back pool once, but ended up back on the bank. I don't understand it, but it's your world. So what's up, Indian?"

"It's about the walk the other morning. The guy was my interpreter twenty years ago in Afghanistan. I just found out he's been dead for over a year…"

The silence would have made her think they had been cut off, but she could hear Thomas swearing in the background. "Sounds like Thomas is struggling with the kill."

"Mmm… Oh. Yeah. I'll need to go help him in a minute. I was trying to remember how to get hold of Red. He doesn't have a phone. You call his daughter, Ona, and she'll drive down to him with the message."

"Do you have her phone number?"

"Why would I have her phone number?"

Nash growled. "How did you get hold of him before?"

"We drove down."

Nash's tirade was almost under her breath. "I swear to everything you hold sacred; I'll beat you within an inch of your miserable—"

He cut her off. "Tommy just fell. I need to go. I'll send you a phone number or address on the Zuni Nation." Even the snick was short.

Nash growled. As the battered old Bronco pulled into the parking lot, she remembered she was only wearing her old BDU olive-drab T-shirt and shorts. Crap. She stood and walked back into the motel room. "Powder. Entertain Zap for a few minutes. I need to dress."

Zap smirked at the clothing disappearing into the door. He had wondered if she relaxed in the starched white shirt and leather pants. The combat-looking boots were optional. He turned off the

Bronco and pulled up some paperwork. Two paragraphs later, he traded the paperwork for his new Ute words for the week.

A few minutes later, the tap on the window was soft. He looked at the hardened face and orange aviators.

"Breakfast." Nash stepped back and looked at the Bronco. "We're taking my ride."

Zap tried to give her a stony stare through the window. He had practiced the sort of face he remembered his mother had used on him as a boy.

"I said breakfast. We're leaving." Nash turned toward the FBI vehicle.

Ch'iidii. He pulled the keys from the steering column and opened the door. "I was studying my Ute."

Nash nodded as she opened the black SUV. "Ya, huh? Breakfast." Powder jumped into the truck and scrambled up onto the center console. Nash stuck her leg in as she watched Zap saunter past the front. "Did I mention how homicidal Paiute women get when they're hungry?"

He stopped and looked along the other three cars nosed toward the rooms. He blinked slowly and deliberately. "How many places do you suppose there are to bury a body between here and Yah-Ta-Hey?" His head slowly ground around to watch the woman halfway into the truck.

Powder danced her front paws. The woof was nothing more than a breath fluffing her lips. Nash got the point. "Ya'át'ééh, Deputy. I'm just hangry. Where's breakfast?"

"Whiteman or Mexican?"

Nash looked at the sky. "Outside."

Zap opened the passenger's door. "Mexican. The Dons."

"Don what?"

"Don have this. Don do that. Don take credit cards. Don come back. The Dons. Just like home."

"You're kidding."

Zap shrugged as he buckled his belt. "You'll see."

The verbal abuse started the second his face came through the door. "Ay, Mama, the pendejo is back."

Even the busboy laughed and contributed to the fun. "Hey, Mama, the roadkill snuck back in."

The three men smiled at the favorite butt of the joking. The greetings were soft, but with smiles, especially the older man who hung out his hand at the edge of his table. Nash noticed the almost low five as Zap washed the hand with his own in passing.

As they turned at the end of the counter, the older woman cooking banged her spatula on the high serving counter. As they looked over, she pointed two fingers at her scowling face and then at Zap. He laughed and blew her a kiss as he pushed open the screen door to the patio.

Two men sat in the far corner of the covered patio. Nash looked up at the thin poles covered with reeds. She recognized the peeled upright logs and poles as black locust, like the kind she had grown up around. Too hard to saw or do anything else with, but perfect for patios. Drill and screw... or just lash together. She noticed some screws for a combination of the two construction binders. It was comfortable.

Zap noticed Nash examining the cover. "They have a drip system on the top. When it's hot, it works like a swamp cooler. It's the most comfortable place to eat lunch or dinner." He smirked. "Unless you like the white man's air-conditioning."

Nash smiled softly as she watched Powder crawl up into the other chair. "Just like home."

Zap nodded at the large waitress coming through the door with a carafe and two mugs. "There isn't a menu. What do you feel like eating?"

Nash looked up at the woman scowling at Zap as she poured Nash a cup of coffee. "I'll take any breakfast your mama feels good about. My dog likes a machaca burrito without beans or lettuce.

Mild and cut up in a bowl. The other dog... well, whatever you usually throw at him."

She set the carafe down next to the empty mug. "He gets last night's plate scrapings." Her face softened. "I see the working vest. Is your dog a pet or a no-pet?"

Nash shrugged. "It's her world. I'm just the driver. Bribing her with jerky goes a long way."

The young woman held her hand out for Powder to sniff. "I'll bring the jerky in a moment."

Powder gave her hand a tiny-tongue touch.

Nash laughed. "Whoa. A kiss on the first date."

The waitress scowled at Zap and turned back to the door. The screen door slapped softly.

Nash studied the man. "Family?"

"They lived next door. I lived mostly in their backyard. The family teased me about Mandy and me being a thing, but there was nothing there either way. We were both just hiding from my mother or the world, who didn't let her be that tall in the sixth grade. She was the lucky one. She got home-schooled. Well, local public school."

"You went to boarding school."

He nodded as he glanced over to see who the two men were. None acknowledged the other.

Nash laid her glasses on the table. "Who do you know down in the Zuni lands?"

"Some. Who are you looking for?"

"A shaman by the name of Red."

"I've heard of him. But I don't know him. What's the interest?"

Nash studied the man who was used to his mother reaching out to him from the other side. "The spirit world and how it works."

Zap folded his dark glasses and gently inserted them into his black uniform shirt pocket. "I think it's kind of a personal thing. Mine is like a Volkswagen bug with a busted muffler, and yours might be a Chevy. The rules are different."

"Dodge. Dodge Hellcat."

His one eyebrow crept up. "Don't invite me into your spirit world."

"No. It's what I drive. A Dodge Challenger Hellcat. It's red."

"Why am I not surprised?"

8

WHAT'S WRONG?

Oz strolled through the office space, passed Muna staring into her dark web computer, and continued into the forensic lab part of the general lab. He stopped to take out a sack from his shoulder bag and looked back at the back of Muna. The thick black braid looked softer than her usual sleek, tight knotting. The tactical vest was the same level three she had adopted for the summer weight. Cocked on the roller arms of her chair, her boot heels showed.

He shrugged as he carried the small sack back to the breakroom refrigerator. Stowing it, he turned to the coffee. The pot was half-full, but the tiny light was out. He felt the pot with the back of his hand. Pulling the glass pot out of the machine, he felt the bottom with his entire hand. Cold.

Pouring the old coffee out, he made more and pushed the button.

Stepping out of the small room, he stopped and studied the backside of the small black woman. Something was wrong. She hadn't moved. The stacked screens displayed what appeared to be older, typed documents with handwritten notes added. She scrolled to the following document.

Oz recognized the title block along the top: Department of Defense.

Turning, he walked into the autopsy room. Mike stood at the wall-mounted computer and small desk. The screen displayed a detailed view of the skull they had been working on the day before.

"Something wrong?"

Mike didn't move. His stance on his two prosthetic legs always seemed welded to the floor. The black scrubs and shorts had become his uniform of the day. The hand-painted Day of the Dead skulls varied, but were usually just a single colorful face. His week in Guadalajara the year before, to celebrate the day, had changed his outlook about losing his sister decades before.

Oz stepped beside the younger man. "What's so interesting about the detail?"

The finger traced along the one edge of the crack in the skull left by the killing blow. "Why isn't this edge rounded over like the other side?"

Oz leaned in. They had boiled the head to remove everything from the bone. They could see the long strike wound in the head, but only the clean bone could give them the definitive answer. He touched the screen and tried to rotate the view.

Mike chuckled. "This isn't one of Muna's screens." He worked with the mouse, rotated the view, and pushed in for an even closer look. "We're the old school. We must use the mickey thing. But see what I mean. The clean edge forms a perfect ninety-degree angle, unlike the other, which is mashed and rounded."

Oz thought about the view. "They sharpened the blade only on one side." His finger ran along the screen. "Where are the pictures of the machete?"

Mike clicked on the shrink line and then clicked on an icon. The file structure ballooned. He scanned down the list and opened the images list. Choosing the weapons list, he clicked on the machete. The screen expanded with the view of the weapon laid on a white background.

Oz grumped. "Edge view?"

Mike clicked on the right caret and stepped through the images. Stopping on the one taken with the blade standing vertically on the back of the blade, the view showed the ground bevels on the two sides of the blade. "Double-sided. Wrong blade."

Oz hummed. "Not so quick. If the blade isn't perpendicular to the skull, but is the same or close degree oblique to the grind on the blade, it's still the prime suspect."

Mike turned and studied the older, former teacher. "The oblique angle should create a slight arch in the strike's path…"

Oz dipped his head. "Do we have a good enough perpendicular image?"

"Should." Mike wiggled the mouse and returned the skull image from the taskbar at the bottom of the screen. "We should be able to align this Pana-Scan…"

He clicked into the tools above the image. Choosing a tool, he clicked on the inner edge of the skull, and then the outer edge. A red dotted line appeared with a zero-zero at the end. His next two clicks were at the edge and a small distance along the skull. The zero-zero changed to eighty-seven degrees. Mike clicked on the eight-seven and typed ninety. The image shifted slightly. He smiled back at Oz.

"Gotta love the new toys."

Oz grumped. "The old tools may have been messier, but were just as good."

Mike smirked. "Down, boy. We'll use the OG tools to check Ludwig's quick and clean version."

"Who's Ludwig?"

"Muna's name for our computer. Professor Ludwig von Drake was Donald's nutty professor uncle. It goes with the three printers, Huey, Duey, and the nutcase needing replacing if Chips can't make it work right."

Oz groaned and pointed at the image. "The strike line?"

Mike clicked three points along the cut. He assigned zero to the one end. And one eighty at the other end. He turned toward Oz with his one eyelid drooped in a visual groan. "Straight."

Oz hunched up his one shoulder and scrunched his face. "Quick, Robin. To the old gangsta tools. But first, I need coffee." He turned and then looked back. "And check to see if Muna has moved."

Mike frowned. "Is she asleep?"

"No. But when I came in, she was doing what the kids call death scrolling. But it was only DOD records or reports."

Mike snorted softly. "You're really getting old. The term is doomscrolling. And I seriously doubt if Muna ever resorts to mindless, negative news."

Oz chuckled. "Yah, she gets plenty here at work. But it's still not like her being oblivious to me coming in. Is she working on something for you? She's on the dark side of the computer."

Mike rolled his eyes. "You mean the side that never rests? The top one has run the facial recognition program, at least for the last two years. When I came in, she was still at the range. The range master said she's been shooting two hundred shells each gun since coming back from the Olympics."

"Yeah. And quieter than usual."

Mike's one cheek flinched. "'Tis the season. Summer can do that in San Francisco. Nobody to play with, and work is rationed to one skull at a time."

"What do you suggest?"

Mike stretched his face and eyes. "I'd order her to take some vacation if I thought she'd go."

"She'd just spend it at the shooting range over at Mount Diablo."

"Check her coffee." He lifted his mug and handed it to Oz. "Mine's so cold it's probably supporting algae growth. Thanks."

Oz stooped over Muna and lifted her empty, insulated pink thermos mug. She didn't flinch. He looked at the after-action report filed twenty years before in Afghanistan. The signature at the bottom was Lieutenant Running Bear.

A few minutes later, Oz laid a plate of cold cuts next to the washed and refilled thermos mug. "You need to eat more than just pork rinds."

The response comprised a mumbled, mindless, "Yeah. Thanks."

Oz's eyelids lowered. "Your mother and father are in town. They just called from the hotel. They're on their way over to take you to the wedding in Berkeley."

"Okay. Thanks."

He shuttered his right eye. "And Nash just went to work for Homeland Security because Powder couldn't work in the field anymore."

Her hand waved loosely in the air. "Okay."

He turned and took a step away. "And PGE said the power would be off for only four days. So we're moving the bodies to a hospital with its own power and then shutting down the building. We'll get you a hotel or something."

He almost made it to the break room.

"Wait. What? What's wrong with Powder?"

He looked back. "I don't know. She didn't say." Turning, he stepped quickly into the autopsy lab.

As Muna turned the corner, Mike and Oz were already leaning against the bank of cadaver storage drawers, sipping their coffees. Mike arched one eyebrow.

She stood in the door—caught.

"So there's nothing wrong with Powder and Nash didn't change jobs." She scrunched the left side of her face. "And there was something about my parents... Okay. You have my attention now. What?"

Oz sipped his coffee and slowly blinked. His voice was more avuncular than his usual academic. "Care to explain what is so all-consuming about decades-old Department of Defense records?"

Mike held the back of his hand to Oz's chest. "Hold on. Let's go all the way back to the grumpy invasion after the Olympics."

An angry storm swept slowly across Muna's face. This wasn't

work interrogation. This was a family intervention. An invasion into personal territory her parents could never go, because of culture, but these two meant a different culture. This wasn't men on the floor of a mosque and women in hijabs sitting in the balcony. Here was thermal nuclear pork rinds. Shooting barefoot in Hello Kitty pajamas and a flak jacket, next to men in irreverent scrubs and flip-flops. A black man braiding her hair while he told her stories of braiding his father's horses' tails. Dad and Uncle jokes she secretly transcribed and sent anonymously to the boys at Deep Six. Or falling asleep at her computer, only to wake up hours later with a blanket over her. Having a kick-ass Paiute big sister, and a fuzzy-faced little sister who was no less ass-kicking. This was about having applied for a job and her life turning out beyond anything she could have imagined. Right down to a dummy in a space suit now keeping her company in the office.

Her shoulders slumped as she backed up to the doorjamb and slid to the floor.

She didn't want to cry. It wasn't about crying—but it hurt.

Muna sniffed, long and wet. "I'm sorry." Her knees rose, and she hung her arms on them, dangling her hands. "I've been a butthead. I just didn't know how to snap out of it. We took fifth place as a team. But I wasn't even the best in our team. And it wasn't about the weird headgear for better targeting or any equipment. Just seriously great shooters. The Yusuf guy from Türkiye. He walks in like he's bored and ready to order a venti espresso just to wake up—and rips off nines and tens like I eat rinds. And the chick... she's in a whole different universe."

Oz sipped the last of his coffee. "But what is their job? Shooting, or something else like you?"

"I overheard she runs a thousand rounds through a 9mm every day. I saw her hands. She had scars on her hands. Scars. Real honest to gosh, scars. But it wasn't that..." Her lips furled as she thought and then looked to one side. "I just hate losing."

She chewed on her lower lip. "I was getting adjusted. I remembered one of our high school students. He was valedictorian or close. Really smart. He ran cross-country. There were a lot of blue ribbons and trophies. But we were in a small school and competed with other parochial-type schools… Then he went away to college on a scholarship to George Washington. I heard later he ran next to last in track and was on academic probation by Christmas. The next I heard, he had slipped into obscurity by joining the Air Force."

She looked up at the two men. Her eyes flooded and reddened.

Mike's eyes slowly blinked over the three beats of his heart. His voice softened. "You said you almost adjusted or resolved… what happened?"

Muna wiped the heel of her hand over her eyes and then wiped her nose wetly along the sleeve of her starched white shirt. She shrugged.

Oz realized it was the white shirt that was different. No appointments—only office work. But she had dressed for the field. "We have nothing but time. It's Muna day."

Muna glanced back at the sound of the phone ringing. She realized the phone had rung several times. Neither of the men moved to pick it up. The recording answered. She realized they truly were about her… her family.

"Nash."

Mike leaned forward and placed his empty mug on the autopsy table. "What about Nash?"

She looked at his face. The man who had taken her into his sanctum sanctorum, taught her his craft, shared his knowledge, and space with her. Not once had he asked her to give up anything. "I've always done her research. Her go-to—her person. Her backup."

Oz's voice flowed softly from under the large white mustache. "I hear a but in there."

"She called Ming instead."

9

BUSH IS BUSH, NOTHING MORE

Nash stood in the doorway—looking out at the street creeping past. Even the rare car seemed to be weary from the heat. The nose pushed against her crossed legs. Nash looked down and waved her hand toward the sidewalk. "Go ahead. Go run around. Show me how this heat doesn't bother you."

Powder pushed her nose at Nash's leg.

"What? You can't go pee by yourself? You're a big girl. Or do you need me to find a plastic bag?" Nash smirked as she pulled some latex gloves out of her back pocket. "Hah. Fooled ya. I have gloves." She uncrossed her legs and let Powder out the door.

The two stopped between the two SUVs. Powder squatted.

"You have no shame. What is Zap going to think of you defecating next to his truck?"

"Same as I think of most tourists wandering around pueblos, taking pictures they'll never look at again. Or buy rugs they hang on their walls instead of using." Nash looked back at the man with a piece of paper in his hand. The black shirt still looked starched, like it was barely more than cool in the sunshine. He held up the paper. "I've got her phone number when you want to go down."

Nash stooped as Powder walked away. Standing, she peeled the glove, so it became a bag for the poop. "Let's do the interviews first. Work before play."

He nodded and turned back into the office with no air-conditioning.

Nash stepped into the office, holding up the inverted glove. "Where can I…"

Zap pointed at the trash can next to his desk. "Trash goes out tonight." He shrugged. "I don't smell most things other people find wéh."

"Way?"

He looked at her, and his face cleared as he bounced his small wad of keys. "Wéh. W-e-h. It means nasty or disgusting. Much about our jobs to other people."

Nash snorted softly. "It's why they pay us the big bucks. White guy or… first?"

Zap grimaced. "I have a feeling. Let's go see the white guy before he starts day drinking."

"Good call."

Developers built the neighborhood less than twenty years earlier. If the house sat in parts of the upper Midwest, Nash knew the sand around the house would be an acre of lawn requiring at least two hours and three beers on a riding lawnmower. The single tree and yellow geraniums in the Midwest front yard, where here was a stunted saguaro cactus with a single arm, and two large barrel cacti.

Nash pointed at the barrels. "Aren't those protected?"

Zap shrugged. "All the cacti are protected on federal, state, and tribal lands. If you're caught removing them, the sentence…"

The front door opened. The t-shirted and gym-shorted man walked out barefoot. "Imprisonment for up to ten years is possible, thirty if you brought two or more friends. Which is why we bring the local law when we plant our sprouts." He pointed back at the door. "I have a camera and microphone." He held out his hand. "Mac. Mac Richardson. But you're probably here about the heist."

Nash shook his hand. "Your saguaro is missing an arm."

The man winced. "Yeah, it's one risk of trying to bonsai a cactus. They don't grow right. After ten years, I gave up and just stuck Prickly Pete out here. He's looking better, but I don't give the second arm much hope."

"You raise cactus…"

He chuckled softly as he looked around the wide-open neighborhood. "Around here, it's a lot more successful than orchids or cymbidiums."

Nash held out her finger. "Cymbidiums… poor man's orchids."

The guy laughed. "I haven't heard that term in a long time. But I guess in a way it's true. Cymbidiums you can do pretty well with in your house if you keep the temperatures in range. But orchids…" He shook his head. "Hot house only. Or around here, it would require a monster ton of air-conditioning. I don't miss them."

"You used to raise them?"

"I tended the greenhouses at the college. It was work study. I needed work so I could study. I was going to be an English teacher. But life changed."

"And you ride in the back of an armored car."

"Until I get my certification as a paralegal. There's a demand in the immigration system. My wife is an immigration judge. We're both bi-lingual, so I'd start higher, but even that's bullshit."

Nash looked back at Zap. The man was stoic and just listening. She looked back at the man in the smudged white T-shirt. "Why bullshit?"

"We speak Spanish. My wife is Castilian. Her parents came from Spain. I speak Southern California Mexican Spanish, which really isn't the same as any Mexican south of the tip of Baja or Ixtapa. They speak Mexican. People from Colombia, Venezuela, Guatemala, Nicaragua, and other countries are crossing the border. So they all speak their own form of Spanish. So when you're dealing with legal matters, precise words matter. In East Los Angeles, we drove a Chebby—with a B. But in Orange County, they drove Chevies. And in the nice sections of Mexico City, they might drive a Chevrolet." He rolled his eyes. "Nah. I'm just kidding about MC. There, they drive body armored Mercedes G Wagons. Or Suburbans. It depends on how high up the cartel chain they are. I just made some coffee. Do you guys want any? Either way, I need to keep packing seeds. The mailman will be here soon." He fished the air with his hand and walked back into the house.

Nash looked at Zap. The deputy shrugged and held out his hand toward the door.

"Just close the front door and come on through."

They followed the voice to the large, covered patio in the back. Rows and rows of tables lined the space, almost the size of the house. Each table stood filled with rows and rows of small plastic square pots with a single barrel cactus.

The man scratched his messy short hair. "Ten thousand eight hundred. Give or take a few dozen. The pots we make out of shredded documents and newspaper. They're good for about five years on the tables, but once we stick them in the desert, they'll break down and become part of the dirt in two. The Fishhook cactus doesn't like to have their roots disturbed once they get established. Each seed begins its life in its own pot. Next year, we'll plant them all over the desert and start all over again. But right now…" He glowed like a proud parent. "They're an amazing sight."

Nash stepped closer. "So, what are you mailing?"

He smiled. "About five million seeds." He turned and fished a small envelope off the table. The tan envelope reminded Nash of the one her replacement dog tags came in. Mac opened the envelope and poured out a large thumbprint of black pinpoints into his open hand. "This is a thousand seeds. With about a hundred extra, just because it's so damn hard to count them." He pointed at a small electronic scale. "One gram is what I ship. Fifty bucks includes the shipping and handling." He held up an addressed envelope.

"And you ship them… where?"

"All over the southwest. Some grow for nurseries, but most do this." He pointed at the rows of little cacti. "Renewal of the ecosystem. The Fishhook in the wild only lasts about twenty to a hundred years. But drought and floods can wreak havoc on them. Then there are the pirates. And the social media idiots who found out you can eat the red fruit. So they get pissed when they get stuck and kick and destroy the cactus." He looked up from his passion. "Oh. I offered you coffee..."

Nash held up her palms. "We're good. But we need to talk about the robbery."

He pointed at the scale. "Can I...?"

Nash shrugged. "As long as you can work and talk at the same time."

He turned and opened an envelope and stuck it in a stand that held the mouth open. Taking a small white plastic spoon, he dipped it into a half-pint canning jar full of microscopic seeds and then poured it into the waiting envelope. Sealing the envelope, he stacked it in a half-full Velveeta box and started over.

"There's not much to tell. Amir and I knew something was up when the driver turned the truck off. They're never allowed to turn the truck off. When I peeked out of the back window, the guy was putting something up to the door. Next thing I knew, something hit my hip." He pulled his gym shorts down to show the large bruise surrounding the four-inch square bandage. "It spun me around, and the next thing I knew, the guy was pulling me out of the truck. They motioned for us to lie on the ground and face away from the truck. They pulled the money out and put it into some black bags. Then an SUV, I think it was a Ford, drove up. They loaded up and drove off. I think if I had a stopwatch, I'd guess start to finish in under five minutes."

Nash blinked a few times. "Did you get a look at them?"

Mac shook his head as he filled another envelope. "They were wearing like gas masks. Except they didn't cover their eyes. Dark hair, black eyes, and olive skin. Middle Eastern. More like Iranian than Lebanese. Maybe Turkish or Kurd. But not the lighter skin like Palestinians or Egyptians." He looked up. "In L.A. and Orange County, we had all of them… and I like ethnic food more than I would eat fast food or a burger." He shrugged. "I'm just sayin' shawarma tastes better than a burger and fries."

Nash chuckled. "I'm not arguing. Your partner…?"

"Amir? I don't know much about him. He just started with us about two weeks ago. Quiet guy. He came, he worked, he went home." He shrugged. "Some people are like that. Some people talk too much, and you want to gag them. But at the end, you get a paycheck and go home."

"How was his English?"

The man straightened. "Like he'd been in the country for several years. But there's still that accent, and the grammar is broken. You know what I mean?"

Nash nodded. "Yeah, the prepositions become past participles or verbs."

He turned around too fast and sprayed tiny black dots across hundreds of little pots and Nash. "Oops. Sorry about that. But you understand. Some people are here for a year and really work on their language. And others… can be here for decades and never get a grasp on it."

Zap moaned. "And then there are those born here and die old, having never tried."

The man looked back at the deputy like he had suddenly appeared. "Yeah. Kind of like that."

Nash pulled out her business card and laid it next to the stack of sticker addressed and stamped envelopes. "If you think of anything more. Call my office. They can reach out to me here in the field."

He looked at the card. "D.C. You must have a large territory."

Zap snorted. "To the moon and back."

Mac frowned at the strange reference.

Nash waved him down. "Ignore it. We have some spaceman

history together." She pointed at the envelopes and baby cacti. "Keep up the good work. Our forests and deserts need our help."

"Yeah. Smokey isn't alone. The struggle is real." The man held up a peace sign of two fingers.

As they climbed into the SUV, Zap mussed as he buckled his seat belt. "Do you think the guy smoked any of those seeds?"

Nash grimaced with an open mouth as she ran her hand over Powder's head and neck. "Powder would have triggered. I think he's that way just from contact with all those prickles. But he's not wrong. The deserts are dying and need a lot more help than just more cacti." She started the truck. "Let's go find Amir."

10

CHASING SAND

NASH CHUCKLED at the rock-chucking distance between houses she had grown up with. At least with her childhood distances, there was a reasonable chance of hitting a tree with the rock. The years of living on top of other people, under others, and sharing the floor with three other condominiums had jaded her toward having neighbors. It was days like these that reminded her about how a lot of the country lives.

The house probably looked worn out right after its 1960s construction. When the hippies dreamed of land, sun, and not much else. The oil embargo of 1973 had changed all of that. Housing tracts springing up across the Southwest froze in the heat of a gas shortage, which turned to a lack of jobs, and the dreams of the Southwest desert withered and died.

The sunbaked door was visibly warped an inch at the top and a finger's distance at the threshold. But the lock held the middle firmly to the doorjamb. The three floating panels split before the Middle East disrupted the American dream and led to the towers falling.

Zap knocked again.

Nash leaned over and looked over her dark glasses. Looking

through the half-inch crack in the center board didn't show her much, but at least she could see there wasn't anyone quietly hiding behind the door. The white floor tiles lead into a living room carpeted in what looked like long green shag. The short hall turned right into the rest of what Nash had estimated as a three-bedroom house.

"They're not there."

Zap and Nash turned at the sound of the man's voice.

The balding man with a walrus mustache stood at the end of the walkway near the street. What remained of his sleeveless T-shirt had holes sprouting curls of hair. The shorts had been some kind of cargo shorts before the pockets committed suicide into embarrassing shards of hanging torn cloth. The toes hung out of the ends of the rubber Hawaiian slippers. His right hand dug into a large bag of potato chips and drew out a chip that fit whole into his mouth. Small flakes of detritus fluffed out as he spoke. "They moved out in the middle of the night almost a week ago."

He devoured the next chip as he waved his hand at the house. "I thought they'd just gone to work early, but I had to chase down my dog behind their house. The back door is wide open. You can look for yourself. They're gone."

Nash glanced at Zap and then back at the neighbor. "Any idea where they might have gone?"

Two chips filled his mouth. The mouth closed and munched twice. "Nah. They were here for a few months. Kept to themselves. Never talked to any of us beyond the occasional hello and a wave."

Zap twitched his head. "How many lived here?"

A small stack shoveled into the furnace as the man took a couple of steps forward. Nash was aware of Powder leaning against her leg and agreed about not wanting the man close enough to verify the lack of hygiene.

"Three guys that I ever saw. Arabs. They didn't wear those towels on their heads, but the one guy wore the white skull cap thing you see some of the Hollywood types wear."

Nash lowered one eyelid behind her orange aviator glasses. "What did they drive?"

"The one guy drove the Honda thing. Kind of like an SUV, but smaller. He was a security guard or something. He wore a uniform, but I never got a close look, so I don't know where he worked. Mostly, I saw him get back in the late afternoon." He transferred two more chips as he thought. "The skull cap guy. He had the jeep. Painted desert camouflage like our stuff in Iraq. The other guy must have worked with him because they always came and went together. Maybe the one guy didn't know how to drive or something."

"License plates?"

The man looked in the large bag as if it might have a hole in the bottom. No more chips came out. "Plates? Sure. The Honda was just New Mexico. But the jeep had Arizona and Mexico plates. I figured they worked back and forth across the border or something. But I know the New Mexico tags had expired."

He noticed Nash's eyebrow raise.

"My dog gets out a lot. I have to catch him and drag him home." He half turned to wave the bag in the general direction of the tan house across the street. "I live over there."

Nash licked her lower lip. "Anything else you can remember about them?"

"Nah. That's pretty much it. Three guys, kept to themselves, never talked to any of the neighbors, and thems the cars they drove. I just came over to tell you the back door is wide open. You can see for yourselves." The bag waved toward the house. Nash wondered how long the man would mourn the emptiness and continue to carry the bag around.

Nash hitched up her imaginary belt buckle and nodded at Zap. "Shall we go see what's left?"

Zap nodded at the helpful citizen. "Thanks for your help. We'll take it from here."

A small square of concrete with crumbling edges gracing the

back of the house would fit a small table and a couple of chairs. The rest of the so-called yard was an acre of more rough sand, rocks, and an attempt to build some kind of edifice with larger stones. The sliding glass door was pushed back to the stops.

Nash frowned at the lack of a screen door. "No screen door? Don't you have bugs?"

Zap shrugged with a wan smirk. "We have hungry bats and lizards for that. Don't you have bats and lizards back home?"

Nash looked over the tops of her aviator glasses. "In Washington, D.C.? The lizards are in and around Congress, and they keep the bats in their belfries. And besides that, we have a doorman who would keep anything like that at bay." She took a fencer's stance with her index finger as the sword. Her reward was a soft smile. She could sense the eye roll behind the dark glasses.

Both removed their glasses and hung them from their shirt pockets as they stepped into the living room. A low coffee table sat close to the sofa. There seemed to be more legroom for the side chair. Neither looked comfortable, but more serviceable for a rental. The three objects looked as if movers had placed them there to be staged later, but never came.

Nash pointed at the table and four chairs in the area between the living room and the kitchen. The counter wrapped around and provided a higher eating area designated by the three stools under the overhang. They studied the four chairs pushed to the edges of all four sides of the faux black wood table.

Nash reached into her left back pocket and pulled out a wad of blue nitrile gloves. Splitting the wad in half, she handed Zap two of the gloves. "Just in case we need to dust." They both blew into each glove and absently slid them on as they continued scanning the dining room and kitchen.

Nash ran her one gloved finger along the surface of the table and noted the fine, darker trail. Bending over, she looked across the smooth black surface. The fine dust was uniform. She stepped to the counter and drew her finger along the laminate made to look like marble. Looking obliquely, she saw no trail. "They never touched the table. My guess is they ate at the coffee table. It was closer to what they experienced back home."

Zap harrumphed softly. "Eating in front of the television."

Nash shuddered her head. "In much of what I saw, there was no furniture. If anything, there were pillows to sit on. But the food was on the mats between everyone. Every meal was communal. You ate what you could reach, and what little they had was in reach for even a small child." She pointed at the counter and table. "This was a cultural thing."

She put her finger on a cabinet door to open it.

"Wait!"

Her finger hadn't moved, but her shoulders had twitched. She looked back around at Zap. He had his hand out. "What if they… You know. Those IED things. Bombs."

Her eyebrows ticked up a notch. "Booby traps?"

"Yeah. Those."

She stepped back. "Powder?" She frowned and listened. The sound of her nails on the ceramic tiles wasn't forthcoming. She turned and moved into the hall, looking toward the bedrooms. "Powder?"

The dog sat at the end of the hall. Two bedrooms lie off the hall in each direction. Nash and Zap approached and scanned the rooms.

"Show me, girl."

The dog granny crept into the smaller bedroom. At the sliding doors of the closet, she sat.

Nash hesitated to touch the door. "Boom-boom?"

Powder didn't move.

"Bang-bang?"

The front paws pushed up and down in her soft dance to a question.

Nash pulled her keychain out and found the tiny but bright flashlight. She shined it in the crack separating the sliding doors.

Nothing appeared to be a trip wire of any kind. She snapped her fingers and pointed toward the bedroom door. Powder moved and sat in the hall. Nash looked at Zap.

"What?" His face lit up. "Oh." He followed Powder's lead.

Nash flattened against the wall. Reaching her hand around the edge of the closet doorjamb, she moved the sliding door two inches. Then four more. And finally opened it halfway. Sticking the flashlight into the compartment, she looked. Then she stuck her head in. A moment later, she opened the other door and waved at Zap as she took out her phone and took a photo.

"Someone royally screwed the pooch." She gestured toward the lone 9mm bullet lying on the closet floor, next to the doors where they converged. "In a rush, and possibly in low light, it's the minor details that count."

"Maybe fingerprints?"

She smirked. "Got a bag in your pocket?"

He thought and held up his one finger. Turning, he moved back into the hall and disappeared. A moment later, he returned as he opened a zippered plastic sandwich bag. "The joys of a stocked rental property. If they don't use them, they don't think to remove them." He held out the bag.

Nash took the baggie and pushed her thumb and index finger against the bottom of the bag—inverting it. Grabbing the bullet at the edge of the rim and the tip of the slug, she lifted the bullet into the bag. Zipping it closed, she handed it to Zap.

He held up his palms. "I've never dusted anything. The closest I get is wiping things down in my house with a dirty T-shirt and throwing it in the wash." He looked at the stone face. "What? I'm a bachelor."

"No. You're good. I was just trying to remember how we dusted the condo."

"Don't you have a wife?"

Nash glared. "She dresses nicer. But she's no more domestic than I am." She frowned. "I think we have a vacuum cleaner."

"Maid?"

"I'll have to ask. We only got married twelve years ago." One eye closed as she looked up. "I think. The pandemic really screwed up remembering how long-ago things happened."

Zap laughed. "Time to have some flowers delivered."

Nash shook her head. "The doormen have us covered."

"Doorman? What do you live in? A Castle?"

Nash shrugged. "Kind of. It's a D.C. castle, but just as safe."

"And cleaned by magic."

Nash gave him a hard look. "Anything else, Powder?"

She didn't move. Nash shrugged. "Check the other room. I'll toss this bed and nightstand."

"Toss?"

"Have you ever searched a place before?"

"I don't have a remote or a TV. But no. I'm not a detective. I push paper and drive out and pick up strange bodies in ghost town saloons."

"Then pay attention. I only teach this class once." She walked to the side of the bed and the nightstand. "Check the lamp and shade. Then the drawers." She picked up the lamp and ran her finger inside the top of the shade. "Always work top to bottom. If something falls, and you miss it, you'll find it when you get to the bottom. But if you start at the bottom, you'll miss it because you think you already searched there." She turned over the lamp to show the bottom. Nothing.

She pulled the single drawer out of the cabinet. "Old school spy craft or old black and white movies would have you believe people tape important information or stuff to the bottom of the drawers. And it's possible. I've never seen it, but it's always good to check."

Standing the drawer on its back, she set it on the floor next to the lamp. She picked up the small cabinet and turned it over. "When it's light and small, check the bottom. Some lazy people just tip it back and slide the hundred thousand dollars underneath." She gave Zap a hard look. "Don't laugh. I worked on a case where they were counterfeiting twenties. We knew the press, the person, and when they were printing, but we couldn't find the plates. Then I noticed the trash can next to a desk never got fuller, and never got emptied. We were there three times in five days. The trash was always the same. I picked up the trash can."

Zap smiled. "They were under the trash can."

"Nope. Taped in the can's bottom, under the black plastic waste can liner. So even if a janitor tipped out the trash, they wouldn't find the plates. Now, about beds. Everything gets peeled gently and one at a time—cover each blanket, and then each sheet. Flip the mattress after. Then check the floor."

11

BETTER ZUNI THAN LATER

"No, sir. We tossed the entire house. All we found was a single 9mm bullet."

The deputy director mused. Nash figured he was trying to find something on his desk.

"I'll find it later and send it to your phone. So where to now?"

"Wind, sir."

"Wind?"

"As in, they appear to be in the wind. I did a rudimentary dusting of the kitchen, bathroom, and bedrooms. They had wiped everything. My guess is with a micro cloth and hydrogen peroxide."

Tony stalled. "Uh… why hydrogen peroxide?"

"When amateurs clean up a bloody mess, they use alcohol. It looks good, but when we use the black light, the blood trace glows like a whore in church. Alcohol is a decent cleaner. But you need oxygenation from peroxide to remove the DNA enzymes. Also, it doesn't leave a smell. But they had wiped the backs of two dining table chairs, but not the dining table. There was a thin film of dust on the table. So we knew they had wiped everything else."

"Where's the bullet?"

Nash looked to her right as the sheriff's Bronco eased into the parking lot. "I sent it to the boys in San Francisco. Mike and Oz will disassemble it, even without fingerprints, and tell me the copper mine and the mining date of the brass."

"So now what?"

Nash waved at Zap as he nosed his Bronco next to hers. "I've got a couple of things I need to run to the ground southwest of here. Then we'll see what the bullet says. Are you missing me?"

"Where's Powder?"

"Lying here next to my chair. She's bored to tears, or just soaking up the heat. Farmer's Almanac says to horde firewood deep and high. Long hard winter ahead."

He snickered. "And the tribal wise man says…?"

"Long hard winter—white man hordes firewood."

"Yup. Good old jokes never die, they just get retreaded. Keep me posted."

"Will do, sir. We'll talk tomorrow."

Zap eased out of his Bronco. "Yah hey?"

Nash smiled, but didn't stand. "Yah hey, Zap? You look like you got some sleep last night."

"Went to bed at sundown last night. Not a single dream. I think it was the cushy seat in your new Bronco. It didn't beat me up." He looked around, and his voice dropped to almost a whisper. "And I still haven't heard from my mother." He looked back at Nash.

Nash thought about the man as they held each other's gaze. Finally, she dipped her head. "That's a good thing. Maybe she's holding off until you and she can talk."

A slight snicker snuck out of the side of his mouth. "Talk would be a lot easier if she'd learn English."

Nash stood and looked down at the man. "It's not good medicine to talk ill of the dead."

"Well, she's the only dead that I know who wants to talk to me. It's a two-way road."

Nash growled. "There aren't any schools with ESL classes in the spirit world. Trust me, I've walked that road many times." She looked down at her olive-drab USMC T-shirt and running shorts. "I'm gonna change. Keep Powder company."

She didn't close the door to the room. "What are we having for breakfast today?"

Zap sat in the chair, looking out at the parking lot. He looked at the damage twenty years had done to his Bronco and the new shiny grill of the FBI unit. "I called that woman down in Zuni."

Nash stepped to the door in her leather pants and pulled her white shirt over her Level 3 body armor. "Yeah? What did she say?"

He glanced up. "She'll meet us at the airport at ten and lead us in. Her father isn't a simple guy to find. From what she said, he's somewhere out in the hills on the edge of the old reservation."

Nash walked out with her boots in her hand and sat in the other chair. Sticking her right foot into the boot, she peeked at Zap. "There's a new reservation?"

"Try no reservation. There's the Pueblo and the territory, but reservation is kind of a white man's term. Anyway, he's somewhere off the beaten track out there with the road runners and Gila monsters."

Nash paused, tying her boot. She glared at Zap. "Those are real?"

"So they say. Personally, my mother yammering at me from beyond the grave is more real—for me."

Nash cinched the second boot and sat up. "Breakfast?"

"White man's shack. It's on the way."

NASH WASN'T SURE ABOUT WHAT SHE HAD EXPECTED, but it was more than a mile of narrow runway and a small parking lot for planes to tie down. She kicked at one ring bolted to the asphalt. It flipped over, but stayed bolted. "Is this all a plane needs not to blow away?"

Zap shrugged. "I wouldn't know. I've never flown. But there are many of those, so I guess they work. But I guess it's BYOR."

Nash snickered. "Bring your own rope." She scanned the blank desert around the landing strip next to the highway. "Sounds like a Mel Brooks movie." She glanced at her large, orange-faced dive watch. "She must be on Indian time."

Powder ran out of the clump of brush and sat next to Nash's leg, looking back at where she had just been. She leaned against the leg.

Nash bent and stroked the side of Powder's head and neck. Her voice was only for her daughter. "What did you find, girl?"

Zap pushed on his lumbar as he leaned back. "Probably scared a rattlesnake in the bush. It would take a stupid rattler to move or strike out into this sunshine. They'll stay there until the sun goes down, then hunt before it becomes too cold to move."

The three turned at the rattle of a formerly red truck slowing and turning onto the minor road to the plane parking lot. Nash wondered if the trucks, other than their starting color, looked the same—worked hard, but cared for.

The woman with graying hair, pushed back with a beaded leather barrette and faded jean shirt, rolled to her elbows, and slowed to a stop beside them. "Yah hey. You must be Nash and Zapata. I'm Ona."

Nash stepped over. "We'll follow you."

The woman ticked her head. The conversation was over. Niceties were short in the heat.

As they drove slowly down the dusty road, Zap harrumphed. "Woman not marry. Too talky-talky. Man gets no quiet."

Nash chuckled and glanced over. "Why, Zap. Those classes are doing you some good. You just made an Indian joke."

He solemnly pointed ahead at the dust and peekaboo of brown red. "No joke. Woman not married. She no marry."

"Did you ask?"

He hung his head and growled. "No need. When she drove up, mother told me she's single and to ask her out."

Nash didn't have to understand Ute—but she understood mothers. She immediately knew what the battering conversations from his mother had all been about. There was no sign of any grandchildren.

The jean-clad arm hung out of the window, pointing. The aged truck never slowed down. But Nash saw the small hogan set on the small mesa. The rough road led around the cleaved barranca and over to the mesa where an even older truck sat in the sunshine.

Nash slowed and turned. "Yup. She'd talk your arm off. Never let you get a word in edgewise. You'd hate it. Want a divorce by the second child. Probably up and move out into your own hogan by the seventh kid."

Zap snorted softly. "Does your wife ever get to say anything?"

Nash turned off the truck. "More than your wife." She glared over and then smiled. "Ass."

The deputy smiled.

The old man moved around the wall of the hogan. It wasn't clear if the long pole was a cane, a walking stick, or just a long stick he was holding. He shaded his eyes from the bright sun and then waved them to come. Turning, he disappeared around to the other side of the hogan.

Nash leaned back against the seat. "Do we leave a trail of breadcrumbs and follow?"

Zap moaned. "Only brain problem, white children do that. We know the birds will eat everything, so we break twigs on the bushes, so they bend down. Nobody will look for us, anyway. We're too old and don't taste good. But just in case the old man is fast, we'd better catch up. Just because our first fella was lying on his back doesn't mean the next guy is going to be so easy. They don't always wait for us to creep up on them."

Nash drew the gold-tinted aviators down her nose. "Seriously, though. Are you okay with this?"

"I only hear my mother. You get to see both your parents and your uncle. Maybe this guy has answers for me, too. Maybe I'm not happy with her yammering on, but I could use some guidance about how to talk to her on my own terms."

Nash pulled the handle on her door. "Calling the shots can go a long way with being okay about a conversation—living or dead."

Zap bobbed his head as he stepped out of the Bronco. Slicking his hair back with his left hand, he notched his hat midway up his forehead and let it drop onto his head. "Time to learn things."

The old man was stirring a small pot over an even smaller fire. He pushed a few more twigs into the flame as he leaned forward to smell the aroma from the pot. As the three rounded the hogan, he never looked up. "Tea's almost ready."

Nash smirked. The man was an older version of Uncle. Or maybe just more weather cooked. The watery eyes moved from the pot to the dog and two people. "Yah hey."

Powder moved forward to the lounge across from the man. The man's face pulled back on one side. "Smart dog. Must be a reservation dog." He studied the two standing just under the shade of the stick-woven awning. His head bobbed as he pointed at the two chairs. His right hand picked up another stick, and he broke it into hand-width pieces, feeding one into the flames. "You found me, okay. Ona didn't have to lead you here like little children. You never know about people from the cities. They wander around like dehydrated rabbits. You tell them to turn left at the cactus, and they're turning at everything not moving—rock, bush, yucca, signpost, and don't even see the cactus."

Nash rumbled as she cleared her throat. "We let the dog drive."

The old man squinted his left eye and studied her with his right. "It took you long enough to get here."

"I've been busy." *State a cryptic statement and get a cryptic answer. Or smartass.*

The man, grabbing the remains of a leather glove, pinched the edge of the pot and poured tea into two mugs. He hesitated over the third and looked at Zap. "It's squaw tea, sage, chicory, lemon balm, and mint. It won't get you high, but you'll pee better for a day or two."

Zap shrugged, and the old man poured the rest into the third mug. Reaching into the pot, he pulled out a small packet and set it in the middle of the tiny fire. The smell was exotic and comfortingly homey at the same time.

Half standing, he held out the two mugs. "People call me Red like the color. I think when I was a little boy, I was redder. I don't know or care. Real name is Oren. I never knew what the bird looked like, so I never cared for the name." He softly landed back on the stick-woven chair. The seat was a worn piece of sheepskin with half the wool rubbed off.

Nash sipped on the tea and thought about the ingredients the man had recited. None grew within hundreds of miles from here. She smiled. She wasn't the only person Uncle mailed his gatherings to.

"Uncle told me you'd have answers for me about the spirit world."

Red rocked as his smile grew behind his mug. He hooked his right hand in the air. "I thought I recognized you. You were the one in a coma. You got blown up or something."

12

INFORMATION COMES AT A PRICE

THE YOUNG GIRL nervously chewed on her thumb, a habit she had yet to fully outgrow. It wasn't like still sucking her thumb, but it was close enough—when others could see. Though she was too old for such a habit, she couldn't help herself in moments like these, when she felt exposed and judged. But that didn't stop her from striving for acceptance among her peers.

Her uniform of the day was black leggings and a T-shirt, varying on what she was interested in that day—whether it be studying, reading, or gaming. Today's choice was a shirt featuring a raven picking at the head of a bust of Edgar Allan Poe, a nod to her secret love for all things, dark and mysterious. But it was as dark as she was willing to wear.

Sweet Thing was told she was an integral player on the team, but she always felt she was there because of her mother, an adjunct to bring your daughter to work.

She peeked across the computer room at her mother. Bunny was bent intently to her closest monitor. The other five screens displayed the rest of the shipping port nobody had dredged since the early 1950s—a dying port—passed over by the newer interstate and trucking. But shipping and energy changed. Now the port needed a major overhaul. Enlarged docking came at the cost of a deeper port for the larger ships. It was a dance Sweet Thing's mother loved to figure out. To her, it was a complicated recipe she loved to cook.

Sweet Thing ground her head around and looked at the glass-enclosed office. The two curved monitors reflected off the dark windows behind. Only the void of black in the middle confirmed what she already knew. Ming was in her office.

The small fingers of Sweet Thing's left hand played with the small brick of silver metal. Petey and Chips had created the block as a joke, but Sweet Thing had turned it into an amazing tool that she called her cricket. It monitored what Sweet Thing was working on, but if she carried it to another workstation or Ming's office, the Cricket brought Sweet Thing's work with it.

The original joke of walking up behind someone with the cube would change their monitors to the cricket's captured work—or funny video, meme, or game. Then the teams hadn't played with it for a few days, and the shining block sat abandoned in Chips' work-room. Sweet Thing quietly adopted the system and asked permission later; however, anyone whose monitor changed knew Sweet Thing had a question. She almost never watched funny videos, read memes, or played games other than team games.

Sweet Thing tapped her cricket softly on the window separating the large computer room from Ming's office.

Ming laughed. "I saw you coming, Sweet Thing. What's up?"

Sweet Thing rolled on her shoulder around the doorjamb. Ming frowned, already scanning the six monitor panels. Every panel was a government form. Some were in the Department of Defense. The other forms were outdated and covered immigration, marriage, adoption, and other Southern-related topics.

"Muna's dump from last night. I had Dana Point Marina and breakwater on my boards this morning, so I only started looking an hour ago. I don't see the thread she's trying to pull here."

Ming took a deep breath through her nose and slumped

forward. "Okay, let's take this chronologically. Where's your oldest chip in the pile?"

Sweet Thing pointed to the top right. "Department of Defense. The manifest. It's a C-130 with a bunch of those army vehicle things—semis and wrappers."

Ming smirked at the young girl's lack of understanding of steaming testosterone, metal, and diesel mixed with burned oil. "Ah, yes. Hummers and two MRAPS. Looks like they flew out of Fallujah on the... Okay, just after I gave up riding my tricycle." She grimaced at Sweet Thing. "What's connected to this?"

"Nothing. The next in the chronological order is this." She tapped the monitor. "A requisition for billeting." She scrunched her face and one eye in a shrug. "Whatever that is."

Ming swung her smile toward the young girl. "When we got you two off the street, where did you live?"

The blonde giggled and pointed at the ceiling, suggesting the fourth floor of barracks and bedrooms. "Heaven."

Ming chuckled. "And still is Heaven. But in the military, it's called billeting—a place to stay or sleep. In the military, they have communal bathrooms and a commissary nearby. We have private bathrooms and Chef's Café. But a delicate woman with comprehensive needs designed ours." Her eyebrows bounced at the younger girl's giggle. "So what's next?"

She pointed. One form lay on top of the other, interlaced.

Ming raised her head dramatically. "Ah, yes, the infamous form 4187." She leaned toward the screen. Reached out and slid the form sideways to reveal the next form. "With the conforming nefarious form AF77." She looked out of the side of her eye at Sweet Thing. "Did you look these up?"

Sweet Thing rolled her eyes. "Natch." Her eyes half closed as she recalled the information from an hour before. "This one," she tapped the screen, "the 4187 is a request for identification papers, and I think what they call dog tags." Her smile was hesitant, but reminded Ming they needed to have her and Bunny talk to an orthodontist.

"The Form 77 is a request from the Air Force to have this guy," she tapped the screen at the name, "temporarily assigned to duty and put on the payroll."

Ming leaned forward. "Abdul Aziz. Right. I offloaded a couple of things to Muna a few days ago. I didn't know why Nash even called me. Other than it was the middle of the night... and I was here and working..." She rolled her eyes at the younger blonde.

Sweet Thing rolled her eyes back in a mirror. "Well, Muna dumped this metric butt load back on us. But I'm just trying to make sense of it all. Like this guy, Aziz. He died, like, years ago. So what's the gives?"

Ming smirked at what she liked to believe was a younger her. Enthusiasm chopped up in the salad of frustration of information that isn't as linear as math. "You worked on the Mississippi bar last year. How much water passes the port of New Orleans every minute?"

The blue eyes half rolled into the upper lids. "Averaged over the year, there's one and a quarter billion gallons a day... which works out to sixteen point seven cubic meters a minute..."

Ming touched her hand to stop her. "A mind-boggling amount. Where does it start?"

"Lake Itasca in Minnesota. Well, technically, the small feeder rivers and streams building Lake Itasca. But most just say the lake itself. And it's not a small lake."

Ming pushed back into her large chair with her hands on the armrests. "But nobody stands on the bridge at the edge of the lake and points to the river to say this is the mighty Mississippi."

"Well, the confluence is nothing to sneeze at. In the winter, it's down to only ten feet deep, but in the spring, it can swell to eighteen and twenty feet deep." She pulled her head sideways and took on her southern accent. "It ain't no crick in the middle of the road."

Ming laughed at the corny accent. "Okay, but that's where the

Big Muddy starts." She leaned forward and tapped the two forms. "This is where this starts. But we need to know where it goes before it ends in a grave in..." She looked back at all the information. "Where is all this?"

"Oklahoma. Does Nash even go to Oklahoma?"

Ming shrugged. "I don't know. But...," she tapped the screen, "...this Mr. Aziz went there. Lived there and died there. Let's find out why, and then maybe we'll understand why Nash asked us, and Muna dumped it back on us."

"Oh... kay." Sweet Thing's shoulders slumped as she turned to leave with her cricket.

"And Sweet Thing?"

She turned. "Yeah."

"Not everything we do is the fun stuff. But everything we do is important, as is the next thing and the things we did before. It may not look important to us, but it is, or will be, to Nash. But clean up the timeline and any other research you and Bunny can add to the information, then send it back to Muna. Only Muna. Whatever the pissing match is between those two, they need to get their house in order, or we lock them out of communication with us. And if it comes to it, I'll send a truck and guys up to pull Chips' domain out of there. And if anyone asks, that is exactly what I said. We're not getting paid to be in the middle of anybody else's family crapping fest. Am I clear?"

"Yes, ma'am."

Ming smirked. "I'm not a ma'am. I work for a living."

Sweet Thing smirked as evilly as a fifteen-year-old could. "Gotcha, Commander."

Ming waved her away as she looked back at the small chat box that had never been silenced. Tree sat licking her lips with a map of the world behind her. The center of the map was Amsterdam. Ming knew the map intimately. It was the boardroom of their biggest client and early benefactor.

Tree leaned into her laptop and growled. "If you go all Detective

Pounds and Jazz on those two, I want to be in the room. And I also get to keep Powder in the divorce."

"I don't think she comes with the First-Class pass vest without the FBI attached."

The blonde shrugged and scratched at the tight bun on her head. "Then I guess I'll have to keep renting space on the corporate jets."

Ming leaned forward. "Where did you pick up that suit?"

"Last month in Singapore. You like?"

"It's badass, girl. And with your hair in the bun, you almost look as grown-up as Jazz."

The blonde laughed. "But not old like Frankie. But I found a new pair of leggings. They are a medieval suit of armor. Now we need Baby to design a retro logo of serfs digging a ditch or something for a T-shirt to match."

Ming looked around through the screen. "Where are Jun and the boys?"

"We finished the meeting about an hour ago. They went off to do some stuff, and then we're going out for a midnight dinner under the stars on a riverboat. I love summer here." She wagged her finger at the computer. "So what's the pissing match about with Nash and Muna?"

Ming sipped on her coffee mug. "I don't know. A few days ago, Nash called in the middle of the night. It must have been early there in Washington as well. She looked like someone had just hammered her out of a deep sleep. Her hair was also pulled apart. But anyway, she gave me a name and some locations in Oklahoma and Afghanistan and asked if I'd track the guy down and what had happened. He came over about the time she cycled out of the Marine Corps and into the FBI. He was her interpreter, but he's multilingual. So the Air Force made him a citizen and gave him a secret squirrel job. He married an American, worked for the Air Force or CIA—I'm not sure which—and died of cancer a couple of years ago."

"So, what did she want to know?"

"Beats me, girlfriend. She did the brain dump, and I haven't heard squat else. I got busy and pushed it over to Muna. She massaged the shit out of it and sent it back to me. Well, to be fair, she jacked it to Bunny, who fobbed it off to Sweet Thing. But, not to Nash."

Tree's eyes rolled into enormous. "Shit, girlfriend. That doesn't sound like Nash or Muna. You sure you weren't getting punked by Powder?"

"Right?"

"Bijslapen! I wouldn't touch that with a ten-pound kipper."

Ming giggled. "You've been hanging out with the Dutch boys too much. But, ya, dis is why I told Sweet Thing to work it up, add what she and Bunny can, and then ship it back to Muna. Let her play slap the sleeping bear on the butt by herself."

Tree pointed at Ming with a broad smile. "Time for some rijsttafel and plenty of shots of Jenevers."

Ming groaned. "Go play Dutch stuff with Jun, Nels, and the boys. Give them my best."

"Hell no, girlfriend. I use you as a threat to back up my sweetness. I keep reminding them who holds the keys to their computers, and you're only a short jet away."

"Short, my ass. It's twelve hours to Amsterdam. Go have fun. Mommy needs to beat the children down in the sweatshop."

"Tot ziens!"

13

LUCK ISN'T PLANNED

Clement and Sam sat in the lieutenant's stopped Bronco. The rise of the dirt track where they sat was slightly higher than the flat they were studying.

"Remember the time the Shoshone kid stole the headmaster's car?"

"The one who couldn't stop talking about his dad working at some casino in Reno? He stole the headmaster's car?"

Sam dipped his head. "They found the car out in the desert. The kid had taken the thing half apart with the tool kit in the trunk."

Clement frowned and looked over with his face screwed up. "That was him? He flunked almost every class. I remember the backs of his hands and arms were always raw where the nuns beat him with the rulers."

The lieutenant rocked as he looked out over the desert. "Yup. He works for Harrah's car museum. But this time, he's putting the cars back together."

Clement looked out across the desert at the mound of disturbed sand, brush, and a lot of truck tracks. He waved his hand and finger at the tracks. "So, what does the headmaster's car and the Shoshone have to do with this?"

The lieutenant squinted behind his dark glasses as he looked off to his left. "Do you remember when they brought the car back to the school?"

Clement snorted a chesty harrumph. "Which truck? The tow truck or the two pickups with all the doors, quarter panels, hoods, and seats?"

The lieutenant nodded rhythmically as the smirk grew on his right cheek. He looked over his dark glasses at his friend. "Sundown Towing doesn't have a four-wheel-drive flatbed tow truck." He waved his finger out toward the tracks in the sand. "When they towed the jeep from the front, the whole thing broke apart. I understand that even the engine came back on two trucks. They used the tow truck's boom to crane the parts into the back of some pickup trucks. I haven't seen the invoice, but from the two charges, it sounded like four trucks and seven hours of recovery towing. That's a lot for a little jeep."

Clement studied the mass of confusing tracks in the distance. Licking his lips, he blinked and ground his head around to face the officer. "Who's on the hook for all that?"

The two paused before the childhood snickering started.

Sam pulled the door handle and swung the door open with his boot. "Come on. Let's see if the white guys missed anything."

Clement nodded as he dropped to the sand. "We already know they missed the two and a half million in cash."

Sam adjusted his hat to shade his face as he walked around the front of the truck. "Let's not tell them just yet. The Albuquerque bank is supposed to get back to me this afternoon. It'll go to voicemail, so I'll pick it up when we get back to town. Let's scout the edges of the track. I want to see if anything fell off the trucks as they came out."

"You know it's shorter for them to go out the other way."

"Didn't you tell me the blown-in sand, down in the wash, was still fluffy?"

Clement winced. "Yeah. But not too fluffy for a four-wheel-drive and an experienced driver."

Sam chuckled. "There's a lot of difference between four-wheel-drive and four-hoof-drive. And there's nothing uglier than calling your competition to come pull you out of getting stuck in the sand on a government tow. They had both of their four-byes up here. And you know how prickly Cactus Towing can be."

"Jason or Justin?"

"Either. They're both half-triggered to pissed off most days than not. What's that?" The lieutenant pointed at a small piece of metal half buried in the middle of the track.

Clement moved it with his toe. "Bullet hole on the one side. It looks like a gas cover. They must have shot the hinge."

"Leave it for now. We'll pick it up on the way out."

The silence settled down on the two, hesitantly stepping as they scanned. Both had spent a lifetime hunting small game in the desert. Even something as small as a half-broken twig on a bush could lead to meat in the pot. As they circled back to the torn-up knoll where the jeep had sat that fateful day, their shadows stretched before them.

Clement stood with his hands on his hips as he looked back up the rise to the Bronco. "I don't suppose you'd have a screen or sieve in your rig, would you?"

Sam sneered. "Have you ever seen my arrowhead collection?"

Clement chuckled. "You mean all the confiscated contraband you gathered off those trophy hunting tourists? Sure. I've sat in your hogan a few times. Why?"

The lieutenant harrumphed. "How lucky do you think those city folk are—wandering around out there where the trading post told them to look?"

"Do they find anything?"

Sam pushed his hat back as he burped a sharp laugh. "Sure. And the kid from Flagstaff at the post is getting better at knapping some nice deer hunting arrowheads. But he still breaks too many smaller bird heads. So they throw them out in that area. The flatlanders are excited, but there are better-looking arrowheads at the post. So, they come back, show off the broken ones, and buy the nicer ones."

Clement hung his head and looked sideways at his friend. "And…"

"So, for most of my collection, I've found around the grinding holes. But you need to dig a few centuries down in the sand. It pays to have a kitchen screen or two in your truck."

"Why the grinding holes?"

"What do men do while the women shop?"

"Sit out front and swap lies?"

"So, when the women ground the seeds and nuts, the men spent their time knapping the arrowheads they would always need."

Clement's eyes closed as he rocked. "Are you saying you have a screen or two?"

"Sure. But, why?"

Clement smirked at his friend. "Don't you think it would be nice to figure out what all those modern arrowheads came from? And I don't mean the ones flattened and fucked up by shooting the shit out of the jeep; but the ones buried into the soft, forgiving sand."

Sam smiled and shrugged. "Let's go play tourist."

<hr>

NASH SCOWLED AT HER CELL PHONE.

Mina looked up from her laptop. "Oh, I've seen that ugly face before. Are we getting new phones again?"

Lele snickered as she looked up from the crossword puzzle. "You got new phones last year."

Nash held her hand out to Mina. "Let me try your phone."

"Who are you calling?"

"Deep Six. Well, Ming."

Mina smiled as she scrolled through the contacts and hit the number. The tone wasn't from the phone company, but the message of the nonworking number was consistent. "How could a multi-million-dollar company lose its phones?"

Nash leaned back. "Exactly. Who else do you have?"

Mina held her phone up. The tinny recording sounded weak from the small speaker. "Jazz." She pulled it back and tried another number.

"The number you have—"

"Frank." She frowned at her wife. "Any other suggestions?"

Nash looked at her phone for a moment and then called up the internet search. The listing for the bar had a phone number. Nash held her finger on the number, and the phone accessed and dialed.

"The number you—"

Nash looked at Lele. "Are you on our plan?"

"Nope. I still have the nurse's package through Assurance Wireless. Why?"

Nash grabbed at the air with her hand. "Do you have any of the Deep Six on speed dial?"

Lele pushed out her lower lip as her head vibrated. "No need. I could always just call you."

Nash looked up Ming's phone number and dialed Lele's phone. The phone only rang twice.

"Deep Six, this is Ming. How can I be of assistance?"

Nash growled. "Let's start with why your system blocked our phones."

The silence was only momentary. "Same reason the moving crew pulled Chips' computers from San Francisco."

Nash sat silent. She could feel her pulse in her neck. Her breathing was soft and slow. The counting in her head had reached past ten. "What happened?"

Nash could hear Ming's chair make the smallest of squeaks.

"When you say what happened, didn't you mean to ask who screwed the pooch and how deep it went?"

"I'm guessing it wasn't you or your team."

"Correct."

Nash sat silently as her eyes moved about the table to the back of Mina's laptop. Her eyes glanced up at the four eyes listening intently to her conversation. A conversation she knew would become extremely uncomfortable. She stood. "I need to walk the dog. I'll call you back in a couple."

"The system will block this phone number in ten minutes."

"Got it."

The snick was metallic, but sounded more final than usual.

Nash snapped her fingers. "We're going for a walk."

Mina gave her a hard look over the laptop, as Lele leaned back in her chair. "Kind of hard to do when your daughter is at the spa. You can't pick her up for another hour. Today is her shiatzu massage day."

Nash froze and then turned to the front door. "I'm going for a walk. I'll be back shortly."

She kept checking her watch as the elevator took its time opening and then creeping back to the ground floor. Her left hand pushed open the glass door as the young doorman turned. Nash's right hand thumbed the green icon to dial.

"Okay. How did I fuck up and how do I make it right?"

Ming slurped as the call caught her drinking coffee. "Mmm." She wiped her mouth with the heel of her hand and looked at her T-shirt. *Shit*. "You called me."

"I said I would."

"No. Over two weeks ago. In the middle of the night."

Nash turned the corner and hoped the traffic would be quieter. "Go on."

"Abdul Aziz? Tinker Air Base in Oklahoma? This is Nash, isn't it?"

"Of course it is."

"Well, the caller ID doesn't come back to you or even the Eastern Seaboard. It says Pueblo, Colorado, and the provider is an

NGO called Assurance Wireless. It provides phones for indigent and below-poverty people. What are you doing with this phone?"

"It also provides the phone service at a deep discount to nurses. It's Lele's phone. You blocked ours. I would have gone to the office and used a landline, but I figured you had the FBI blocked as well. What the fuck did I do?"

Ming's voice was calm. "Like I said. You called me."

"I've called you several times."

"Stick a pin in that for a moment. Is this guy Abdul Aziz, who is now dead, a person of interest for the FBI?"

Nash stopped and leaned against the brick wall of the alley. She had only scanned the wall for obvious filth. "I don't know. He was our company interpreter in the sandbox. I really don't have solid knowledge beyond that."

"But you knew he came to America, and the CIA granted him citizenship for his work in a mobile listening station aboard a C-130. Just that is top secret squirrel shit even I can't research."

Nash looked out of the alley at the afternoon traffic. "It's complicated."

"But you knew."

"No. Until the other night, I knew nothing. We shipped out, and he was waving us goodbye from the tarmac. That was the last I knew of Scissors."

Ming sipped her coffee. "Until the other night?"

"Until the other night. Yes."

"Who contacted you?"

Nash sighed. "That's where it gets complicated."

"How complicated can it get?"

"Scissors reached out."

"When you say scissors, you're talking about Abdul Aziz."

Nash looked down the alley and realized how sketchy the neighborhood she had walked into was. "He had a strange walk. He crossed his legs, misaligning his footprints. It looked like his shoes were on the wrong feet. Our guys and I adopted the scissor stride, so all the footprints just became a confusing mess. Look, what does this have to do with Aziz?"

"If the guy has been dead for two years, three months, and seven days. Explain how he reached out."

Nash scratched at her forehead and then smoothed her hand back over her hair. Her breathing was shorter. Her eyes jumped from the crushed beer can to the cigarette butt, to the lump of what might have been a rag. "He came to me in a dream."

"That's one vivid dream. Or should we say spirit walk?"

"It was. But how would you know?"

Ming blew out a small breath as her nails clicked on her keyboard. "You've got over four hundred air bases to choose from. But you nailed Tinker out of Oklahoma City. You told me he had married an American, and she had a granddaughter. Does any of this ring a bell?"

"Vaguely. I was still asleep. And I've been busy lately."

"Yes. I called you last week—many times. We didn't do what we did lightly. But your phone immediately went to voicemail."

"I was in a dead zone all week."

Ming sounded distracted. "Yes. You were near seven cell towers. I pinged your phone. It never moved, but it was off or died. Even your boss didn't know where you were. We wondered if you were alive. Lack of communication goes both ways."

"I was on the Zuni reservation. Well, on the edge of the reservation. It was very remote, and there was no power. So yes. My phone died. But back to Scissors. What did you find out?"

"Ah. And we finally get to the point."

Nash could sense the diminutive Asian was holding up her index finger. "Which is?"

Ming's voice took on a steel edge. "Was this research of an FBI concern or just casual Nash shit?"

Nash stepped out to the street and a cleaner sidewalk. "I don't know. It was something about his wife's granddaughter. He felt she was in trouble or something. Like I said, it was only a dream. But if this is going to cause a rift in our relationship—"

"You have a team member who does your research. You need to figure this out. She's your backup. She's your partner. When you need answers, your thumb should dial her... not stick it up your ass. I don't have time to get in the middle of whatever happened to you two to get a divorce. But if it ends up with her quitting the FBI, I'll be on the first charter to bring her home. And that's not a threat —it's a fact and a promise. Tree and I have already voted on it."

The metallic snick was sharp and final. Nash's head flinched at the sound. Her hand lowered, and she looked at the screen. Looking up, it took a minute to get her bearings. She was only a few blocks from the condo, but nothing looked familiar.

14

GETTING DARKER

THE WIND WAS GENTLE, but pure import from the Bering Sea. Russia's Kamchatka peninsula siphoned off any hint of warmth as the wind circled out of the Arctic Ocean. The Aleutian Islands of Alaska sniffed for anything they could use and passed it in a straight-line message of frozen death to the San Francisco Bay. Welcome to the deep freeze of summer. The icy rain lashed the windows facing west.

Nash studied Oz. The large mustache drooped on the left, and his hair, while usually fluffy and wild, lay flat on his head. Then she noticed the collar on his white dress shirt. No scrubs, T-shirt, or Hawaiian shirt. "What's going on out there, Oz? Muna's phone and station go straight to a cryptic voicemail directing back to the CJIS in West Virginia. It doesn't even loop to special operations?"

The man twitched his head. "I wish I knew. A week ago or so, I walked in and found a set of crates stacked next to Chips's tower of computers. But no Chips. She turned off all her computers. I've worked some creepy, spooky cases before, but the dark in that corner creeps me out."

"What did Muna say?"

He stood and started walking out of the autopsy lab and into the

95

office. "I'll show you. Maybe it makes sense to you." He stopped in front of Muna's computer empire, and then Nash watched the large finger fill the screen. Her phone flickered, and the scene was Muna's station. All six large monitors were grayish black except for the screen-filling FBI logo. The yellow sticky note was a physical piece of paper stuck in the middle of the logo on the lower center monitor. Oz pushed the phone in.

Gone home to think. Muna.

"Back up, Oz."

Nash could hear his voice; he had stuck his phone on speaker. "Yeah. That showed up the next day. But I never touch her computer."

The computer graphic of a yellow sticky note pulsed in the upper left corner of the top screen of the computer Muna used for the dark web. Nash thought about the meaning and placement of the icon. All their interconnected communications were always located in the upper right corner of the screen. Same for the D.C. office, same for their laptops, and same on her desk. Except this was on the other side of the screen.

"Tap on it."

Oz's phone pulled back to show the clean desktop. Not one keyboard or mouse.

Nash frowned. "Is there a roll-out tray mounted under the desktop?"

He lowered the phone to show the construction of the 1940s desk hadn't changed. Oz pulled open the drawers one by one. Paperwork, figurines, and a half-eaten bag of pork rinds. He found the bottom right drawer locked.

"That's her weapons drawer. Touch the icon on the screen."

He pointed the phone at the screen and touched the sticky note. The entire screen opened on a stacked document. Oz touched the edge of the next page, and it became the top.

"Stop. Move in a bit more." Nash read the Department of

Defense document and pressed her side button to screenshot the image. "Go back one, Oz."

"It must move this one to the bottom now." He touched the screen, and the edge became the top document.

Nash screenshot the image. "Okay, next. Next."

They walked through all seventeen of the documents.

"What is all this, Nash?"

"It's the research I asked Ming to do for me. But she sent it to Muna instead." She didn't mention if it was to the light side or the usual side of Muna's tower of information. She didn't want to guess why it was sitting on the dark web computer.

"Ah."

Nash had heard that *Ah* before. It didn't fall from her old teacher's mouth lightly. "Talk to me, Oz. You know more than you're telling. Don't make me come beat it out of you."

The image changed back to the usual FaceTime. She watched the perspective change as Oz sat in Muna's desk chair. "We may… well, you may have a problem. I say you because I think only you can fix or make some of it right."

Nash slowly lowered her boots off the corner of her desk. She noticed the quick peek of Donna, noting the shift. She leaned into the desk and changed the phone from FaceTime to standard phone for privacy. "What happened?"

"A couple of weeks ago, Muna was acting strange. No, even strange for Muna. Mike and I trapped her in the autopsy, and what we thought would just be a talk…" He cleared his throat. "It became an intervention of sorts. We knew the outcome of the Olympics weighed on her mind all winter, but we thought maybe she doubled down on target practice to do better next time."

"But that's not the problem."

"No. Just the setup. She doesn't make a big deal about winning. I mean, remember when she had you make us clear all the little trophies off her desk…"

"Yeah. But that's Muna. They raised her with ingrained humility. It's her nature."

"Exactly. But she's not that person anymore. All teasing aside, she emulates you. Braid, shirt, gun, leather pants, etcetera. Everything, but she wears different boots."

"Someone pointed it out to us."

Powder sat up and put her paw on Nash's leg. Nash shifted the phone to her left hand and stroked Powder's neck.

"Well, she idolizes you. Or at least looks up to you."

Nash squirmed at the obvious that she wished wasn't. "Look, Oz. I need to walk Powder. Can I call you back in a few minutes?"

"I'll be here. There's nothing else to do. It's San Francisco, cold as hell, and I'm all alone."

Nash frowned and looked toward Donna. It wasn't the weekend. "Where's Mike?"

"Mexico. He took a month off."

"Mike? He works on Christmas Day. He never takes time off."

Oz rumbled his throat. "Talk in a few. Go walk the little bladder."

Nash slid the phone into her pocket. Standing, she stepped over to Donna's desk, where she was holding a travel voucher.

"I don't need..." She stopped and thought for a moment. She was dealing with Donna. "Where am I going?"

Donna's smile was almost enough to show her teeth. "I'm sure you'll tell me when you know. Some days it can really be a crap shoot with you."

Nash dipped her head at the truth. "Meanwhile, can you get me information on Muna's parents in Philadelphia?"

Donna smirked as she tipped her head. "Sure... if they had moved. But I'll get you the contacts in Pittsburg. They live on Polish Hill, and he still drives for the metro. Go walk the dog. She's losing her patience. I'll have it when you get back." She held out the voucher.

Nash drew her breath in through her nose. "Hang on to it until I figure out what I'm doing."

"Yah hey, Indian."

Nash snickered. "You've obviously talked to Red."

"He visited the other night." Uncle groaned softly. "We talked like old times."

"He never leaves New Mexico, so he must have spirit-walked?"

"Nothing better. He said you need more training, but you're coming along like a ten-year-old should. How does your friend feel about the spirit world?"

"He doesn't see things, but I think he found a new friend in Red. We woke up one morning, and Zap was already making the fire for the tea. That reminds me—Red needs more sage. We kind of made a large dent in his stash. You might want to send him more Squaw tea while you're at it."

Uncle groaned again.

"What are you doing? Did I catch you sitting on the throne?"

"Nah. Junior and I went hunting yesterday. I'm just stretching out my legs and getting ready for when Junior gets off his macho trip and decides it's time to go down and soak in Bone Creek. I thought he was going to cry before we made it home."

Nash stooped and grabbed the poop. Turning the glove inside out, she pulled it off her hand. "You two need to dial back the macho shit. His back is older than you. And you're no spring chicken."

"It's all good fun. So why the call?"

"Just to thank you for turning me on to Red."

"And...?"

She thought about everything between Uncle and her. Growing up, he understood the world from a different viewpoint, as he was the only family member who could truly understand her. "Have you talked to Muna lately?"

"Not since the Olympics. Why?"

"I'm trying to find her."

"The boys in the city?"

"She left a note over a week ago and went dark."

His voice was soft. She could feel them sitting on the edge of the front porch when she was a little girl. Her new soft white moccasins were dangling over the edge. "Good luck with that, Indian."

"YOU COULD TRY HER FOLKS' PLACE IN PITTSBURG. BUT I have a feeling she didn't go there. Maybe down in Orange County with the Deep Six people."

Nash sat on the concrete bench in the atrium. Powder jumped up and lay down next to her, resting her head on Nash's thigh.

"No. I know that place would be a nonstarter. Until I work this out with Muna, we are persona non grata. I just don't know why they didn't pack Chips' stuff up before she left."

Oz snapped his finger. "Oh. Before I forget, the bullet slug they sent from New Mexico. They fired it from a short-barreled .30 caliber machine gun. Probably a mini gun. The striations showed deformation consistent with continually overheating the barrels. Unprofessionalism tends to hold the triggers down and run off all nine yards in a single expression of misplaced testosterone. But if it's a drug cartel, they have plenty of money to buy new machine guns. They only cost what, a hundred grand a pop?"

Nash watched the two men in black suits walk from the FBI side of the atrium to the Homeland side. *Homeland.* "What slug?"

"Wait a minute."

She listened to him rummage through paperwork, obviously piling up on the forensic desk. Mike's absence appeared longer than

Oz wanted to admit. As well as the neat filing freak in the front office.

"Here it is. Lieutenant Samuel Ochoa. He's with the Albuquerque sheriff's office. Huh. It wasn't you. I just assumed you were there for the same reason."

"What was it connected to?"

The slug went from Albuquerque to the Los Angeles major crimes lab. They just sent me the findings report. I'd guess since the slug came from a bizarre paramilitary case in the desert, they assumed you'd oversee it and sent reports to your West Coast branch.

Nash rolled her eyes and leaned back against the cool concrete wall. "So, who do I reach out to in Los Angeles?"

"I can't read the scribble. Why don't you reach out to Maggie? She'd know who to transfer you over to." The silence made Nash almost ask if he was still there. His usual booming voice dropped to a shy child. "What about Muna? Now I'm worrying. You're calling Deep Six for the research instead of Muna, which really shook her to the core. More than losing the Olympics."

"I'm getting her folks' contact information. If I need to, I'll drive up there. Trust me when I say I'll make this right. I don't know what I was thinking, or not thinking that night... but I'll make it right. And you're right, she's family. She is my person. I should have stayed more in touch after the Olympics. I just figured her radio silence was her needing quiet time to process."

"She did. But none of us saw that she also needed reassurance about her being important."

"Got it. But besides all the above, Powder and I need our wing person."

Oz's formality cracked. "Go find her."

15

TOO DARK TO SEE

REFUELING the Hellcat and lunch was outside a burger stand on the border of Pennsylvania. The tree offered shade and a grassy spot. And quiet. Far from the angry woman, who didn't understand her lack of control over another person's service dog, ended far behind her yappy mouth. The grass was a bonus for Powder.

The midweek drive was clear of any heavy traffic. Nash smirked as she parked against the curb twenty minutes sooner than the GPS on her phone had predicted.

Various colored flowers guarded the wide front porch from the small, neatly trimmed front yard. The iron chairs on the deep porch, Nash guessed, got painted the same dark green every spring. The tan brick house was western New England blue-collar. Humbly blending with the rest of the street. Even the yellow marigolds mirrored the ones across the street.

Nash raised her knuckle to knock on the wood of the screen door as the inner door opened. "Nash. How wonderful to see you." Mrs. Al-Faragi pushed open the screen door. "Please, come in."

Nash pointed at Powder, who was sitting next to her leg. "Your allergies…"

The woman wiped the air with her hand. "I am never allergic to family. Please, Powder, come bless my home. Come, come." Her waving hand became more demanding. "The neighbors will talk if you stay on the porch in this heat. Come."

Nash and Powder stepped into the quaint front room, where every piece seemed to tell a story. The well-worn couch bore the unmistakable mark of Mrs. al-Faragi's favorite spot, next to the knitting basket and the small end table. The stout brown leather recliner stood like a silent sentinel, flanked by its own matching end table, completing the room's cozy symmetry.

"Come. I'm in the kitchen preparing dinner. Ari will be home shortly. You two will stay for dinner, of course."

Nash found her protesting finger rising to empty air. Her mouth closed in a furled frustration.

"Does Powder like lamb? I'm making biryani."

"I didn't mean to stay. We just dropped by… Mrs. al-Faragi."

The woman fluttered one eye as she looked back. Her voice dropped into mother's mode. "Please, I told you in Paris, it's Nettie. And you were just in Pittsburg on what business?"

Nash could feel the woman channeling her dead Paiute mother. Nash sagged. "I wasn't."

The woman turned and moved the large glass bowl of water and rice to the sink. Washing her hand through the rice and water, she felt the texture of the rice-soaked water. "See. Isn't the truth easier than duplicity?" She looked up from washing the rice.

Nash rolled her eyes. "Muna never got away with anything, did she?"

Nettie poured the rice and water through a strainer. "If it was unimportant, I didn't ask or tell like her pork rinds. I left the bags where I found them. They never affected her grades or her beliefs. So why would I? But this isn't about Muna…" She turned around as her eyes narrowed. "Or is it?"

Nash clenched her lips and swallowed. "Yes."

The woman set the strainer in the sink and leaned her back

against the counter. Wiping her hands on her apron, she studied Nash. "What happened? Or does my husband need to be here?"

Nash tossed her head gently. "Maybe it's best if we keep this... dar mian zanan." Among us women.

Nettie's right hand floated to cover her mouth. "She's not..."

Nash put out her palm. "No. No. This isn't that kind of visit. I just need to find her. She left a cryptic note on her monitor a week ago about going home to think." Nash licked her lips. "I haven't talked to her since..."

Nettie's hand dropped as she rocked in understanding. "The Olympics. Yes. She was glad to see us, and we could tell the weight of not telling us about her shooting was lifted... but there was something else. And we didn't pry. But we could tell."

"Evidently, it weighed on her. And then I screwed..." Nash's eyes snapped wide. "I mean—"

Nettie smirked. "Screwed up? Or screwed the pooch?" She held her palm out toward Powder, lying on the linoleum floor. "Sorry, Powder. But yes, dear, I live in Pittsburg. I've heard the term before. I'm an adult. What did you do?" She turned the rice and water out into a strainer.

"It was the middle of the night. I needed some research done. It wouldn't be easy..."

Nettie dipped her head as she drooped her right eye. "Muna is your research person, yes?"

"Yes. And I should have left a message on her phone..."

Nettie turned and raked her fingers through the wet rice and ran more cold water as she continued to rake and wash the starch from the soaked rice. "I'm hearing a butt in there."

"I called Ming."

The woman turned off the cold water and stood calmly looking at the rice. As her eyes moved to study the backyard, the voice became as soft as the water dripping from the bottom of the strainer. "You took Muna's job away."

Nash's chest rose and settled with the weight of the statement. "Yes."

Nettie slowly turned. Her eyes tracked the floor and then looked up. "And you hoped she came home… here."

"Yes."

Nettie poured the rice into the large earthenware pot. "It makes sense… the only homes she's ever known were here and the FBI."

"And she's left there… Oz checked the dorm rooms. None of her clothes were there. She's decamped, in a tactical jacket and body armor, right down to her skivvies and Hello Kitty pajamas."

Nettie giggled with the back of her knuckles covering her mouth. "She still wears those?"

"Skivvies? I assume…" Nash winked and burped a laugh. "Every morning she would go down and shoot in her Hello Kitty pajamas, body armor, and barefoot or with the pink fuzzy slippers."

Nettie leaned against the counter with her knuckles at her smile. "I don't think I will ever get that image out of my mind. After watching her shoot at the games… it just seems so… incongruous."

Nash shrugged. "Her not wearing body armor under her Olympic uniform shirt surprised me. After getting her jaw broken and shot up in Colorado, I wouldn't have been surprised if she showered with her level three armor."

"Jaw broken?"

"Oops."

They both turned at the back door opening. The man in the bus driver's uniform looked up at the sight of a dog in his kitchen. "Nash. What a wonderful surprise. And… Powder? Did I get the name right?"

Nash nodded.

The man stepped to the sink and gave Nettie a peck on the cheek as he set his lunch box on the counter. "I'll unpack it later. Faghat zabaleh." Just trash.

Nettie patted his hand. "You remember Nash speaks Farsi, do you not?"

He looked at Nash like a shy schoolboy. "Sorry."

Nash shrugged. "I learned most of the cruder terms first. Trash was the second tour in the sandbox. When I had to pretend to be a lady or something."

He nodded his head up. "Ah, yes. The other life."

Nettie gently ground her face around in a circle. "Yes. Speaking of other lives. Nash and Powder are joining us for dinner. She was about to tell me about an important part of our daughter's other life... and it wasn't about computers." She leveled a hard eye at Nash.

Ari frowned. "Muna isn't here?"

Nettie pushed her finger on his shoulder. "No. Go wash up. We'll catch you up on everything over dinner."

Nettie leaned to her left to watch down the hall. At the sound of the bathroom door, she leaned back. "Except the broken jaw. What happened?"

Nash glanced at the entrance to the hall and understood that each family had their secrets. "Short answer. We got blown up and spent time in the hospital. Then we recovered and are still working on the case. Muna was closest to the double agent. She got shot, shot him, he pistol-whipped her, and broke her jaw. But she tracked him down and... well, let's just say, she did better than she did at the Olympics." Nash blinked as she waited for the mother's response.

Nettie bobbed her head once and turned for water from the faucet. "Good."

Nash grimaced. "Good?"

Nettie turned with the four-cup measure of water and poured it into the pot. "Yes. You don't practice every day to be good at something, and never use it. You speak Farsi. Did you use it?"

"As best as I could in Afghanistan. But speaking another language and shooting with deadly outcomes are different things."

"Are they?" She placed the meat in the rice and layered the vegetables. "I cook, and Muna does not. You speak Farsi and…?" She raised an eyebrow as she looked at Nash.

"Enough Spanish, Japanese, Russian, and Swahili to get in trouble. And enough Chinese to stay out of trouble with my wife and her mother."

"And do you shoot as well as my daughter?"

"Um…" Nash heard the bathroom door. "No. But I have my dog. And her nose is better than mine."

Nettie held out her open hands. "Well, there you go. I've never heard of a bomb-sniffing kitty cat."

Nash stifled a snort as Ari walked in. "But I've met a few attack cats."

Ari pulled open a drawer and pointed back over his shoulder at the conversation. "Never trust a cat. They have sixteen little razor knives and aren't beyond using them. I won't even get into those teeth."

Netti leaned toward Nash. "Ignore him. His sister had a cat when they were growing up. He's still mad that the cat would only sleep with her. But Abyssinians can be very fussy about who they are affectionate with. It's why the pharaohs kept them around to guard their palaces."

He counted out the silverware and looked back at Powder. "I'm guessing she doesn't need a fork or spoon. Knife?"

Nettie slapped the air near his shoulder. "Behave. Set the table, please. We have guests. Four places. Power eats like a civilized adult."

He grabbed four place mats and scurried from the spousal abuse. "How much news do I get?"

Nettie looked at the pot. "Half-hour, maybe a little more. Go watch David. I'll let you know."

Nash frowned at her watch and then at Nettie.

Nettie shrugged as she turned the lid on the pressure cooker. "David Muir. He tapes the news and watches it the next day." She plugged in the pot and pushed the buttons. "I love these pots. This used to cook for hours, but now… it comes up to temperature and then cooks for four minutes. Come, we can talk on the back patio. Would you like some iced tea? It's green tea, no caffeine."

"Sure. Please."

They settled under the awning. "You can sit on the swing so Powder can be with you." She held her hand out at the porch swing. "Muna used to love sleeping out here. She called it Pittsburg camping. We worried, but she ignored any talk of danger. I'd like to think of it as the innocence of youth. But I think sleeping out here meant more to her than the safety behind a locked door."

"Muna said it wasn't the best part of town…"

Nettie sipped on her tea. "But Pittsburg, in general, has some of the lowest crime rates on the entire Eastern Seaboard. We've had the occasional break-in or car stolen from the neighborhood, but overall, on this block, nothing. So what else do I need to know about my daughter?"

"Colorado was the second time she saved my life." Nash held the mother's gaze.

"And now… she's gone missing. Have you tried calling her phone?"

"A few times. When was the last time you spoke to her?"

"Last month. I called her yesterday. It went right to voicemail. But then, it usually does. She gets the message and calls back in a day or three. She's terribly busy. And she has the important job running the two older men and their important work with the dead bodies and all." Her face pulled down as her one eye rose with doubt.

Nash leaned back in the swing as she clawed her fingers in Powder's fur under the tactical vest. "Exactly."

16

BUT WHOSE BULLETS?

"I'LL BE HOME in two hours. Nettie made biryani, and it would have been rude to say no."

Mina sighed. "Biryani. Goat or lamb?"

Nash checked the mirrors. "I didn't ask. It wasn't roadkill."

"Was she there?"

"No. Nettie hasn't heard from her for almost a month. I'm guessing widespread radio silence. Even Oz said some days, Mike and he felt alone. The work got done… but…"

Mina rolled over. The sound of the phone changed. Nash smiled at Mina's unique sounds. "My sense says she's working on more than just the Olympics. Your calling Ming occurred as a final push. She'll surface. How much personal time has she accrued?"

Nash snorted as she took the off-ramp. "Probably more than a year. I don't know, and I'm damn sure not going to call HR. Technically, that would be Mike's job."

"Okay. Bring our daughter home. Lele and I changed the sheets today."

Nash remembered an esoteric conversation in the past year with someone else. "Just for clarification?"

"Yeah?"

"Who washes the sheets and clothes?"

Mina laughed. "We've been married for how long… and just now you're thinking to ask?"

"No. Someone asked several months ago."

"What did you tell them?"

"I told them we did the laundry on the third floor."

The silence was long. Nash almost asked Mina if she was still there, but she could hear the rustle of the sheets. The conversation was muted. "Hey, Lele? Is there a laundromat on the third floor?"

Nash snickered at the red light as she scratched Powder's neck. "Your mother is so silly."

The snicker came through the speakers in stereo.

Nash laughed. "What did she say?"

"She'd ask in the morning. Which part of silk, leather, or starched white cotton did you want to throw into a regular washing machine?"

THE QUIET OF THE BULL PEN ROOM WAS NASH'S favorite time of the afternoon. Summer, more than any other time of the year, stimulated agents to check out early to do some field research. It was the same research they hadn't done for the previous hours after the long lunch, but with some alcohol.

Nash initialed the box and closed the folder. Some days, the number of folders used for fewer than five sheets of paper amazed her. The entire case could be a memo. She threw the folder into her famous wire *out*-box and looked at the even more famous *in*-box. The dark stain of the oak stared back at her.

Checking the orange face of her DOXA watch, she tilted the seat back and rested the leather of her pants and boot on the corner of her desk. The sound of an office phone rang. Her eyes closed.

Donna's chair squeaked, its rare complaint of being tilted back. "It's your line, Nash."

Nash hung her arm over her eyes. "I'm out of the office."

"Suit yourself, but I'm not answering the bull pen line. My badge doesn't stretch that far."

The new agent's answer was barely more than a grumpy burp. Nash wanted to record him sometime and play it back to see if he dropped any of the syllables. His FBI Special Operations and Investigations unit seemed like what an ordinary person would consider asking "excuse me" to.

The man mumbled more and then hung up. "Coming your way, Nash."

Nash peeked out from under her arm. "I'm on my break."

"It's the deputy director of the office in Albuquerque. He sounded like his pants were on fire about you not getting back to him last week."

Nash straightened her arm and pointed a single finger at the ceiling.

"Exactly what I said. One week."

Nash's gaze jumped to the movement in her boss's office door. Commander K-BAR stood with his arms folded. "If he has to call me, I'm calling your wife."

Nash's arm slid from her head and landed on the phone. "Running Bear."

"This is Deputy Director Don Quixote of the Albuquerque field office. I'm getting sick and tired of tilting at the windmill of people who think they're more important than the little office stuck in the middle of the desert."

"You accepted the job. Where was your last posting?"

The quiet wasn't what she expected, but then she figured if you start with a smartass statement...

"Anchorage, Alaska. The left armpit of the northwest."

Nash closed her eyes as she lifted her left leg up and onto her right.

"Other than the cold, was it better than Bismarck, Montana?"

"Bismarck is in South Dakota. And yes, the heat is better than the food you can't get and the long dark."

Tony turned in his doorway. "If that's Don Quixote, tell him he still owes me dinner when he's in town."

Shit. Nash sat up and googled the Albuquerque roster. *Shit.* "Is this about the slug from a machine gun? The squints sent the report to the wrong coast. And Tony says you owe him dinner and a bottle of fifty-year-old scotch."

"Tell him to keep sitting on his thumb. I never go to D.C., and there's no such thing as a fifty-year-old."

"I guess I'll just have to have him back over to dinner and share my two-fifty." She hung up the phone. If the man was who he said he was, the next phone call would be on... The phone buzzed on Donna's desk. Nash noted the small single chuckle. But the redhead didn't answer the phone. It didn't buzz again.

Nash's phone vibrated on her desk. She flipped it over and looked at the caller ID. "Yah hey, Zap?"

"Yah hey, Nash. We found the money. Well, the guys down in ABQ did. Along with three bodies."

Nash crushed her forehead into her left hand. She spiked her elbow on the desk. "How much crap do you think the deputy director at the FBI in ABQ gets about his name?"

"No more than I do about little shoes. Zapateos Mateo. Why?"

"He's talking to my boss. I gave him crap and then hung up on him because I figured I was getting trolled or punked."

Zap chuckled. "He's probably used to it. Last Halloween, someone parked a donkey in his parking space. While everyone was laughing about the donkey, he walked into the office in a suit of armor with a lance in his hand. It was his second month in the Q. I don't have to deal with him, but I'm guessing he's got a sense of humor."

"So, where was the money?"

"The three guys had it in a jeep out in the desert. We figured they were making some kind of buy. But someone showed up and hosed them down with a few thousand rounds of thirty caliber."

Nash shifted her hand so she could peek at the deputy director talking to Donna. "Yeah, armor-piercing, high-pressure. We're guessing it got pushed out of a mini gun. But then you need to ask the twitchy question of who the hell has a helicopter outfitted with a mini gun or two. And is it a door gun or belly mount?"

Zap muttered something.

Nash frowned. "Did I just hear you say shit, Zap? I think those anger lessons are doing you wonders."

"Nah. I've been spending time with Red. His daughter is a bad influence. She's kind of like you, but swears a lot. Maybe if I up my game, she might have me over for dinner. Or let me ride one of her horses."

Nash chuckled. "Ride her horse. Is that a euphemism for something else?

"Man, you women have nasty minds. No. She has Appaloosa ponies. You should try them sometime."

"I do occasionally. My wife has a hot-rodded Mustang. If we don't take her car, we take my Hellcat. Either way, we kill a lot of dinosaurs. So, what happens next with the three bodies and money?"

"You tell me. My scorecard says the bank robbery is FBI. People killed on a reservation are FBI. Acts of terrorism are FBI and Homeland Security. They weren't close enough to the Mexico border, so Homeland is only iffy. But they might come sniffing around with the idea of machine guns mounted on airships on civilian land. What's your take?"

Nash let her face slip down in her hand to look at the top of her desk. "What part of the shitshow was straightforward?"

"Well, an armored truck heist is pretty straightforward... but with bombs and an inside guy..."

Nash rocked her head in her hand. "A couple of years ago, my boss and I had just finished probing a bombing range. He turned to me and asked if I always got the strange cases."

Zap cleared his throat. "If it's a bombing range, isn't it normal for bombs to be there?"

"Sure. But the two twenty-six cubic foot freezers that were full of frozen dead bodies... well, it's not your usual murder."

"What were they doing in a bombing range?"

"Certain people consider cars, freezers, campers, or anything else in a marked bombing range as fair game for a few rockets or two hundred pounders. Duds or boom-booms, they'll still fuck something up if they hit. In the sandbox, we watched an F-15 who had run out of ammo, wind it up to supersonic, and fly about forty feet over a contingent of ISIS. He caught a few holes, but the fighters turned to red mist."

Zap mumbled something under his breath. "So, do you think you're going to draw the short straw again?"

"My name is already on the folder. The Albuquerque deputy director just talked to my boss. I suspect that his secretary will hold up my travel voucher any minute now. I'll pick up the Bronco again in ABQ and call you. Maybe we can spend a little evening time with Red. Well, I'll talk with Red. You can go ride the little pony with his daughter."

"I like my desk, but I'm intrigued where this case might go. When the FBI comes knocking, I need to hang a note on the door and heed the call. But the thought of machine guns in helicopters scares the heck out of me."

"Too scared to ride shotgun?"

"I don't think a shotgun would make it a fair fight. But I'm game. I'll just pack a spare set of pants."

"They help, Indian. They help. Yah hey." Nash thumbed the phone and glanced over at Donna. Her head twitched toward the door.

Nash looked down at Powder, sprawled on her side, snoring. Even her ardent wing girl was no help.

Nash strolled into the deputy director's office and slumped into the chair. "They think we'll need to K-BAR the shooting site."

Tony's one eyebrow raised, but his attention was still on what he was reading on his computer. Nash waited.

"What does high-pressure mean? I know what armor means. Well, I think I do. But high-pressure?" He looked over at Nash.

"In larger calibers, like thirty and up, there are low-pressure loads and high-pressure loads. The load is the gunpowder, what it's made of, and how much. Fast-burning powder, and with a lot in the shell, results in a higher speed, or what we call muzzle velocity. In this case, supersonic. Combined with the armor jacket, it is for penetrating any and everything. Big armor, like on tanks and MRAPs, resists penetration, so standard full metal jacketed rounds, such as copper rounds, cannot penetrate it. Then there are armor-piercing bullets that have a copper jacket but with a soft lead tip. The tip splats and stops the jacket, which forms a brace for the hardened center, which does the actual piercing. In the first Desert Storm, they had tank rounds with a core of depleted uranium. The radiation would do its own damage, but over a long time. But the real reason was for the uranium core to penetrate through the tank armor. But doing so heats the uranium to thousands of degrees by the time it enters the enemy vehicle. Instantly turning the air in the vehicle into an incinerator, leaving the tank intact. Because we wanted to know who supplied the weapons."

"So, just a fancy way of saying supersonic. Don said there were thousands of rounds…"

Nash nodded slowly. "Tore the hell out of a jeep and three guys who robbed the armored truck in Ship Rock. My guy says the money is on the three who were there to buy something expensive but got ambushed by a helicopter outfitted with mini guns. Not the usual for cartel or drugs."

"Sounds like a Nash case. Keep me posted. Donna will have your travel vouchers. And for god's sake, don't go off somewhere else and start a gang war like you did in Orange County."

Nash didn't move.

The deputy director frowned. "Is there something else?"

"A week ago, Muna left a Post-it note on her monitor. It said she went home. Nobody has talked to her since."

"Her folks are in…"

"Pittsburg. I drove up yesterday. They haven't spoken to her in the last month."

"Her cell phone?"

"Off. I'd have it pinged, but she probably has that blocked as well."

Tony steepled his fingers at his mouth. "What about your friends in—"

Nash shook her head. "It's complicated, but she's not there."

"I'd reach out… but I don't know who to."

"Same."

17

DO YOU SPEAK MUSKOGEE?

NASH HAD FORGOTTEN what it sounded like flying military hops in a C-130 cargo plane. Or that she had to get up and get her own coffee.

She peered out the window at the patchwork below. *At least there's coffee.* A step above instant granules, but coffee. She thumbed through the series of screenshots. Pinching them open and closed, she worked from Scissors stowing away to get to America, to working for the CIA and Air Force Intelligence. She smiled— remembering how smooth he was at talking the team in and out of situations.

She sipped on the old-school paper cup as she read through the document for a green card. Nytah May Woods. Mother of two, and grandmother of one. Nita Anne Cloutier, born 2009. *Sweet sixteen and already in trouble?* Nash looked up as the pilot called for landing stations. Belts and braces. The pilot would learn about slicking on a landing when the plane had a company name on the side of the fuselage. The teeth-jarring double-hit confirmed the pilot had a few years left until retirement. She didn't look out the window as they taxied. Air Bases, domestically, all looked the same. Gray and drab.

As they stepped out of the back end of the plane, a woman in a ramp rat uniform pulled up, driving a forklift with a train of flat trailers behind. "You're the two FBI agents?"

Nash squinted at the sun behind the woman's head. She flashed her ID wallet.

The young brunette snickered and pointed. "I spotted the badge on your boss from the shack. Well, okay, when she cleared the tail. If you don't mind a trailer, I can give you a lift to the K-9 toilet and then the human toilet... er... command shack. Rumor has it you need a lift into town to the FBI office. They don't have one out here. We only rate secret squirrels and other whack stuff, ma'am." Her salute could have passed for wiping her brow of sweat. The heat helped carry the illusion.

"How long have you been here?"

"Since oh-four-twenty this morn... oh. This was my first duty station. Six years, ma'am."

Nash laid her head over to the side as she shifted away from the sun. "How well did you know any of the Tube Rats?"

"The Squawk and Die club? A few. They're mostly vampires. But a few are nice, ma'am. Why?"

"Anyone nicknamed Scissors?"

"Grandpa? Sure. He was a real human. His wife used to host the base Christmas Party, Fourth of July, and something about reading. I heard it was for kids, but there were some of the force who learned a lot from her and the other teachers. A lot of us thought they should have held his funeral here on base. They touched a lot of lives. Did you know him?"

"Afghanistan. I'm looking for his wife."

She pointed at the first trailer. "Get on. I'll introduce you to the right person. Your kid's potty is next door."

The colonel's darkened armpits almost touched the middle of his back. Grease marks camouflaged the front. His crooked smile matched the shirt buttoned wrong. But the trimmed mustache still matched the black curls on top. The brown eyes twinkled at the mention of Aziz.

His hands were busy in the middle of a large rag, as greasy as his hands. "I'd shake, but unless you're here to help me fit the heads back on the Piper…"

Nash held up her palms. "We're good. I always leave the grease to those who understand it. I track, point, and shoot. Did in the Corp, and still do."

"You look like a Marine."

"Teams. Lieutenant in the sandbox. I'm a reserve. But because of the FBI, I'm detached. Probably got a letter, but I never paid much attention. I'm busy enough."

"And you're here looking for Aziz's widow…" He squinted in recall. "Nita…"

Nash bobbed her head. "Nytah May Woods. I guess she kept her original last name."

"She worked at the base outreach. They're a volunteer group to help the families who need help with rent and making ends meet—"

Nash nodded. "I'm familiar with them. Many of the lower ranks have families living below the poverty line. The kid who barely made it out of high school or a GED goes home first chance, and he's wearing his uniform. The girl who couldn't get a date to the prom catches his eye, and the next thing he knows, he's a daddy. All on his beginning pay. It's an old story, and it's on every base."

"Well, the base misses her." He gave up on clean hands and pitched the rag toward the half-naked airplane. "How are you getting out to her place?"

"Uber, I guess. After I talk to her, I need to get to Albuquerque, so I'll probably catch a puddle-jumper from the domestic."

"Do you need a GPS?"

Nash squeezed one eye shut and winced at the colonel. "Uber usually has their own…"

He waved his hand toward the back corner of the hangar. "Only Willy isn't automatic, but he does come with a Thomas map book. Her house is on page twenty-eight. The front gate is on twenty-seven. If any guard gives you grief when you bring it back, just shoot them for being too stupid to recognize the camp's mascot. Someone can run you over to the other airfield if we don't have a hop going to New Mexico."

"I'd appreciate that. Anywhere I can park my rucksack until I get back?"

He waved his hand at the small orange airplane. "Throw it in the Piper. Nobody but me goes near the old plane. They're all afraid it'll fall apart if you talk loud around it."

Nash smirked at the Piper Cub, older than either of them. "What year?"

"My father stole the Piper from an airfield south of Inchon when the armistice broke out. He was only sixteen. He flew it to Japan, took it apart, and shipped it here piece by piece. Some parts reference to 1942, but serial numbers say 1947." He shrugged. "I should scrap it for something I can get genuine parts for, but my dad and I kind of bonded over putting it back together in the seventies. I blame my going into the Air Force on her. She was my first for a lot of things. I flew before I could drive."

Nash slipped into the ancient Willy's jeep. Amused by the simple dashboard, she put her hand on the gear stick. Even Thomas's antique 1964 Chevy truck in high school had an oil temperature gauge. She grabbed the small silver key with a white rabbit's foot hanging from it. She turned it the single click and then remembered about the stomp button on the floor. Wiggling the shifter in neutral, she pushed her left foot down on the silver-dollar-sized button. The engine coughed once and then settled into a pampered purr. Powder ticked her head toward the large hangar door as Nash felt for the seatbelts hanging on the sides of the seat.

Easing the jeep forward to the smiling man, she stopped.

Nash pointed at the large round speedometer. "Has it ever pinned the speedometer's sixty?"

"You can hit the freeway, but it would be a way out of your way.

The locals frown on you terrorizing the neighborhoods at forty-five in their twenties. So don't go nuts and you'll be fine."

Nash waved her hand behind the left side of the enormous steering wheel.

The colonel laughed as he stuck his left arm out and then cocked it. "The kids just think you're waving at them, but the old folk will recognize the jeep and steer clear of you, anyway. The gas tank was full yesterday, but don't trust the gauge. I just haven't looked on eBay lately for a replacement sending unit. It takes a Model A sender."

"How are the brakes in an emergency?"

"Better than the rest. Straight off a 1968 Ford Mustang. Someone in the motor pool did the conversion during the Vietnam War. About the time I was trying on my first diaper. But who knows when they'll need new shoes? She gets babied a lot."

Nash pulled her gold aviator glasses down her nose and looked at the ancient Piper Cub. "Yeah, I don't think she's alone around here. I'll be back later."

"When you come back, tell the gate to let me know. We'll make appropriate arrangements then." He glanced at his watch. "But a warning about Nytah. Be ready for food."

"We're good."

He hung his head to one side with a laugh. "Uh, huh? We'll see."

Nash glanced at the Thomas Guide pages and shoved it down beside her seat. The corporal at the gate gave her a snappy salute, and she returned a wave. She glanced at Powder and the lack of any doors. From what she could see along the smooth top of the windshield, there had never been a top either. "No jumping and chasing anything. You hear?"

Powder gave her a patronizing look and then resumed looking down the street. A mile away from the base, she took a left and then a right. Pulling to the curb, she gave Powder a hard look. "No telling anyone."

She pulled the map book out and oriented herself. Thumbing through her phone, she found the address. And started looking for the street on the map. It had been a long time since she had used the guide, and she had to find the directions in the front.

Her finger slowly traced down the streets on the second page when she heard the slow-moving car behind her. She glanced up for a mirror and looked at the glass and a metal crossbar. No mirror. She looked for a mirror to her left as the gray car slowed to a stop.

She turned at the sound of the side window rolling down. The sergeant, with a touch of silver at the temples, smiled. "I heard you were looking for Nytah's place. You've been sitting here for five minutes. So I'm guessing it's been a few minutes since you used a book map."

Nash bit her lower lip. "I was looking for an off-leash dog park to take my dog before heading over there."

The man smiled. "Is he tied down?"

"She. And no."

Silently, he pointed behind her. Nash turned and looked at the large wooden sign. *Red Creek Off-Leash Park. Please pick up after your dog.*

"Is that the one you were looking for?"

She could feel the heat around her collar. "Yeah, it just wasn't clear on the map."

"Yup. They only built it recently. Just before I got out of high school on the other side. After she takes care of business, you can follow me over to Nytah's. It'll save you some daylight. Willy doesn't do good at night driving."

"Why?"

"Take a look at the lights."

Nash turned off the engine and pointed Powder at the park. "If you can't go, fake it."

She stepped out of the jeep and walked to the front. The headlights had a mask over the glass, top and bottom. Walking to the rear, she stared at the single two-inch taillight over the historical license plate.

"Yup, she's that old. The last of a dying breed of getting around."

She turned back toward the sergeant. "Why would they ever have blackouts in Oklahoma? It's the middle of the country, for god's sake."

He pointed at her. "You said it. God-fearing folk who had the bejeezes scared out of them by those Kamikaze crazies. People just knew they would fly those Zeros twelve thousand miles just to commit suicide on their house, here in the suburbs of the center of god-fearing heaven. Well, some think it's heaven. Most of us just know it's better than living down in hurricane bay or out where the earth shakes and turns to dry mud, then opens and swallows you whole."

Nash snorted as her eyes rolled back into her closed eyes. "Which do they fear most?"

"Ever since they've fracked the hell out of Oklahoma, we've been getting little shakers all the time. You'd think people would start getting used to them, but it's not so. Want to clear a diner, shake your table, and scream about little baby Jesus coming to take you this second? You'll have the place to yourself before you can order the cherry pie à la mode."

Nash didn't hide her amusement. "And you have first-hand knowledge of this, how?"

"Oh, not in the last few years... but I probably owe for a few dinners I skedaddled from in an earthquake or three."

Nash glanced back as Powder jumped back into the passenger seat. "Did you just pee, or do I have to go find some poop also?"

Powder looked through the windshield at the street ahead.

Nash turned back to the man. "So they're more afraid of the earth moving."

"Sure. Hurricanes are just wet tornaders. We get those all the time. But the fear is of the unknown. So shaky dirt is scary stuff.

But then, your accent says you're from earthquake country. So to you, it's just an amusement ride while you watch the scared tourists."

Nash stuck her right foot back in the jeep and pulled her left in behind her. "Something like."

"You want to follow me?"

"I don't think I can keep up with you."

The man barked a laugh. "I'm not old, but even my dad gets frustrated when I drive."

Nash turned the key and stomped on the starter. The engine burped to life.

18

WHEN THE RIVER RISES

THE NOTE PINNED to the screen door was direct. *Go round back, I'm canning.*

Nash stepped back as she reached for the high gate and watched it pull away. The woman wasn't what she had expected. Some freckles on the dark face had turned to black skin tags. The eyes crinkled at the corners. Her mane of natural hair was a blend of silver-white and pepper. The arms wobbled from the sleeveless muumuu printed with fish, dolphins, and whales.

"Oh. I didn'st hear y'all coming up the walk."

Nash mirrored the warm smile. "What are you canning?"

"Hah. Taint me. I'm just the neighbor who eats the canning." She held up two jars of dark something. "You be wanting Nee-tay." She half turned back. "Missy Nee-tay? Youse has a visitor and her dog. She done brung that there Willy jeep."

Nash stuck her hand out. "Nash. And this is Powder."

The woman's hand barely folded in Nash's. "Weenie. Edwina. She be Powder as in powdered sugar, or gunpowder?"

Nash slowly ground her head back and forth. "That's between you and her. I'm just the driver."

The woman giggled and bent forward with her hand out for Powder to smell.

Nash looked past the large woman's shoulder. At first, Nash thought the woman standing with one fist on her bib overall'd hip at the corner of the house was a child.

"Weenie, stop jawin' and let the woman through. If she brung Willy, she's here on business." The short hair enhanced the pixie look of the petite woman. Nash didn't think shoes would bring her up to Muna in bare feet. The silver hair glowed in the afternoon sun like one would imagine a pixie. She turned on her heel, and the arm with the large wooden spoon scooped the air as the pixie disappeared. "Come on back."

Nash had seen canning before, but not on such a serious scale. A half-dozen tables stood filled with cooling jars. Three tables contained two large pots of water on heaters. Three more tables had large pots of bubbling food to be poured into the jars sitting on two other tables. Five women moved from table to table, filling, capping, and bathing the jars. Another woman watched over the cooling jars to put them in worn wooden carrying trays stacked against the back wall of the house.

The pixie glanced back. "If you're hungry, grab a bowl. The chili is ready to eat. None is spicy hot. We have too many who think the ketchup at McDonald's is too spicy." She held out a bowl. "What does the colonel want now?"

Nash held up her palm to refuse the bowl, but her stomach growled at the smells of home-cooked food.

Nytah bumped the bowl in the air. "I heard that. What's your dog like?"

"Jerky or anything I'm eating. Broccoli gives both of us gas. And I've seen her bury eggplant and okra."

The woman rocked in agreement. "I may be southern, but I'd bury those two myself. Grits is another roadkill I can't understand. But sweet tea is the only way to make sun tea." She pointed at one of the already canned jars. "Feel them. Maybe one of them would be the right temperature for your dog."

"Thanks." Nash took the two bowls and stepped over to the cooling tables. The woman was feeling the temperatures with the back of her hand. She held out the jar and a spoon. Nash nodded and opened the jar. Talking over her shoulder, she poured out the chili into the two bowls. "I'm not here at the behest of the commander. I'm here because Abdul asked me to."

Every hand in the backyard froze. Every face and eye turned to look at Nytah.

The woman gently turned from the large pot as she rested the long wooden spoon on the edge. "When?"

Nash looked back and turned, taking in the attention of the women. Her voice lowered. "Maybe we should talk in private."

The small woman gently banged the spoon on the side of the pot and then handed it to another woman. Stepping down off the wooden box, she sank to her actual height. The tabletop hit her about her armpit. She rested her elbow and arm along the table's edge. Her other hand and finger wound around in the air, indicating the other women. "Look at these women. I'm Creek, like a couple of others. We have Oglala Sioux, Chumash, Mohawk..." She pointed at the woman who had given Nash the jar of chili. "And Tammy is Pontiac. We all grew up with people who could speak with the dead. When did you talk to my late husband?"

"A few weeks ago. I didn't know if it was real or not, so I... We've kind of been busy."

The woman pointed at Nash's pants. "He called you on your phone. If so... it was a bullshit call. He's been dead for—"

"Yes. Two years. I know. I also didn't know he was even in the country. The last time I saw him was when he was waving our plane goodbye in Afghanistan. He was our interpreter."

The pixie smirked. "What did you call him?"

Nash recognized the challenge to her authenticity. "Scissors. Because of how he walked. His feet crossed over the center track ever so slightly. My team learned to mimic the walk, and we left a single confusing track."

Nytah nodded. "You were the LT. He had a tough time pronouncing the difference between the *ent* and *ant*. It was just easier to use the initials. So what did he say?"

Nash watched as the beehive of work resumed, as if it had never stopped. "He said his granddaughter was possibly in trouble. He wanted to know if I could still find people."

Nytah directed her hand at the cheap aluminum snap chairs. "Please."

As they settled, Powder looked at the chair and then at the bowl on the patio.

Nash snickered. "Trust me, baby girl, you don't want to get your leg caught in the webbing on these chairs. It's not an attractive look."

Powder went back to delicately eating.

As the woman crossed her legs, Nash spotted the narrow gold ring on the inner toe. Nytah scratched the sleeveless T-shirt under her bib. "Cooter fell off the grid about a month ago. She's had a problem with alcohol and smoking weed since the seventh grade. This last year, high school lost any pull for her, and she spent more time at home than earning more detentions. My daughter works two jobs and is just trying to keep up. Cutting meat for a market who won't pay for a certified butcher, and waiting tables for little more than tips at the Waffle House doesn't go to the end of most months. If it weren't for Medicaid, they wouldn't have any help. Oklahoma doesn't believe in welfare for anyone who isn't lily white or coal black. So those of us in the middle suck the tail end of tornado alley."

Nash winched her one eye as she finished chewing and swallowed. "Did she report her daughter missing to the police?"

"Not worth the bother. The second the words Creek or Muskogee fall out of your mouth, the words alcohol and tribal are louder in their heads. No matter where you live, the first thing they ask is what the tribal council said. The council doesn't look after missing girls. They be busy running the casinos and oil wells." She looked down at her hands clasped between her knees. "So, it would seem, it's up to dead men and lieutenants of the US Marine Corps."

"FBI."

The woman scoffed and swatted her hand backward through the air. "Fuck them suits. The only thing worse than the KKK of the police is the men behind those locked doors. They wouldn't give a tribal woman the time of day. Much less a teen runaway." Her face darkened, and she pointed her finger and pounded it in the air. "And that is all they think happens to an Indian girl."

Nash rolled onto her right hip and pulled the thin flat wallet out of her left pocket. Dropping the wallet open, she pointed at Powder. "She has her own badge. And if you couldn't tell, we're Northern California Paiute. And she's a full-blooded reservation dog."

"Oh." Nytah's mouth was a small circle as she looked around at the other women, suddenly finding other places to look and work.

As the other woman squirmed, Nash put away the wallet. "Now. Would you like to tell me how an Afghani man can show up in my spirit world?"

The eyes narrowed. "How well did you know Scissors?"

"He was our interpreter for two tours. We didn't shower with him, but if we bivouacked out in the desert or up in the hills east of Kandahar, he was just as muddy as we were. If you're at a base and making motorized patrols or sorties, he would have his own place to bunk. But a lot of times, we were out in the hills, trying to woo the hearts and minds of the natives. You get to know people…"

Nytah stood with her hand out. "Excuse me." She stepped to the table and leaned over toward the offered wooden spoon. Slurping some of the chili from the spoon, she grimaced. "Give it about twenty more minutes. The beans are still firm, but I can't taste the celery yet. The next pot is in the kitchen. You can take the lid off and get it started in there. Thanks, Poly."

She sat back down and reached for the quart jar of iced tea.

Sipping, she smiled as her eyes danced around. "A lot of hungry families will have chili for a few months."

"How many gallons of chili?"

"This round, we'll put up about six hundred quarts. And when the hunting season brings us more meat, we'll put up over a thousand quarts. Hunger never ends."

"Why chili?"

The woman raised her eyebrows and looked at Nash. "Why make jerky?"

Nash squinted. "Because it tastes good and lasts."

"Yup. Except when the families are hungry." She held her hand out to the cooking committee. "That's where the aunties come in. We've all been there. So now, we can help those young people who haven't overcome."

Nash wound her finger in the air. "And Aziz?"

"It wasn't like a shaman. But did he ever tell you which trail to take or street not to go down?"

Nash bolstered her lips as she thought about her sergeant calling Scissors their lucky charm. "Yeah. He would look at the map and run his finger down one track we could patrol. We rarely got hit or engaged in firefights. Others who took the other routes ran into IEDs and insurgents. My sergeant called Scissors our lucky charm."

"Same with traffic here. Sometimes he would turn up into neighborhoods we'd never been. The next thing I knew, we were across town. Then we would hear radio reports of traffic jams where we had been going."

Nash dipped her head. "I guess I never thought much about it, because my father had been the same way. He'd be coming home and taking a different route. Whatever the roadkill was, it was still warm. He would bone it out on the side of the road and leave the rest for the animals. I didn't think about it, but it was his connection to the world."

Nytah pointed at the chili. "When we started the chili years ago, some truckers had hit a group of deer. They brought them to the base, still warm. It was a lot of meat, and the commissary said they couldn't serve it. But one cook said he'd butcher them out and give us the meat."

Nash pointed. "It always comes down to jerky or something you can freeze…"

"Or can."

"So, Scissors was maybe a shaman but didn't know it?"

Nytah shrugged. "How much do you know or understand about the spirit world? Because I know nothing."

"I'm still learning. But about your granddaughter…?"

The shrug was tired. "Some of us looked. I talked to the girl I thought was her best friend. But she said she hadn't talked to Cooter since last fall. I guess they had a falling out. I couldn't tell if she was lying or not, but I went and asked around, or seemed to. There were a couple of houses… drug houses. I don't know. It was draining, but we showed her photo around. It was as if the ground had opened and swallowed her whole."

Nash rocked softly. "It happens a lot. Much too often with indigenous people. Sometimes you think the reservation is small enough to be a tight group, and then someone just wanders off or disappears. Or worse. We've started a clearinghouse on a national scale. I'll get you the information, but hundreds of kids are no longer in our tribes. Kidnappers, murderers, or other people cause both women and men to go missing. But with our declining populations, it's too many." She leaned forward and pulled out her wallet. Pulling a couple of her business cards, she handed them across. "You can email me Cooter's information—whatever you've got." She remembered what she didn't have in research. "I can't make any promises, but we can try to help. If it goes to voicemail, I'm probably out in the field. But you can call the general number and ask for my supervisor. He's all in on the missing person profile. He was there when I started it, and he's been a tremendous help."

Nytah rolled her head. "Tammy, this pot is done. Go ahead and bring out the other one. Thanks, hun." Her head rolled back. "It's just good to know you're not out here alone. I'll send you what we have." She leaned forward and rested her fingertips on Nash's knee. "And... thank you. You don't know how much it means to me. You put someone into the ground... and..."

Nash wrapped the hand in both of hers. "He looked good. I see people in their different ages. I think he still looks like he's only fifty. But he seemed happy, or at least content, except about Cooter. Is that her real name?"

"Nita Anne Cloutier. Her father is a French Cajun. I think it's someone who makes nails. Like the kind you build with. But he liked to hunt ducks. Not kill them, just take pictures of them."

Nash stood. "Let's see if we can bring this little duckling home."

"I'd like that."

19

WITH MORE EFFORT, WE CAN GET NOWHERE

"No, Donna. I've seen that guy in action. A brainless sheep chewing bubble gum would be more impressive. I don't care if he claims he knows the dark web like the back of his hand. The guy's brain and penis are dressed center. It leaves space for whatever opinions he might stumble upon later."

A sudden warm silence buzzed like a hand covering a phone to stifle a laugh. Donna cleared her throat with regained composure. "Have you tried poking around Quantico or even, heaven forbid, Langley? I hear Langley's building quite the cyber army these days..."

"And luckily, our enemies are facing the same hurdle. The tech-savvy kids lounging in their parents' basements aren't ready to trade home-cooked meals and free laundry for anything as exhausting as working." Nash squinted out the expansive windows at the increasing noise. "But it's sparked an idea. I might need to head to San Francisco to make it happen." The windows rattled with more urgency. "Gotta run. Sounds like my ride's touching down."

Nash and Powder walked out onto the apron of the tie-down. The dirty gray of the three Pave Hawks did nothing to diminish the serious visage of incoming Valkyries. Rotor wash pounded the concrete expanse as they nosed up gently and settled as one. The stationary nature of the rotors' plates made them visible to see the tips were only twenty or thirty feet of separation. This was a highly trained and practiced team. The center leader was only ten feet forward of the wingmen.

As the engines cycled down, the pilot leaned forward slightly to check something. Nash smiled. She couldn't read the lettering on the helmet, but the small children's toy rotor stitched to the helmet was all she needed to see. The pilot looked over at her co-pilot and then out at Nash and Powder. She smiled and waved.

The two walked over after putting the helicopter to bed. "Special Agent Powder and her wing girl, Nash."

"Cotton, Trouble, good to see you two. But you're kind of far from home, aren't you?"

As the other two teams walked up, Cotton did the introductions. "Special Agent Nash and Powder, meet Vapor, Sidewinder, Thunder, and Flash. Rounding out the triad of the Air Force. We wow the crowds, and then talk to the girls. Our home this last month has been at air shows in Orlando, Tampa, Atlanta, and Little Rock. We do formation flying and then talk to kids about flying."

Nash finished shaking hands. "So why here? There's no air show coming up."

Thunder nodded. "You're right. But we have one coming up in Phoenix, and I have a harmonic in my tail rotor. So tonight, it gets looked at and maybe replaced, and tomorrow we fly some bigwig VIP across the desert."

Vapor smirked. "It's an American story. Our ponies don't have names, so what better way to cross a desert?"

Trouble looked up from hugging Powder. "Where's your other sidekick?"

"Uncle?"

The pilot stood, chuckling. "Well, the boys were fun too. But I thought you and…" She snapped her fingers a few times.

"Muna."

"Yeah. Muna. I thought you two were inseparable." She peered into the windows of the building.

Nash looked around. "No. She's… well, it's a long story."

Cotton ticked her head up. "Did she ever shoot at the Olympics?"

Nash groaned. "Part of the story… What about over dinner?"

The other four pilots touched Cotton on the shoulder. "We'll catch up later."

Cotton glanced at her watch. "Circle back about eight and we'll see what's up with the rotor."

THE FOUR RINGED A TABLE UNDER A RAINBOW umbrella. The only one not making a mess of the tacos was Powder.

Cotton hung her head sideways as she tried to control the soft taco, the juice, and everything falling out on the plate. "Any thoughts as to where she might have gone?"

Nash shrugged her face and swallowed. "If she had checked out one of the rigs, she could be local or traveling. But Andy said he didn't even see an Uber or taxi pull up. It's as if she turned into a wisp of smoke and disappeared."

Trouble wiped her hands on the wad of napkins and then wiped her mouth. "How much stuff did she have to pack?"

"She stayed in room three. I looked. Nothing was in there. So I'm assuming here, but I think it all fits in her rucksack. Other than her Hello Kitty pajamas and fuzzy slippers, she only wore her body armor and uniform." Nash plucked at her white shirt. "White shirt and leather pants."

Cotton hung her finger out in the air. "Yeah. I've always wondered… how many pairs…"

Nash held up her thumb and two fingers. "Stay clean. Corn-starch the insides. One is at the cleaners, so you wear one and pack the backup. It's the dirty little secret that makes the debutants throw up and mothers gag."

Trouble frowned half her face. "But why...?"

Nash's smirk was slow to grow. "Remember the first time you put on a helmet with a heads-up display?"

The pilot's smirk showed the hint of a tooth. "Yeah..."

"Remember how badass it felt?"

The smile grew. The eyes reflecting the cars going by on the street twinkled.

Nash pointed. "That. That right there. First time you put on a pair, you'll buy three."

"It can't be cheap."

Nash shrugged. "It isn't. But you sit in the little dressing room, and know deep in your soul that wool, cotton, or silk will never make you feel that good ever again."

Trouble looked over at Cotton. "I need to go shopping."

The three laughed.

Cotton looked at the last third of the taco on her plate and then pushed it over to Powder. Wiping her hands and mouth, she dropped the paper on the table. "Have you checked with HR?"

Trouble rocked as her hand flopped out with her finger pointing at Cotton. "If we walk off into the sunset without an okay, it's AWOL. But I don't know what the civilians call it."

Nash sat blinking at the two pilots. "I don't know civilian terms. Technically, I'm still a Marine. Just reserve detached or something." Her one eyebrow rose. "Hell, it's been so long. I don't know what rank they think I hold. But yeah, I think some kind of AWOL if she doesn't have somebody's sign-off. But hell, I'm sure Oz and Mike would produce some sort of competition to figure out which uncle gets to cover for her."

"So, who's your human resource person?"

Nash yawned. "We have those?" She thought about the time differences. Rising onto her left butt cheek, she pulled out her phone. She scrolled through to the number she almost never used.

Her thumb covered the green icon and then found the speaker icon.

The squawk told them where she had dialed. The echoes on the stainless-steel drawers, tables, and equipment confirmed the squawk.

"My hand is playing handball with this guy's heart. Tell me what I need to know or shut up and go away."

Nash chuckled at Cotton's raised eyebrow. "Getting kind of testy in your old age there, Oz."

The second groan was younger, but no less edged. "Nash."

"Happy to hear you're still alive as well, Mike. You guys sound like you're filleting a large fish or something."

Oz's voice was softer. "We tried out our new... um... equipment."

Mike coughed as he tried to cover his laughter. "Oz found Amazon. He ordered one of those French hot bath cooking things."

Trouble softly muttered into her fist. "It's called sous vide. You put food and meat into a pouch. Seal it and stick it in a water bath to cook it at a low temperature."

Nash's one eyebrow ticked. "What did you cook?"

"Oz got a screaming deal on a four-pound prime rib. Well... okay, the calf died."

The older man's voice was quiet. "Oh, Momma. Look at that meat. It's just like uptown."

Nash recognized Mike's approval whistle. "Hey, Nash. We're kind of busy here, and it's after hours. What can we do for you?"

"Did either of you two check in with HR?"

Oz cleared his throat. "What's HR?"

Mike wasn't going to be easy. "Health Register. No, Nash. The calf was dead when they butchered it. Something about the lack of resilience when a four-hundred-pound calf tangles with a three-ton truck. Why?"

Nash sighed at the other two women, laughing. "No children. Human resources. About Muna being away without leave."

The silence was unmistakable. Nash was sure the two boys were checking with each other about the question and what to say. "Okay. So you guys don't know who to call either."

Oz growls with a short throat clearing. "I've never heard of anyone running away before. If you figure out who to call... um... call us first, please?"

Nash slowly counted to five. "So you can write her a parental excuse note?"

Mike interceded. "I would think, as her supervisor, that would be my job."

Nash raised her eyebrows and held her hands out to the phone on the table as she rocked. *See. What did I tell you?* "Okay, you two can draw straws or break a rib bone or something to see who gets to write the memo. I just wanted to see if she had made arrangements we didn't know about. But I've had my dinner, so I'll let you get to yours."

"Good night, Nash." The snick was pure stainless steel.

Cotton eased her arm over the chair back. "And these men have how many higher education degrees?"

Nash's eyelids closed with a slow nod. "Between the two? Probably half a dozen or more. I know Oz has at least four doctoral degrees. But he also has a sailboat, which seems to spend a lot of time out of the water."

"So they wouldn't know who to call either."

Nash ruffled Powder's ears. "I'm not laughing. The smart one on this team probably can't tell me who to call, and I've never thought about it. But I think I know who might."

Two of the other pilots wandered up. "Tail rotor is being installed as we speak. Must have picked up a rock in Little Rock. But we're good for an oh-dark-thirty lift off. As soon as the VIP gets there."

Cotton pointed at Nash.

"Oh."

Trouble chuckled. "Oh-dark-thirty is when she drives 9mm slugs through paper. But chow is at oh-six hundred. With a new rotor, I don't want to lift off in the dark. But go get some sleep."

The two gave her a two-finger salute.

Nash studied Cotton as she turned back around. "How long are you going to be in Albuquerque?"

"The air show in Phoenix is Saturday. Why? What have you got going in Albuquerque?"

Nash closed one eye in a squint. "You've seen combat. Or at least trained with mini guns..."

The southern drawl pulled out longer as the head tilted. "Yeah...?"

20

RED STRAWS AND LOTS OF SAND

"I'M WAITING for the Albuquerque office to come get me. Their motor pool's bringing me a Bronco they hate because the pig doesn't have freezing air-conditioning, and the paint isn't shiny."

Donna's boohoo matched the two pilots, rubbing their knuckles at their eyes. "Then what?"

"We're going to meet Zap at the sheriff's impound yard. It's connected to their forensics barn or something. But he promised to buy me lunch if it doesn't impress me."

Donna snorted a quick chuckle. "Has he seen your poker face before?"

"Yes, and those are big words for a man of few words. So I'm guessing it's worth the drive. But I have some tough backup. I've got two combat-experienced Black Hawk drivers with me. We're going to vote on who pays."

"Any word on Muna?"

Nash looked across the small general aviation parking lot. An Explorer followed the Bronco. "That's why I called you. How do I reach out to HR?"

The woman snickered. "We have an HR department?" Nash

could hear the phone being covered and something said to another person. "Sorry. Just pulling Tony's chain. He just got back from an obviously useless meeting with Homeland. Let me make some soft inquiries with HR. If there's a delicate situation, barging in with your number twelve combat boots could make matters worse."

"Okay. Our ride just showed up. I'll touch base in a couple of days."

"I should know something by Friday."

Nash and Powder led as the two vehicles pulled to the curb. The special agent stepped out of the Bronco with the engine running. Nash mentally shook her head at the black suit in the summer desert. He gave the white shirt and black leather pants a second take. "Agent Bear?"

"Running Bear—it's a single family name. Where do I bring this back?"

"Same as last time. Call us and we'll come to get it. Just don't leave it shot up in the Southern Ute Reservation."

Nash looked over her gold-tinted dark glasses. "That car wasn't yours. And as far as I know, it's still in Colorado. The investigation is ongoing, but not FBI's need to know."

His Cub Scout salute was snappy. The man had gotten the gist of the lesson.

Cotton walked around to the passenger seat as Trouble slid into the back. Both snapped their buckles in unison. *Once a team…* Nash smirked as she thought back on those days.

"Do you leave many cars all shot up in the Ute Reservation?"

Nash glanced over at Cotton as she scratched Powder's neck. "Southern Ute."

"What's the difference?"

Nash eased the truck out of the parking lot. "What's the difference between officers and a captain? All get saluted."

Trouble snickered in the back. "Mostly. Some with a single finger."

Cotton's index finger pointed back at her partner. "So, is there a Ute Reservation, or a Northern Ute Reservation?"

Nash dipped her head as they turned onto the highway. "If I remember my education right, the Northern is mostly in Utah. Some of it reached out to allow trading with us, the Northern California Paiutes. Then there are the Ute Mountain Utes. We got ambushed on our way there. So the car ended up a Southern Ute problem, as well as a local sheriff. Nice guy, but I don't think the former Marine wanted to know what had happened."

"How bad?"

Nash glanced back at Trouble, who was leaning forward to hear better. "A total cluster fuck for them. You met the boys. Little Felix has a Barrett he loves tweaking with. Between Felix's and my evasive training in vehicles, their armored van and SUV never stood a chance. It was all scrap metal at the end. But it sold me on the durability of the Hellcat and the engine. It's my private car as well, now."

Cotton acknowledged the shift away from a past case, which wasn't their business. "What are we going to look at here?"

Nash turned up the on-ramp. "My guess is a certain jeep. Shot to shit and needing answers. I saw a report on a slug. It's thirty caliber, but armored and armor-piercing. They sent the slug to Los Angeles for a second opinion. The second opinion stated that a poorly maintained mini gun fired the slug. At least, the gunner was overheating the barrel." Nash glanced over at Cotton's low whistle. "Yeah. Those are kind of hard to carry around in your hip pocket."

Cotton glanced back at Trouble with raised eyebrows.

Trouble chuckled. "Heavy on the thumb can do mucho damage. Quick bursts allow you to aim better instead of the fire hose. The continuously overheated barrel anneals. Then the crisp edges of the lands and grooves start to round over, and it loses its effectiveness. But if you have the money to fire hose everything, you aren't caring about accuracy as much as sending a message."

Nash pointed her left finger at Trouble. "Which is what I gather we're going to see."

Cotton focused on the highway ahead. "We're fliers, not forensic people. Why are we here? I mean, besides lunch."

Nash smiled as she turned into the parking lot of a large building with a flagpole in front. "Just in case I need some open-door time with altitude."

Trouble laughed. "Now we're talking."

The red rods sticking out of the jeep looked like someone had turned a first-grade class loose, maxed out on a sugar high in an ice cream parlor. The massive cluster was in and around the body of the jeep. But the kids had taken the extra box of straws and had fun with the engine compartment as well.

Trouble commented under Cotton's low whistle of amazement. "At least they weren't tracers."

Zap turned on the pilots, still in their Air Force flight suits. "Tracers?"

Nash interceded. "Incendiary bullets. The movies show tons of them, but they never explain them. Most people think it's so the pilot can see where they're hitting. The movies show them so the audience can see where the bullets are going, or not going. But the real purpose of the incendiary load in the bullet's butt is to ignite any gas or fuel. Holes are just holes. Sometimes they get lucky. But the tracer ignites anything it passes through."

Cotton continued as they walked over to the jeep, positioned at the far end of the cavernous building. "The old days of dogfights used lead bullets. But especially in World War I, the planes could come back riddled with holes. The bullets passed right through the painted canvas. The only hope was to kill the pilot, shoot holes in his gas tank, or shoot the engine. There are records of pilots returning and gluing on patches, some fresh paint while they had lunch, and off they went again. A fresh load of bullets and a full tank of gas. But with the next war, they came up with the tracers. Huge game changer because the gas tanks were in the wings."

Zap blew up his hands in an imaginary explosion. "So stand over here." He circled his finger at the floor.

The four gathered. Powder looked at Zap for the new game.

Zap pointed at the front of the jeep. "By the way, those rods are ten feet long."

The two pilots looked at the ends sticking only two feet out of one side. Nash nodded. "Armor-piercing and went all the way through. Look on the back side."

The two stepped to the left. Two feet of red porcupine quills stuck out on the other side.

Zap nodded. "Some of those also went through the soft targets as well." He walked over to the porcupine mass on the original side. "But this is the part about Nash buying lunch." He thumbed small switches on the ends of the rods. Laser beams snapped into being between the jeep and the far wall. The dots on the distant wall clustered just below the high ceiling. "The distance is a hundred and fifty feet. And the ceiling is forty feet." He turned on the last of the rods and stepped out of the way.

The dots clustered within ten feet of each other. Lowest to highest was less than eight feet.

Cotton leaned toward Trouble. "Could you hold that steady?"

"A Cobra could, but they're always moving. The angle would change and therefore the height." She turned to Nash and Zap. "I had twin minis under the nose of my Hawk. But this isn't our kind of warfare." She waved her hand at the jeep. "This is unloading the whole nine yards in one go. I came back with yardage to recycle— most days."

Looking back at Cotton. "Did you ever have a door gunner?"

Cotton rocked in thought. "Yeah… but… we never tried to stand still. But I'm looking at the dots on the wall. That's what? Thirty or forty feet? Ground wash would be a bitch to hold still. Getting so low without turbulence would take a trouble bubble. But a mini would buck a bubble around something fierce."

Nash thought about what they were evaluating as she walked over to the jeep. Studying where one rod entered the panel near the door jamb, she looked at another on the rear quarter panel. She pulled the rod out of the back panel and handed it to Zap. "Go ahead. Turn them off. We have what we need." She pulled five more.

Kneeling, she looked along the panel and then stuck her little finger into the holes.

Cotton frowned as she leaned over to look at the holes. "What are you thinking?"

Nash pointed at the red dots on the wall. "That's too low, and too close." She wiped her hand along the metal panel. "I've seen what thirties and fifties do to metal up close. These slugs had burned off most of the kinetic energy. They're just passing through. No concussion." She pointed at the distant red dots. "But what else do you see about the pattern?"

Cotton studied the distant spread.

Nash pulled out one rod and used the laser light. She circled half the cluster, and then the other half. In the middle, she circled a small oval.

Trouble put her hand on her head. "I'll be dipped. They had a mini strapped to each side. If you're sending a message, do it in a quick text instead of a long, drippy love letter."

Cotton looked back at the jeep. She waved her hand around in the air. "Even if some went high and some hit low or short, this isn't a full nine yards of shells. This was short and sweet. But running twin side saddles, they would knock you back, but it would be stabilizing." She looked at Trouble.

The younger pilot shook her head. "Too much for a bubble. You'd want more like a Bell 429 or an Agusta Koala. That's not too much weight, but the torque would twist the bubble out of whack damn fast. But the Bell or Agusta are relatively common and solid platforms."

Nash smiled at Zap. "Do we have the coordinates?"

He fished a piece of paper out of his shirt pocket. "Do I talk to my dead mother?"

Nash snorted. "No. But you're getting there. Have you taken the daughter out for a ride yet?"

He flashed his eyebrows. "No. But I'm getting there."

Nash smiled and turned to the two pilots. "Lunch and then a flight?"

21

DIG MY DRIFT

THE PAVE HAWK hovered over the sand wash. Nash and Zap sat with the side doors rolled back, with Powder between them.

Zap felt at his throat for some kind of button. Nash leaned forward and rested her hand on his arm. "There's no button or switch. I made sure your helmet is lit up. Just talk."

"Oh." He rolled his eyes and looked back out of the large opening. His arm pointed at any of sixty square miles of desert. "The little stake with the orange ribbon."

Trouble's crisp retort on the radio was more obvious and different from Cotton's southern drawl. "Got it. How close do you want to be?"

Nash pulled out her spotting scope. "Let's start with a hundred and see how far we need to back out."

The helicopter shifted closer.

"Okay. But you need to be about twenty feet lower."

The helicopter settled. The rotor wash caused sand and dust to cavitate into the air.

"Y'all are going to need that twenty to see anything. Even if it's a Koala, it's still going to kick the desert up. The Bell is worse."

The helicopter moved up and slowly shifted away from the marker.

Nash watched the level and angle of the slope in the spotting scope. "Easy... easy..." She lowered the scope and looked at the marker. "I've got one forty-five. What do you think, Trouble?"

The helicopter spun, and the nose pointed at the tiny flag half a football field away. "Acquiring..." The helicopter suddenly began to shake and jerk in the air. Nash counted seven heartbeats. *About ten seconds.* The helicopter calmed down and hung in the air. "Cotton?"

"Targeting says your main cluster stayed within five feet of the stake target. You lost a sixteen percent drift above and ten below."

"Nash?"

"Yeah, Trouble."

"So with seventy-four percent of half belts, you get over four hundred rounds through the jeep. Did you want to do a walk-in?"

"It beats the hell out of driving back out here tomorrow. Besides, I think the little bladder needs a bush."

"Tell Powder to hang on. I'll go put her down on the rise off to the right."

The helicopter leaned and drifted toward the small flat away from the target, and where they now knew the shooter had hovered and for how long. Nash watched the target area as they nosed around to land. She had forgotten how lethal a flying platform could be.

Powder nosed at a squat bush as they walked down to the small stake and ribbon. Trouble leaned over and felt the ribbon. "Huh. Cotton."

Her co-pilot turned. "Yeah?"

Nash and Trouble snickered. Trouble growled. "No. The ribbon is cotton instead of the usual plastic."

Zap put his finger in the air at his side. "We stopped using plastics years ago. It's an environmental th..." His voice trailed off at the faces of the three women.

Nash snorted. "It's okay, Zap. It's a woman thing. She was just pulling Cotton's chain. But yeah, good to know about someone looking out for the desert."

Trouble frowned. "But wouldn't plastic be a more durable marker?"

"How long do you think a crime scene is active?"

Trouble shrugged. "I'm just a pilot. But a year or two?"

Nash looked at Zap. "Have they identified the bodies yet?"

He shook his head. "Even all the background stuff on the guy who worked for the armored truck was bogus. I give it another month or three, and the folder ends up in a box on a shelf. The jeep was registered to some guy in Texas who died in an arms raid a couple of years ago. The plates were from a Volvo in Juarez. To command, the handwriting is on the adobe and fading fast. Even the local FBI isn't coming up with anything."

Trouble smiled. "Heck, send all the information and bodies up to…" Nash's glower stopped her. "Oh. Yeah. Sorry."

Zap frowned and looked at Nash. "What about your whiz kid?"

Nash growled. "Long story."

"But she figured out the spaceman and…"

The face darkened. "It's another case of a missing person. I need to go to San Francisco next, to try and figure it out."

Zap thought and then drew his thumb and finger across his lips.

Nash pointed at their feet as she looked at Cotton. Her arm rose to point to the airspace in the distance. "Well?"

Cotton side-eyed Trouble. "Koala?"

"The rotor wash would still be hammering, but the sand wasn't that bad. The Koala would create less wash thrashing, but the fine particles will be there, no matter which. But for an easily available airframe and the most stable, I still like the twin jet on the 429 the best."

Nash thought about something she had seen working a case in the southern tip of Louisiana. "What about an old Huey?"

Trouble glanced east. "Are you thinking about the Slicks they use out in the gulf shuttling to the drilling rigs and stuff?"

"Yeah. I saw several of them in and out of a place called The End of the World."

Trouble nodded. "They're good. Cheap too, but for a reason. It takes a lot of spare parts to keep them in the air. They fly the hell out of them, but they don't make them sweat. Throw six or eight drill rig crews in the back and fly them a couple of hundred miles offshore. The lift is still under five tons. But mount some minis on the sides or even a sling-mounted door gunner, and you've got some serious abuse going on. You run off a chain or two and watch the pieces fall out of the sky. Wrong kind of metal fatigue. It's why most of the ones parked a few hundred miles from here in the desert will never fly again. The metal fatigue is just waiting for gravity to finish the job."

"No new ones?"

Trouble shrugged at Zap. "It depends on what you consider new. Bell stopped making Hueys before I was born. Or at least before I started riding a bicycle."

"So how hard is it to buy a four…?"

"Twenty-nine? Easy. Look in any of the helicopter sales rags or online, and you'll find pages of them. Cash sale would probably make it simpler, but not clean. Governments need to track any craft. For boats, cars, trucks, planes, or choppers, you'll find a CS number. They're all getting registered somewhere."

Zap frowned. "What's a CS number?"

Nash rested her hand on his shoulder. "Chicken shit number. It's how desk weenies justify their existence." She turned to look at Cotton. "Who would have the information on a helicopter?"

Cotton shrugged her face and shoulders. "FAA would be as good a place as any to start. But having a tail number helps with those civilian office weenies."

Nash turned back to Zap. "Did that witness get the number of the helicopter?"

"He never even heard it. But by the time he rode up, it had disappeared. But he said the blood still oozed out of the bodies."

Trouble frowned and pulled down her dark glasses. "How can you be that close and not hear the mini guns? It's not like they can run silencers or anything."

Nash thought a moment and then pointed at the rise the helicopter sat on. "We're only a quarter klick from the chopper. But if I get about twenty feet down the other side of the hill, and fire off my 9mm, I'll bet you can't tell me how many shots I'd fired. The desert has screwy acoustics. I've been to places where we could watch the firefight, but couldn't hear it. Line of sight. But the sound went somewhere else. Other places, you could be that quarter klick away, and hear a quiet conversation. And if the guy was on a horse, he could have been a couple of klicks, and they'd still be oozing when he rides up."

"So now all you have to do is find a 429 or Koala with mini guns and tail numbers."

Nash pointed back at the helicopter on the rise. "If some guys are doing sketchy shit like shooting up a jeep and the occupants in the desert, do you really think they'd bother with a tail number?"

Trouble snorted. "Probably not. But then, that's what they pay you the big bucks for. We're just stick jocks."

"It looks like we have three bodies with no names. On the other hand, there is a helicopter with twin mini guns, and may or may not have a tail number. The smart uniforms here in New Mexico pointed out four routes they could have flown and never gotten watched."

Maggie looked around the large forensic lab. Every head was in duck and cover mode. Everyone knew who she was talking to—and they wanted nothing to do with any bizarre case the FBI agent notoriously dragged them into. "Send me the files. I'll see what I can do from here." Her voice rose. "Even if I have to work late and oversee it myself." The mass of heads lowered even further.

Nash snickered at the mental visual of how Maggie's crew reacted. "I'm also bouncing all the information up to San Francisco."

"I thought you said Muna was MIA?"

"She is. But I'm going to go up and see if I can crack her computer. I'm hoping I can at least get into the Interpol network and ask for their help."

The older agent laughed. "Oh yeah. Good luck with that."

Nash coughed. "Hey. I know which end is the shooting end of a mouse."

"Yeah. Like I said. Good luck."

"Well, if nothing else, there's some notable food up there."

"Some fine restaurants down here in Los Angeles as well." Maggie snapped her fingers. "Hey, what about that enormous giant out there in Fort Mojave?"

"Moose? What about him?"

"Didn't he have a niece or something who was a computer whiz?"

Nash groaned. "Are you trying to get me in trouble? She's like majorly underaged. Like fifteen or something."

"Hey. It was worth a shot."

22
DRIFTING SIDEWAYS

"THEY SAID you would need to come to Quantico to talk to them."

Nash rested her face in her right hand. "I'm on my way to San Francisco. Depending on what I can get done there, I'll be a while before I'm back in D.C. Did they say why I need to physically come there?"

Donna's voice changed and lowered to a whisper. "Personally, the hairs on the back of my neck stood on end. I think they know more than they want to let on. I don't think Muna is as missing as we believe. You might want to make an effort to get back here as soon as possible. Tony also got a call from a peer in Tel Aviv this morning. He didn't identify himself, but I know an Israeli accent when I hear it. And he said they were old friends; it sounded more like Mossad than old school chums from the prep academy."

Nash's hand dropped to Powder's head and neck for a quick scratch. "Okay. I need to go walk the little bladder before we board. I'll check in tomorrow. Try to figure out who the Mossad agent was. And as for the hair on the back of your neck—red hair does that. It's when my braid twitches that I know something is up. And I think it rhymes with Interpol."

"Have a pleasant flight." The snick was soft but left Nash's phone blank.

Nash hefted her rucksack, and they stepped over to the desk. "Excuse me, but is there a four-legged potty nearby?"

The older brunette with six pins of flair looked over the edge of the desk. "What a cutie. Is he trained for a sandbox?"

"She, and how big is the box?"

The woman snorted. "My two Great Danes can use it at the same time. They just haven't installed the fire hydrant or a tree yet. But if she's a she..."

Nash smirked. "Oh, good. Then even I can use it, at the same time."

The raised eyebrow was the effect Nash was looking for.

"Okay, I'll go after we take off."

The senior desk agent turned to her companion. "I'll take them down before we load. Back in a couple of minutes." The man nodded as he kept typing and staring at the monitor. She waved her finger at Nash to follow her through the doorway. "What's her badge for?"

The woman's failure to check their credentials surprised Nash. "We're FBI."

"Oh. I saw yours. I just missed hers. We get every kind of service dog, or compassion pet, from dogs to cats. I'm surprised we don't get miniature donkeys and Gila monsters around here. We have our share of spoiled passengers. I have three more years and then I'm out of here." She opened the door to the outside area. The raised bed of 2x4s was eight feet square and filled with kitty litter.

Nash pointed at the sand and spoke to Powder. "That's as good as it gets. Go there or learn to use an actual toilet."

The woman snickered. "I've seen dogs do it on YouTube. Cats too."

Powder looked back one last time as she stepped over into the soft sand. She squatted as she looked away from the two women watching her.

"Jeez." Nash turned her back toward Powder. "She'll brazenly knock you over for half of your burrito, but let her go tinkle, and she becomes a pampered poodle."

"What's her training?"

Nash snorted. "A wild animal named Uncle raised her during her formative years. The only thing he didn't teach her was to drink coffee."

The woman's eye opened larger. "I'd never stand for having to share my coffee in the morning. I even make my husband make his own."

Nash fist bumped the agent. "I would, but it's my wife's nurse who makes the coffee… and breakfast… and dinner…" She looked over at the woman as she felt Powder lean against her knee. "Yeah, we're pampered women."

"Well, at least dog food—"

"Doesn't exist in our family." Nash held the woman's stare.

The woman smacked her lips wetly. "Yeah. Who am I kidding? My husband cooks special meals for the Danes. But they're eleven and still have solid hips. Let's get you on the plane."

Oz MADE IT ALL THE WAY TO THE BREAK ROOM. STEPPING back, he blinked a few times. The wall of computer screens outlined black hair, a long braid, and a white shirt. Stepping back into the breakroom, he put the bag of food into the refrigerator.

Fighting the urge to rush into the other room and give a hug, he poured coffee into his skull mug and added the cream. Stirring slowly, he thought about how to approach the subject.

Mike whirred and clicked into the small room and stopped next to the older man. "I hope you left enough for…" He fluttered his one eye low as he glared at Oz. "Thanks."

Pulling the strainer from the machine, he dumped the old grounds and pushed another filter and fresh coffee into the strainer.

Filling the reservoir with fresh water, he looked at the other man still standing there. Mike pushed the start button. "What?"

Oz nodded his head toward the office area.

Mike hummed. "Yeah. She was there when I came in early. I didn't want to risk it being a hallucination, so I didn't say anything."

Oz fished down the black Hydro Flask with the Hello Kitty laser etched into the side. Tearing open two pink packets, he poured in the powder. Mike reached into the refrigerator and added the half and half.

They waited for the coffee to run through and finish.

Oz carried the flask as Mike followed. They both stopped as Powder clicked her way across the linoleum and Nash turned.

"Did you have fun with Andy?"

Powder looked at the two men in the archway. Nash turned the chair around and leaned back. "Not the person any of us wanted to see."

Mike hid the bag of pork rinds behind his back as Oz held out the fresh coffee. "But welcome back to the correct coast. I see you got the computers working."

Nash pointed at the partially open bottom drawer. "I owe you a scalpel. I don't fly with a knife anymore. Not even one in my rucksack. So I improvised. I figured that if she took her guns, the drawer wouldn't remain locked. I think the old school reusable scalpels wouldn't have snapped so easily." She looked at the drawer. "I guess a weapon locker is a weapon locker—guns or keyboards and mice."

Mike frowned at the six monitors being active. His finger slowly twitched from screen to screen. "What is this?"

Nash sipped on the flask and realized Oz had made the sweeter coffee for Muna. "We have three shot-up bodies in New Mexico."

Oz's face slowly raised as he read snippets of the documents on the screens. "Shot by…?"

"Twin thirty caliber mini guns mounted on a helicopter. My experts think a Bell Twinjet 429. Easy pickings, new or used. And if you have cash, it's almost as easy to buy."

Mike's finger waved back and forth. "And the bodies…?"

"Not Americans. Not in our systems, anyway. They appear Arab, and one worked for an armored truck company and gave an Arabic name. Bogus background, but Arabic. So I came out here to see if I could get into Muna's contacts in Interpol."

Oz grumbled as he rubbed his mustache. "And your success rate was…?"

"Broken leg in the fifth race on a muddy track." She swung around and pointed at the one screen on the dark web stack of monitors. "This guy is in Switzerland. And is reaching out to the D.C. office to verify it's me. I'm hoping once I'm verified, others will join in."

Mike nodded. "You're hoping these popsicles have international records?"

"No tattoos, but I'm hoping the fingerprints and faces produce something. Otherwise, I'm at a loss. Without some guidance, we have three stiffs and a thousand rounds of lead through a jeep. And with that and fifteen bucks, I can get a coffee and frybread just north of Albuquerque."

Oz's voice was softer than his usual booming self. "And on our missing girl?"

"If I had anything, I wouldn't come here. I'd go wherever I needed to go. Seriously, guys, this is just as bad on me as it is on you. And I don't think your dad jokes drove her away. We'll figure out what happened. Powder slept by her door all last night. I left the door open, but she stayed by her door."

Mike frowned. "How did she know which room Muna stayed in? I mean, she kind of moved around up there."

Nash hung her head and looked at him through the top of her eyes. "Seriously? You're questioning the super nose?"

"No. Guess not."

Oz pointed at the small flashing envelope in the upper right corner of the dark web screen. "I think you got a response."

Nash clicked on the envelope, and it opened.

Send information on your bodies.

Will have something for you later that you also need to know.

—Asap

Nash clicked on the file folder and copied it. Shrugging her face back at Oz and Mike, she held the cursor in the middle of the letter and clicked paste. The letter folded up and disappeared.

"What kind of name is Asap?"

Nash swung around to look at Mike. "It's basic Arabic for an Adder or Asp. The viper that Cleopatra used to commit suicide."

Oz mussed as he raised his eyebrows. "Interesting choice of name—the desert viper."

Nash rocked her head. "Almost as scary as the name the Ottoman Empire hung on the British Intelligence officer Edward Lawrence."

"Mmm, yes. Lawrence of Arabia. A nasty piece of work he was."

Mike pointed at the dark screen as he slowly turned back to the lab. "How soon do you hear back from them?"

Nash scratched Powder's head and stood. "Just as soon as the envelope reappears. But now, we're going to breakfast."

NASH STOPPED AT THE BENCH IN THE PARK. SITTING, SHE pointed at the tree as she pulled the vibrating phone out of her pocket. She noted the number. It wasn't the deputy director, Donna, or Max's extension, but it was from the FBI's matrix.

"Nash."

It was Donna's voice. "Just giving you a heads-up. The director just went into the deputy's office. They closed the door, but not before I heard your name."

"Thanks… um…?"

"Carter. Peg Carter."

Nash snickered. Glad she had been catching up on current movies. "Of course you are. And thanks for the warning."

"How are things on the other side of the world? Did the other people remove their computer stuff?"

Nash thought about the wooden crates stacked around Chips' workstation and the other remote dredging station. "No. We haven't heard a thing. I suspect it's the old ploy of leaving the threat in plain sight to make you hurry and do what you're supposed to do. Except I don't know what to do."

"Just don't pack it up yourself and pitch it out the window."

Nash watched the power-walking couple of silver-haired men stride past with pumping arms and fists. "I hate waiting. Every time I suggest a walk, Powder shows me the worn shoe leather of her feet. We might have to get her resoled with Vibram's. I check the screen twenty times a day… It's been four days. I need to go kill something."

Donna snickered. "You're not a vulture. Make like a sniper penguin and chill. Nobody else is coming up with answers either. So how are you killing time in the big city?"

Nash stood as Powder danced her feet twenty feet ahead. Breakfast meant breakfast. "I've been doing all the filing the boys haven't done this last month. They've gotten lazy over the last few years. They laid it on the desk, and it magically disappeared. And when I move on to the next spot, they might need to relearn how to do what they used to do for themselves." Nash frowned. "I didn't recognize this phone number. Whose desk are you at?"

"You know the one nobody ever sits at over in the corner?"

"They call it the draft hole. Ice cold in the winter and the sun beats down on it in the summer."

"I had maintenance heavy tint the window in the limousine tint they use on the SUVs. I wouldn't sit here normally, but it keeps me away from Tony's door. He's been getting twitchy lately about what I know of his sensitive conversations."

"That's why you're the Donna."

"Yup. And the door just opened."

"We're out."

"Have a yummy breakfast."

23

TIME TO MOVE

The gray was winning the battle at the back of his head. His right hand scratched, releasing the cowlick. The Slovak hair was still thick in control, more than the oil, grease, or cream his barber kept trying on him. Max could feel the tuft rise between his fingers. His eyes slewed to the last of the iron phones in New York. No ID panel, no extra buttons, just a surprise when he answered it.

"Dammit, Schnelling, answer your fucking phone."

Max smirked at the jangling ring, and its guarantee to always upset the younger agents in the room. He'd quietly spent $1700 of his own money on an antique push-button phone. The inside was pure twentieth century, and not a single millennial had figured out the handset was the same as the green and red icon on their smartphones.

He scooped up the handset and growled. "Schnelling."

"Fuck you lard-ass. You should have retired when you had a chance."

Max chuckled as he recognized the voice. "Fuck you screw head. You and your wife wouldn't have come to my party, anyway. So I had to take the promotion instead."

"I heard you're only warming the seat temporarily. Holding the desk while they train a twenty-something blond bimbo to clean the toilets and polish the chair. Or does the position of station chief mean general flake?"

"Speaking of flakes, I called down to D.C. They said you're out on the woke coast, soaking up the big bucks and sunshine. Any word on the crab cakes, Nash?"

"They're good, but the Hog Island oysters are better. Come on out and I'll take you up to Tamales Bay and treat your fat ass to a few dozen."

His chair squealed in protest as he leaned back and crossed his legs up on the end of his desk. His one foot shoved the In & Out trays to one side, threatening to tumble them over the edge. "Now that's a low blow. You know how much I love good oysters. I've heard of Hog Island…"

Nash snickered. "Seriously. Exercise some of the high-ranking privileges and come out. Twice a day, at low tide, the two rivers flush the oysters with freshwater. Even the New Zealand lip shells can't come close."

Max raised the right arm and flung it over his eyes. He stared at the stacks of files and paperwork piled on his desk. "Well, work has been kind of light this month… No. Really. Why did you call?"

"Truth?"

Max remembered the strange case where nothing appeared to be what it really was. The word truth had taken on a new meaning between the two of them. Almost on a dare, the other wouldn't believe what they would reveal. "Straight up, Injun. One to the other."

"You're Jewish."

"Aaa… Teepee, temple, it's all the same. It still starts with a T. What's stewing?"

"I'm bored."

The silence settled on the man's heart. The B word was one he had never expected to hear from Nash. His right hand flopped out onto the desk and grabbed his coffee mug. He could still feel a trace of warmth, so he brought it to his mouth. The sip turned into draining the mug.

"You're in San Francisco. The center of the Western world. What's going on?"

"Starting east and moving west. I've got a semi-personal problem with a missing Creek or Muscogee Indian girl. She's only sixteen, but still…"

"What's the personal connection?" Always aim for the center mass of the meat.

"My interpreter in Afghanistan immigrated and ended up marrying her grandmother."

He grumped at the empty mug. "Just a moment." He covered the phone and yelled at somebody. "Okay, I'm back. I needed more coffee. I guess it's great being the boss. So, could she have just run away?"

Nash groaned. "Eight hundred Indian kids go missing every year. Some, they find their bodies. A few they find living elsewhere or come home."

"Got it. Go west."

Nash took a deep breath. "Two incidents turned out to be connected. First, an armored truck robbery. Um… think of it as if it happened in a small town west of Albany…"

"Schenectady?"

"Too close… but Buffalo's too far. The robbery was in Ship Rock near the Northern New Mexico border with Colorado. But they found the getaway car in Yah-Ta-Hey near the western border with Arizona."

Max growled. "Bullshit. Let's get back to honest injun territory."

Nash snorted softly. "No. They really found the getaway car. The robbers dumped and torched it." She yawned dramatically as she ignored what he really meant. "It's a sleepy little town with four exits."

His growl turned from avuncular to more paternal. "Let me

guess. North, east, west, and oh my gallbladder... it must be south."

"Wow. You're good at this detective shit. You ought to consider it as a career path when you finally grow up."

Max chuffed. "Ass. Yah-Ta-Hey is a fucking white guy word. The director John Ford put it in his movies because it sounded—"

"Just like the Navajo words, Yah-Ta-Hey. Except friends just say Ya-hey." She swore as she sipped on her coffee flask. "The town is about five thousand people scattered over an area the size of Manhattan."

He sighed as he took the full mug of coffee from the other agent. "Okay. I'll look it up later. So you're out west in Rome."

"That's in Italy."

"Okay, then make it Cooperstown. I don't give a fuck. Small town. What's it matter?"

"Because we found out why they knocked over the armored truck and where they ended up."

Max groaned as he sat up. He was tired of the guessing game. "Which was where? East Park's neighborhood little league baseball diamond?"

Nash sighed, "Might work, as long as East Park is a neighborhood in the suburbs of Albany."

"I don't fucking know. So they're a hundred miles apart..." His voice changed as the detective gene kicked in. "Two different investigations, with two different investigators. How did they tie them together?"

"The other team dug one of the bullet slugs out of the sand and sent it to the Los Angeles ballistic lab. Los Angeles figured it was just whack enough of a case that I was probably involved."

"So they sent the findings report to you in Washington."

"Close. They sent it to my San Francisco office. But yeah. At first, it made little sense. Just some random report on a thirty-caliber machine gun round buzzed through an overheated barrel."

"Did they shoot up the armored truck?"

Nash realized they were back in the guessing game again. "No. In fact, the only shot fired was one of those nail-setting guns they use for concrete. The robbers shot out the lock on the back door. But they threatened the guards with explosives… sound familiar?"

The air escaping through his teeth almost whistled. "Yeah. A bad movie. Stop. Don't come any closer or I'll blow us all to kingdom come."

"Exactly." Nash hummed the most recognizable tune used while contestants wrote their answers.

"Oh. Shit. The robbers were jihadists."

"Arab. But yes."

Max closed his eyes as he pinched the bridge of his nose. "How did the other guys know there was a slug in the sand, and how did they know where it was?"

Nash mouthed the word *bingo*. "Have you ever shot a fully automatic machine gun before?"

"Yeah. We were at a range in Alabama. They had all sorts of full auto shit. An old water-cooled fifty down to some old M4s from the streets of East Los Angeles. Why?"

"Did you shoot the old fifty? Or better yet, did they have any mini guns?"

Max withdrew his hand from his nose and looked at the red pen in his cup holding pens. Only one was red. "One of the other guys shot it. Watching the belt jumping around as it fed was as close as I wanted to get."

"Did he walk the shots out to the target?"

"Yeah… What a waste of lead."

"And there you go. Now think of two of those strapped to the sides of a helicopter. And the shooter didn't care if the barrels looked like Rudolf's nose. And just so you get a clear image, the slugs hitting the jeep and the three Arabs went through and through. Only the engine had any stopping power. My experts figure they ran half a chain through each mini. Maybe more. But a chain is three thousand rounds. Just to answer your next question."

Max looked up at the ceiling as he leaned back in his chair. His mind raced to catch up to his old trainee. "Jeez... mareez Nash. What the fuck were they flying? A Blackhawk?"

"My experts fly a Pave Hawk. Their consensus is a Bell 429 or something called a Koala."

Max blinked. "They use the 429 a lot around here for executives and ambulances. They have two engines and can fly on only one. But years ago, I held one of those cute little bears. The fucking claws on them are a full squad of Samari swords. Either airframe would work. But mini guns aren't exactly something you can hide at the local airport."

Nash stopped sipping on her Hydro Flask of coffee. "Exactly. I've reached out to the FAA and NTSB in the area."

Max snickered. "Now you've given them nightmares and guaranteed some therapist years of income. Do you think you'll hear back from them?"

"Hell, no. But if we find it, you know they'll whine about us impinging on their turf. So this way, I can point out the fact that they received the information and took no action. Personally, I'd like to find the bugger. I mean, who the hell thinks they need a full-blown assault helicopter?"

"I want to know as soon as you find it. And before you try to go fly it."

Nash chuckled. "Because you want to ride shotgun?"

"Fuck shotgun shit. I want to thumb the mini guns."

Nash turned at the sound of the metal whirring and clicking. "Just a minute, Max." She watched Mike turn into the break room. She put the phone back against her ear. "I thought someone needed me. False alarm."

Max watched the movement of his own office. "Obviously, you're busy out there. So how can I help?"

"Injun to Injun?"

"Injun to Injun."

"Who do you know doing the best research on missing people? And… who can do the best dark web shit on my three Arabs? They're not in any of the usual databases."

"That's easy. Your girl. One hundred percent."

"Can't."

"Why not? Is she in the hospital or dead?"

Max didn't like the silence. At the fourth heartbeat, he started counting.

Nash's voice was softer than he had ever heard before. "We don't know. She went MIA a month ago."

Max counted to five and calmed down. "And you buried this lead?"

"It's still a delicate subject. I'm partly to blame, probably mostly to blame, but I don't know how to make it right. At least not until I find her and can talk to her."

"Didn't you once tell me she had an inner network of Interpol geeks?"

Nash splashed some of the coffee back into the flask. "I reached out over a week ago. It was kind of a one-way deal. They said they'd get back to me. I've been waiting ever since."

"Send me what you have. I'll reach out to my old boys' network in the CIA and MI6. Maybe they'll give me some numbers in Interpol. Are we working on just the Arabs, or the girl too?"

Nash sighed. "Which girl?"

"Good point. Have you talked to HR?"

"In a way. I had the deputy director's personal assistant do the reach out. She said they wanted to talk to me in person at Quantico."

Max groaned. "Oh yeah. Like there are no frightening undertones there at all."

"Yeah. And if I can't make progress out here…"

"Eventually, you'll be told you're off your reservation. And it's demanded you report to the principal's office."

Nash dropped her right hand onto the fur. Powder moaned. "I've been off the reservation since I was seventeen."

Max snorted. "I'll vouch for that."

24

HURT LOCKER

NASH LEANED AGAINST THE TREE. Four of the signs she always remembered. *Hurt, agony, pain,* and *love-it* never seemed to change. The tree was in the forest run. Everyone passed it. With time, most ran a little slower as they passed. Many of the returning, for refresher courses, jogged in place or stopped to think or remember.

Nash glared at her phone and then noticed the fresh sign sneaking in between the two fading signs of *pride* and *attitude*. The new lower square sign extolling *respect* and *loyalty*. The new, fresh sign summed up everything: *family*.

She rolled over and leaned against the tree as Powder walked around impatiently. Her tongue hung out and then slurped back in. Only to hang halfway back out.

Nash opened the text attached to an unknown or blocked number—but the digits were international. Nash closed her right eye as she tried to remember the country code. France.

"The file is in your nasty room. Happy hunting. Asap."

It didn't help her attitude. The only enjoyable part of the day was the drive down from D.C. Even Powder had chilled enough to curl up on the passenger seat and sleep. But Nash had always enjoyed driving at night, especially when it was driving into sunrise. The pleasantries ended at the gate. The guard issued her a visitor's pass and lanyard; she had to keep it around her neck until she requalified on the range.

Her first stop was the range. Nope. Privileges were revoked until she had passed her psych evaluation at Human Resources. Soonest appointment was in three days. The only visitor housing was the transit officer barracks on the Marine base side. Running was her only outlet available.

She slid down the tree trunk and sat. Powder calmed down and sat beside her. At least the coarse hair under the tactical vest hadn't changed. There were four more miles on her usual circuit to run—but to where? She pulled up the contact and pushed the button.

Mike's voice was soft, but with an exhausted edge. "I thought we got rid of you."

Nash looked through the trees. The view wasn't like the view across San Francisco's Sunset District. "I thought you went to Mexico. But some people think I work on the West Coast. Can you check Muna's computer screen, please?"

"They were blank and... oh. Well, when I walked in. Where are you?"

"Quantico. It's a long story, but I'm getting the runaround through every door I open."

Mike yawned. "I know the feeling. Okay. There is one of those yellow envelopes pulsing in the left corner. Do the corners mean anything? I mean, usually we get communications on the interconnect in the upper right corner..."

Powder lay down and leaned against her naked thigh, and summer was running short. Nash scratched her back near her butt. "Muna said something once years ago. I guess I wasn't paying attention. Touch it."

"Yeah. We do the same... a lot. She tried to teach us things, but they were beyond the basics of Oz and my understanding, so it just goes intercranial in a second. In one side and scatters out the other. Okay, it's four files. One is doing that glowing pulse thing."

"Touch it. Muna's mind runs at Mach seven, and she forgets we're just mortals hoping to make it through the day in one piece. What's the file?"

Mike's voice became muted. "There are four folders. The pulsing one is photographs. Four look like drone shots, and three are from across a street. This isn't America."

"Middle East?"

"It has the flavor. One picture is a closer shot of the guy."

"Blond?"

"Yes. The SUV he's getting into looks armored, and there are six armed guards."

"Are there any documents with this, Mike?"

"No. Just proof of life kind of photos. The rooftops are flat, so I'm guessing a hot, dry country."

Nash kicked her heel in the trail's dirt. "Yeah. An update. Just to let you know, they are still tracking his whereabouts. What about the other files?"

Mike was silent for a moment. "They look like rap files on three guys."

Nash pulled her phone away from her head and looked at the reception. "Okay. We'll need to leave it for now. I don't know how to send those files to my email, and I only have an iffy two bars and half a battery. How about I call you tomorrow? We'll walk through all of it, and I'll take screenshots."

"Sounds good to me. Oz will be back, and he can finish boiling the two heads we got in from Modesto."

Nash snickered. "Which reminds me. You had one they thought was a machete, but you said it was only sharpened on one side. Did you ever figure the weapon out?"

"Mm, yes. The killer turned out not to be the man's wife, but his brother-in-law. He's a sushi chef. But I think the wife may be complicit. I think she asked her brother to get rid of her husband."

Nash started walking. "It puts a twist on the old sleeping with the fishes."

"Yes. Yes, it does. I think I need to write it down for Oz. He'll need something to cheer him up. He's going over the survey on his boat today. He said something about renaming it the sieve."

Nash looked at her phone for a moment. "Hey, Mike, snap photos of the surveillance photos and text them to me. We'll do the others later. I want to try something here at Quantico."

"You've got it. I'll take photos, text, and then email backups now. And we can talk tomorrow. Happy hunting, Nash."

Nash hummed as she stood. "Tomorrow."

The library was as cool and empty as Nash remembered her early mornings in training. The young woman behind the counter, sitting at a desk, reminded Nash of the older woman who had been at the same desk. Nash realized she didn't want to remember how long it had been.

Nash held up her phone. "Excuse me. Do you have somewhere I can charge my phone?"

The blonde stood and approached the counter. The few freckles alluded to more strawberry blonde than a true blonde. "Is it an Apple?"

"Yeah. I have an important conference in an hour and don't want to go in half dead. And like a dunce, I forgot to bring my cables."

"If it will charge with a MagSafe, set it on airplane mode and stick it in any of the boxes here."

Nash watched for the green light and the tone.

The young woman looked up with a smile at the tone. "In an hour, you should be at full charge and ready for the day. Is your K-9 regularly off-leash?"

Nash chuckled and looked back at Powder, sitting and waiting. "Powder. The gracious lady wants to know if you would like a cute leash to wear?"

Powder got up, turned her back to them, and sat back down.

The woman blushed slightly as her mouth made a small, pursed mew.

Nash leaned back on the counter. "Leash is a nasty word in her native language. Now I'll have to go bribe her with some roadkill or take her over on the marine side and let her have her way with some grunts."

"She's off-leash all the time?"

Nash shrugged. "I don't know. I've only had her for four years."

"What did she do before?"

"Terrorized an old Athabaskan Indian in Northern California. It's kind of like being raised by crazy wolves, but the sleeping arrangement is better."

"I saw the badge—what does she do now?"

"Bombs, bodies, skeletons, treats, drugs, wayward children. The usual."

The blond squinted. "I thought the training was only to do a specific job like drugs or bombs."

Nash smirked. "Oh. Yeah. You're talking about the white man dogs. Yup. Specialists." She pointed at Powder. "Powder trains the trainers who train the dogs. But then, those guys never grew up on a proper reservation, or they'd know about reservation dogs. They must do all the above from birth, or they get left out for vulture bait."

The woman's one eyebrow arched in skepticism.

Nash snorted at the doubt. "Powder, where does the woman keep her treats?"

Powder half glanced back and rose in her best granny walk. She moved to the back of the counter and then to the desk. At the second desk, she sat next to the drawers.

Nash half-smiled at the woman. "No treats. Not even snacks?"

"Type 1 diabetes. Same as my parents. But why is she sitting at Martha's desk?"

Nash chuckled. "Shall we find out?"

They walked to the desk.

"Show us which drawer."

Powder touched her nose at the bottom drawer.

"Is it candy?"

Powder looked over her shoulder.

"Sweet treats?"

Powder pushed back and forth on her front paws.

"Your sister's pork rinds?"

Powder laid down—bored with the questions.

Nash looked at the librarian. "I won't invade Martha's privacy, but she has baked goods in there."

The woman nodded slowly. "Chocolate cupcakes. But I didn't think she opened them yet."

Nash wagged her head. "It wouldn't matter. Our first case together, she showed me where twenty-some skeletons lay at the bottom of a river. I'm not sure it's all nose, or she's psychic. But she knows."

The young woman smirked and pointed at Nash. "I see what you did there. Now I've gotta see." She opened the drawer. The two unopened cupcakes were in a zipped Ziplock bag. "Well, I'll be dipped."

Nash twitched her head. "It's why she doesn't have a leash. Look at her harness. There's no connection point. And when we fly, the flight crew treats her like royalty. But excuse us. I need to go use the reference terminals."

"Yeah. Over... well, you seem to know your way around. Your phone will be here when you're ready."

"Thanks."

Nash sat at an empty terminal, away from any prying eyes. Powder laid down with her back foot resting on Nash's boot. Nash smiled and relaxed as she entered her codes to open her email file.

Making the photos full screen, she looked at the front of the building and the roof. The differences in construction throughout the Middle East were subtle, but there. Nash was certain Sergei Romanov was still in Syria. She didn't have the other photos, but the street views looked similar. He felt safe there. Safe enough to have stayed in one place for almost a year or more.

"Maybe safe enough to round up or something else," Nash mused. Pulling the thumb drive on her keychain, she stuck it into the computer and copied the photos onto the drive. As she stuck the key chain back in her left pocket, she realized she had nobody to send them to or talk about them. The mysterious Interpol contact, nicknamed Asap, was only available through the computer in San Francisco.

She sat back in the chair and folded her arms over her chest. Her eyes bounced from the strange, generic keyboard to the smaller monitor to scanning around the room. Something was off or wrong, and she couldn't put her finger on it.

She scratched at the side of her breast where the bra was chafing in the heat.

She held up her arm and looked at her breast. The lighter shadow of the bra showed in the folds of her white cotton shirt. Her arm gently descended. With the heat, she wasn't wearing an undershirt. And without the shooting range privileges, her level three body armor was still in her rucksack at the Marine barracks.

She focused on not moving. The weight on her hip confirmed the holster and 9mm pistol. The slight dig at her hip confirmed the badge on its clip holder. She had dressed, but wasn't armored. Only the leather pants weren't regulation.

She backed out of the website and then cleared the search history. She looked down at Powder. "Do you need a potty break before we talk to Uncle Mike?"

Powder moaned and sat up and looked at the windows.

As she picked up her charged phone, she looked at the blonde back at her desk. "Brenda, was it?"

"Yes?"

"Do I need to check out one of the quiet rooms?"

The blond burped a chuckle. "At this time of day? You only need a reservation after about four. Then everyone wants to call home and do FaceTime. Just make sure nobody is in one and jump on it."

"Thanks. We'll be back in a minute." Nash tipped her head toward Powder. "Duty calls."

THE QUIET ROOMS WERE THE SIZE OF A SNUG APARTMENT dining room. Just enough room for four around a cocktail-sized table. No room for cards and chips—just talk and phones.

The white walrus mustache blotted half the screen. "Mike ran to the potty when he heard his phone ring."

Nash snickered. "Oz? It's a FaceTime call. Pull the phone away from your... thank you." The large bruise around a bandage Nash hoped hid stitches. "Jeez, Oz. Have you been fighting with the harbormaster again?"

"No. Just an argument with a bow sprint. The aluminum rail won. Here's Mike."

"Thanks, Oz. Good to see you're still alive."

25
SHOW ME SOME LIGHT

With each page of the rap sheet, Nash longed for the days when she could see such things on large screens. She felt like she was rubbing crayons across paper stretched over bas-relief carvings in Palmyra. Artistic attempts, she hoped, would impress the folks back home.

"Next page, Mike."

The screen had frozen.

"Mike?"

"Sorry. Oz needed something. Are you ready for the next page?"

Nash took a deep breath and slowed down her mouth. "Yes, please."

The next page broke into three sections that overlay. The writing on the pale pink note was in handwriting.

"Oh shit. Mike, can you zoom in on that pink note? Is that French?"

The pink filled the screen in San Francisco and overwhelmed the phone. But Nash could see the words. *Shit. Flemish?* She took the screenshot. "Okay, Mike. It's too large this way. Back it down a bit..." The image shrank in her phone, and as the entire note fit the screen, she took another screenshot and waited for the entire page.

"Where does it look like most of this information has him coming from?"

Oz's deeper voice rattled and then cleared. "He's Somalian. It looks like he started as a pirate and then crossed over to the Houthi. Safer to shoot rockets than to board ships. But this last page... the note is talking about being a mercenary and Saudi Arabia, I think."

"You read French?"

Oz chuckled. "I speak French bread, but no. This is Italian. And no, just enough to pick out some words. You need someone who speaks it. See if Jonathan Smyth is still out at the farm. His family has a small vineyard in Tuscany."

"Okay. Thanks Oz. Any help is still help. I feel like I'm back to napping arrowheads with a deer horn."

"Antler, dear. The Cervidae lose their antlers every year. You're thinking of a bovine who grows horns and doesn't lose them unless Vikings get thirsty."

"Oh, yes. Silly me. Maybe I was just thinking about needing to make a drinking horn to get a drink."

Mike coughed. "Please. Don't remind us how much you cleaned up around here. It just exposes how much is getting backed up again. When are you coming back? Soon? He winks in hope..."

Nash groaned. "Being there, listening to you two rehash old dad jokes, would be better than going stir crazy here. My psych eval is tomorrow at three in the afternoon. I think if I suggest another run, Powder's going to go hijack a plane and run away."

Oz grumped. "Well, Powder is always welcome out here. Is this all the files, Mike?"

The more academic of the two cleared his throat. "Um, no. Speaking of hijackings. Someone wandered the conversation down through the piles of undone work."

The screen changed to a new page. "I'm lost here, Nash. Is this page right-side up?"

"Just a moment." Nash pinched and spread her phone's screen.

"Nope. Upside down. It might be Chinese. But I can kind of read it as second form Japanese." She screenshot the document.

"And last, but not least, we have Uncle Sam's contribution."

Nash recognized the ubiquitous form, which did nothing but confirm the recipient had received the aforementioned documents and had no questions. It had a form number and title, but everyone who had ever gotten speaking training referred to it as the dreaded *Umm doc*. "Oh, thanks, Mike. The file wouldn't be complete without the Umm 765-34B."

"Okay. Are you ready for body number two?"

Nash grabbed the screenshots and moved them to a file she marked as *Body-1*. "One... seco... nd. And ready."

The screen changed.

"I'M TEMPTED. I CAN'T BELIEVE I BROUGHT THE computer bag and missed the weight of the laptop still charging on the countertop."

Mina giggled. "Well, I guess I'm not allowed to nibble on your ear when you're rushing out the door at oh-dark-thirty."

Nash washed her hand over the freshly mowed lawn as she watched Powder rolling ten yards away. "Oh yes. The flash of us getting back to our normal was what made me lose my mind. But it was good to know you're turning the corner. How's your strength?"

"Lele took me over to the Blue yesterday so I could chew some freshman ass. I swear, the new kids bought their jobs. They talk big about how bad DEI hires are, but then turn around and elect a fourth-grade maladroit from the backwaters of clueless county. And then they expect them to do right in running the country."

Nash smirked. "And there's the girl I married. Piss, vinegar, with a black-belt mouth wrapped around a sharp stiletto. Did you at least feed Lele?"

Mina groaned. "The twit stank so high of a five-shot lunch, we left and went to have tapas. Gordo says hello, and you never bring your wife enough. She's having to see another woman on the side."

Nash glanced at her orange-faced dive watch and did the math about the drive. "I think it's too late to come back now. We'd get in after dinner and just in time to turn around to get back here for the psych evaluation tomorrow. Besides, I overheard a couple of agents talking about a few agents who run in the evening. I want to go check it out."

"Don't they always run in groups?"

"Sure. But not all groups wear hijabs."

"Oh. Happy hunting you two."

"I think I'm going to have to rely heavily on Powder this time."

The track could have been at any high school in any state. The bleachers could tightly squeeze less than a hundred people along the four rows of seats. As Nash and Powder climbed to the third row, Nash remembered the seats weren't wooden, but cast fiberglass. The color guaranteed to never fade had only become a softer gray over the years. The junior agents who returned for special classes always found it amusing. Their choice of uniform matched the gray of the bleachers at the track.

Nash nodded at the young couple who were cooling down from running in what some referred to as FBI dating. Smelling like aged gym gear wasn't the sexiest cologne or perfume for romance. But it was the most pervasive smell during the months spent less than ten kilometers from the romantic Potomac River. But it was a shared experience like no other.

Nash lounged back into the next row and mussed as she ruffled Powder's ears. "Kind of like sharing your bedroom with a hundred other people. Not all of them are the same sex." She pulled the head to her lips and snuggled a kiss. Then she pulled the chest of the gray, sweat-stained sweatshirt to her nose. It still reeked of the pimple-marked kid she had given the hundred dollars to for his sweatshirt and ratted, brown ATF hat. The cheap, black wraparound dark glasses were always in her rucksack.

Memento from years before her taste in glasses had followed her wife's.

The first group, turning onto the track, could have been a lost squad of Marines. Each left foot landed flat in a single flop. Nash silently counted the cadence as they double-timed their way around the oval. Not the most elegant, but also not the worst she had seen on a base.

Oh, here we go. Three pink-faced young men turned onto the track. The gray sweatshirts were all darkened in what EMTs refer to as the heart attack stain. Center mass. The sweat spreading the stained spot toward their soft bellies would start shortly after the second lap. Nash and Powder watched as the three struggled past the bleachers. *Where do they get these children?*

The man and woman watched until the trio started into the curve and then glanced back at Nash and Powder. They exchanged a few soft words, looked around the field, and then left. The congestion of eyes being trained to observe nuances can sometimes be overbearing.

Nash paused, scratching Powder's neck as she spotted five women turn onto the track. The t-shirts on the three of them were long-sleeved. Two were baggy, but not overtly so. All the sweatpants were the standard. Gray. Not baggy, but not fitting, either. From across the field, Nash only knew they were women by their stature and the dark gray hijabs. A sight unheard of when Nash was a fresh recruit. Even then, women were not the norm.

Nash pulled the hat hard down over her dark glasses. Her running shoes rested against the back of the next row of seats. She snapped her fingers for Powder to get down on the walkway for the upper row. With only her head showing, at a casual glance, the face might pass for a towel or something.

Powder slipped down and rested her head next to Nash's hip. Leaning back, Nash braced her shoulders on the top seats—reducing her visual profile.

The squad of Muslim women rounded the far end of the track.

Nash's focus danced from one face to the next. Only one face was as light as creamed coffee. They ran in a formation of three and two. The arms were held at different heights, but the feet were in unison. They had been running together for some time.

As the five drew to half a length of the field, Powder rolled back and looked behind them. Nash froze—her attention was on the middle woman of the three. Her sweatshirt didn't move right. There was body armor underneath.

The voice was soft. "Shh. Don't tell your mother she sticks out like a blooming cherry tree in a pine forest. And that she's busted."

Nash looked down at the nose rising in the air. Powder's sign that she wanted nothing to do with the pissing match. "Tell your sister I could smell the pork rinds for the last hundred yards."

The small black woman walked around the end of the bleachers. "Total bullshit. I ate the last pork rind in San Francisco."

Nash studied the new look and realized she had seen the head in the library. The natural curls softly fell from under the FBI ball cap to her shoulders. There wasn't any armor under the light gray T-shirt. But the fit was close enough to hint at the sports bra. The black leggings sank into the scrunched socks and black high-tops. She might have gotten by walking past Nash on the street. But not the super nose.

"You chopped your hair."

Muna shrugged and settled down on the other side of Powder. "Eh. Hair is hair. It got hot, and it was a hassle to braid it long." Her head turned up from kissing Powder's head. "Don't worry. I still pray to Allah."

"And gave up pork rinds…"

"And coffee." Muna looked out at the field. "For now." She glanced back. "I sleep better."

Nash looked out. "Yeah. Sleep is good." She looked back at the agent of mystery. "Have you spoken to your mother? She was worried."

"Not until you showed up on her doorstep. But yeah. Last night. I figured you would hear about the Muslim girls running at this time of the evening."

Nash drifted her chin up and then down. Not sure what to say, or what she could say.

"Are you ready for your psych evaluation tomorrow?"

Nash twitched a half-chuckle. "Was I supposed to study for it?" *Of course, she knew.*

Muna leaned back to the next bench and rested her arms akimbo. "I don't know. They won't let me on the range yet. They've gotten kind of touchy about things like traumatic brain injury and PTSD. I guess they've gotten sued lately."

"Or someone forgot to warn the agents what fieldwork could look like."

Muna rubbed her ribs. "Or feel like. But it only hurts when I laugh."

"Then don't hang out with Oz and Mike."

Muna blustered her lips. "I said laugh, not groan."

"The pile of paperwork burying Mike's desk is spilling onto the floor."

"Yeah. I figured."

The silence stretched out between them.

Nash peeked over. "So they're letting you shoot soon?"

"Not until you pass your psych evaluation. That's why I know it's at fifteen hundred."

Nash hooked her right foot under the next seat and levered her body upright. "I guess I need to go feed the little one."

Muna stood and turned toward the other end of the bleachers. "Yeah. I need to go finish my five miles before prayers."

Nash turned. "Hey, Muna?"

She turned back. "Yeah."

"Who's the hardass in Human Resources who locked down our range time?"

Muna firmed her mouth as her hands rose. Her right thumb rubbed against the edge of her left thumb. Her gaze rose from the ground as her face hardened. "Oz."

26

PAPER

NASH GLARED out the window at the lone, small cloud drifting in the endless blue sky, framed by the hulking government-issued steel window from the post-World War II days. Washington, every four years, talked big about cutting budgets. But they never talked about changing the cold in the winter and the hot in the summer windows in the government buildings. Her hearing shifted to the sound of the shuffling papers. She bet the woman raking through the thick file hated the office in the heat of summer and wore her jacket during the winter.

"It appears getting blown up or shot wasn't new to you."

Nash's eyes shifted focus from the window to the woman behind the desk. The dark near the ears wasn't shadow as much as the woman making a pass or three of mascara where the temples had revealed the truth about the stress of the job. Nash guessed late fifties. But the nature of knowing that everyone you talk with, every day, resents your existence will age you faster than a race car driver forced to race on bald tires.

"No. No, it wasn't."

The woman flipped back through several pages. "In Kandahar, you were…"

"Both, ma'am."

The woman's wide eyes looked shocked, but Nash guessed it was more about not being used to new contact lenses. The woman hadn't blinked more than a dozen times in the last half an hour.

"Bad enough to fly you…?" She flipped through some more pages, searching for the answer.

"It's not in there, ma'am. The dust-off was only to Bagram air base. Once they stabilized me there, I got the jolly green to Landstuhl, ma'am."

The woman looked up from the paperwork and let the pen roll out from between her fingers. Studying the agent before her, she leaned back in her chair. "We're just talking here, Special Agent Bear. You don't have to sit at attention."

"No, ma'am. Not at attention, ma'am."

"Then what's wrong, agent?"

"Nothing, ma'am. And everything, ma'am."

The hazel eyes ticked and danced minutely as she studied the face, starched white shirt, black leather pants, and boots she would expect more on a man. "Let's start with what's wrong."

Nash raised her right knee a half inch—redistributing the weight from the right hipbone to the left. "Permission to speak freely?"

The psychologist dipped her head slightly. "That's what this interview is for. To catch up on what's going on with you. I'm not a superior officer or something. I can't fire you… nor would I ever want such a responsibility. Just the junior shrink."

Nash's eyes narrowed. "Three years, four months, and twenty-one days."

"What's that?"

"My last psychological evaluation. The evaluation took place in the morning. So technically, it was three years, four months, twenty days, and eighteen hours ago. I was still on morphine, with an intravenous drip of glucose and saline. The oxygen was the only appreciated part."

The woman cocked her head to one side. "Why?"

"It didn't hurt."

"And the rest hurt? How so?"

"The intravenous port was becoming infected, but they didn't believe me. I don't like morphine as much as I'd prefer plain aspirin. They made my wife wait outside, and I didn't have my dog with me. But at least the interviewer understood and got my name correct."

The psychologist leaned forward and flipped the folder back to the front. "Your name isn't Bear?"

"No."

The woman frowned. "Who are you then?"

"Bear is an animal. They are only semi-seasonally socialized to reproduce or hibernate collectively. My collective is Northern California Paiute. My clan is Running Bear, not a bear. One is a proper noun, and the other is a pronoun."

The psychologist gently closed the folder. "Do you feel a need to have your wife here with you?"

"I would advise against it. Neither one of us would get a word into the conversation. But I'm curious why you seem hostile toward dogs. Did you have an unpleasant experience as a child?"

"Would you feel more at ease with your K-9 here?"

Nash twitched her head side to side. "It's not me. But she would be more at ease to know I'm okay."

"Is that common with K-9s? Separation anxiety?"

"Not in my experience. But then, those dogs are not my dog. K-9 dogs are trained to work with a handler. A few form a lifelong bond. But most military dogs work with a few handlers as duties cycle in and out."

"And your dog…?"

"No one trained her. We're partners, but also family. She sleeps between us at home. We eat at the same table. She's family."

"And you would feel more comfortable if she were here?"

"Yes."

"Where is she?"

"In the front waiting room, I assume."

"Where did you tie her up?"

Nash softly snorted in derision. "You can't tie her up. She doesn't have a leash, and there's no leash ring on her tactical vest. We have a leash in D.C., but she carries it in her mouth, so we're not technically breaking the law. But nobody in the neighborhood has ever complained."

The woman held out her hand at the closed door. "Okay. Let's get her in here and see if she makes the interview a little less adversarial."

Nash stood and resisted the urge to salute. She stepped to the door and opened it. Looking down, she chuckled and looked back up at the marine sergeant standing at parade rest.

"The dog was unaccompanied, ma'am."

"Yes. It's okay, Sergeant. We've got it from here."

"Yes, ma'am."

As Powder stepped into the room, Nash closed the door. "As you can see. I'm alive, and I'm not bleeding. Nobody is beating me to make me talk. Would you like to come sit with me?"

The dog all but limped her stoved-up granny walk and crawled into the wing chair, not smelling like Nash. She circled and then sat at attention—facing her nose just left of the psychologist.

The older woman looked at Nash, but was also watching the dog. "Well?"

Nash settled. "Where were we...? Oh yes. Getting blown up and shot. Sixty-seven days in Germany and then rejoined my team, who had cycled back while I was goldbricking. The next year, I got offered a job with only slightly less potential for injury, so I took it. I taught here at Quantico and over at Langley. Eventually, it became boring, so I opted for special operations, special investigations." She pointed at the thick folder. "I believe it should all be in there?"

The woman thumbed the edge of the folder. "I only perused it.

There's a lot there. How did you feel about your time in Afghanistan ending?"

Nash's cheek twitched on the right side, and she turned to look at Powder. Her right hand stroked the back of the neck just above the tactical vest. "It didn't. I'm still dealing with fallout from there."

"Flashbacks?"

Nash fluffed her lips. "Wouldn't that be nice? You get a classic triggered psycho, and I never play in the field again. No. Twenty years later, my team's interpreter reached out. Now I'm in the middle of a case involving missing girls, dead bodies, a lot of cash, and a shot-to-shit jeep. I'm missing my research backup, her team, and now, I can't qualify to shoot until you sign off."

"And the sleepless nights?"

Nash studied Powder. "She's getting better. We cut back on her broccoli and garlic. We think it was giving her night reflux."

The woman's eyes narrowed. "And you?"

"When she sleeps, I sleep. Are we good here?"

The woman leaned back with her fingers steepled at her chin. "Is this always a game with you?"

Nash slumped back into her chair enough to mirror the steepled fingers. "My guess is you got my file yesterday. You stuck it in your briefcase and told yourself you would go over it at home after dinner. The wine was superb, but the dinner burned. To get your calorie count, you doubled down on the wine and angry-binged several episodes of whatever is tripping your trigger right now. But the last thing was my file. So at lunch, you tried to sort through everything, but little made sense. You looked for the normalcy in my life and hoped to guide me back there. How am I doing?"

"Go ahead."

Nash wiggled back up to her usual sitting at attention and reached out to the still stiff at attention Powder. "My boss insisted I take a job once. It involved jumping out of an airplane with my dog strapped to my chest. We would land in a bombing range and crawl on the frozen ground, probing for bombs with a knife."

The eyes opened slightly. "And did you?"

"I told him the only way I would take the assignment and pack my dog out the door of an airplane was with three conditions. The first was that he had to be by my side every step of the way."

The woman held up her thumb.

"Second, I was at the top of the incident command structure, and I used my own team. My former sergeant and a friend. Later, it grew to four more box ticks in the alphabet soup, and then a civilian research group. But by then, my third condition was guaranteed. I got everything I needed with a blanket sign-off."

The woman's forehead wrinkled as she tried to raise one eyebrow. "And this is important... how?"

"The morning after he had almost soiled his cold-weather suit, probing for bombs, he asked me if the case was usual for me, or did I always get the strange cases?"

"What was the case, and why did he consider it strange?"

"My former sergeant and his team of smoke jumpers had landed in the bombing range. Almost on top of two large freezers full of dead bodies. Human bodies."

The psychologist's mouth mewed into a microscopic circle. "What did you tell him about your cases?"

Nash pointed at the file. "If you had in fact read the file, you would know I'm a member of one of the smallest tribes in a large nation. I'm taller than most women. My wife is of Taiwanese Irish descent and about the same height. I got named for the car they conceived me in because my father worked the shit hours the white man throws to the lowest person on the railroad. My mother was the woman who sees things. Only recently have I come to the understanding that my father is also a shaman. Even as a small child, I saw things like my sister, who wouldn't be born for another two years. In the Marine Corps, I chose the most macho and high-testosterone job they had. After that, I taught hand-to-hand combat, shooting, and firefight safety and tactics, as well as defensive driving like a spy.

When I got bored, I opted for the most engaged of all the field positions. But when the deputy director asked if I always got strange stuff, I asked how could I know. I don't know what normal is."

The woman closed her eyes and pinched the bridge of her nose. After a few seconds, she asked from under her hand, "What does your wife do?"

"She works at attempting to guide members of Congress to do the right thing and help the country."

One eye opened. "A lobbyist."

Nash's scoff was sharp and short. "Hardly. Those asshats work for corporations whose only interest is lining their pockets and making more money at the expense of the nation. My wife wears a white hat... or wig—as the case may be. She's battling cancer. But she finds the funds to pay for her using her influence. Most of the time it's anti to the lobbyist interests. So, why is what she does for a living relevant?"

The woman sat up straighter. "It isn't. Does it tick any of the boxes? No. But you're right, dinner was a disaster, and trying to get through your file will take more time than I thought, or what we have here today." She glanced at her watch. "But knowing more of the facets of the whole Nash Running Bear can help me understand how all the reports and evaluations come together."

Nash shifted as Powder glanced at her. "Does it get me my range privileges back?"

"That's important to you...?"

"I assume you're probably the person they forced Muna al-Faragi to see. I talked briefly with her yesterday. She indicated she's not released to shoot again until I am."

"So... a competition thing?"

Nash thought about the question and the implications. She nudged her chin toward the woman's watch. "How much time do I have left?"

The therapist narrowed one eye. "This isn't a therapy session.

This is an evaluation. I won't try to make dinner again tonight. So is it a competition? If she gets to shoot, you get to shoot?"

Nash cocked her head. "Sounds petty when you put it that way. Do you have any siblings?"

"Five brothers and two sisters. A good Boston Irish Catholic family."

"Who did you like to hang out with and do things together?"

"My oldest brother taught me everything about hotrods and taking care of a chronically dying Mustang. We called her the palliative pony."

Nash nodded. "So the competition isn't about who can drive the car the fastest. But it's about the shared rebuilding of the carburetor, setting the points, or gapping the spark plugs."

The one eye closed softly as she dipped her head.

"In straight-up shooting for score, Muna's in a league of her own. In Paris, I won't begin to guess what was going on, but it wasn't the shooting I watched her do day in and day out. We shot the tiny plus signs at the corners of the targets. We shot the tiny sniper targets with our pistols as the target still raced away to the end of the rifle range. If I started shooting out the center, she was there one shot ahead of me at the end. It's never about who was better, but a matter of *we*. We shot because we enjoyed it. Shooting calms her. Sometimes it was how we worked out the discomfort coming with a case. But it was what we did… do. Like going to breakfast in a café a mile away. It's a respectable walk and has outstanding food. Sometimes the morning is in silence. Other times, we have complex conversations with our pistols while shooting five hundred rounds at paper targets."

The psychologist took a breath through her nose. She nudged out her chin. "Let's talk about your right hand."

Nash looked at her hand. Flexing it, she frowned at it. "What about it?"

The woman pointed at Powder. "Your other one. You stated she wasn't trained, but she seems to be."

Nash shrugged. "She's a reservation dog. She doesn't know the commands to sit, shake, or roll over. But if you ask her to sit with you, she understands. When our favorite flight attendant holds up his hand, she knows how to give a high five, but she doesn't know what it is. It's something she and James have seen other people do. She wasn't trained to sniff for bombs, bodies, or drugs. But if you have candy, baked goods, or some other treat in your desk, she will show me where it is."

"And you used her, how?"

"The first case I met her on, she showed us where the skeletons were in a creek. Underwater and had been there for years. No cadaver dog can do such a thing. Being a smart ass, James, her flight attendant uncle, told her if she found the body, he'd give her a treat. She walked the length of the plane and then sat down at row seventeen. James asked the pilot if there was a Jim Wilson on the flight. It's the code for a dead body being transported. It turned out there were two servicemen they were carrying back to San Francisco for burial. The coffins lay stowed in the hold at row seventeen."

"How were you assigned her?"

"I wasn't. It was more like she knew she was supposed to be with me."

The silence was palpable. The woman's voice was softer, not on familiar ground. "Is there such a thing as a shaman dog?"

Nash ran her hand over Powder's head and scratched the neck. "First one I've heard of. But, now you're starting to understand both of us."

"And you're talking with al-Faragi?"

"If she'll answer her phone."

The woman opened her desk drawer and pulled out her phone. She scrolled through the contacts and then typed a brief message. She watched for the answer and nodded. Returning the phone to the drawer, she closed it.

She leaned back. "I'll sign off tonight for the range. I think it will do you both some good. I texted her dinner dates were ready.

She'll be here in five. I think you two can help each other work through what's going on between you two better than talking to me. I'll return her to active duty. The classes she's teaching end next week, so she can decide where she wants to be. I'll back her play whether it's here or in the field. She used a term once about being a grown-assed woman. I'm not sure what it means, but I'm more Boomer than Gen X. And the millennials have their own code."

"Thank you."

"I'll text you the information you'll need. But when you know you're going to be around, I'd like for you to check in at least a few times a year. Or call. I know you're all over, but we can even set up FaceTime sessions or Skype."

Nash nodded as she stood. She looked at Powder. "Let's go take your sister to dinner."

GETTING HOME

POWDER LEANED against Muna's shoulder. The head would turn and then look straight ahead.

Nash chuckled as she chewed. "I don't think she's sure about the short hair yet."

Muna threaded her thumbs over her ears. Grabbing two handfuls of hair, she raised them to the top of her head. "It's my covert hair."

"Under cover?" Nash frowned. "Since when?"

"I figured out how to infiltrate the castle."

Nash frowned around the chopsticks. "Castle?"

Muna stirred the air with her ad hoc pom-poms. "It's a gaming reference. Every game is nothing more than a variation of Dungeons and Dragons. Storm the castle, conquer the defenders, and steal the booty."

"Are you applying for a job with Ming and Tree?"

The shy girl blushed as she still held her hair up in wild renditions of puffs. "May...be..."

"So what happened?"

"When?"

Nash studied the junior agent as she lowered her hair and

gingerly picked up chopsticks. "Start wherever you want to start. Doctor Feelgood figured out we're better talking to each other than talking to someone who never shot a gun, got blown up, or shot."

Muna nodded her eyelids as she chewed. Taking a sip of tea, she dabbed at her mouth. "Yeah, she kind of turned white when I started talking about getting my jaw broken. As we got into the firefight and me dragging my guts out onto the mesa to avenge my partners, I had to stop. I almost thought she was going to use the trash can to throw up. My guess is she only sees the recruits and office weenies."

Nash smirked and chuckled. "You used the old storyline from…" She looked at the ceiling. "Shit, I can't remember the movie, but it was about Marines or Grunts, definitely not about Air Force."

Muna tossed her head. "I'd say going to save the Ryan guy… but I know I never watched that one."

"So you already know I wore out my custom-shaped level three armor. Evidently, sleeping in it breaks the isotope bonds in the layers—or something."

Nash coughed into her fist. "*Bullshit.*"

Muna smirked and rolled her eyes. "Yup. Not a fucking inch of slack." She turned her head to within inches of Powder. "What have you been feeding her? Mean girl pills?"

Powder turned the other way—ignoring her.

Both women laughed.

"Well, whatever it was, the back cracked, and duct tape isn't a long-term solution. Then the Velcro let go from the breastplate, and by then, I was here. I checked out some new level two, which is all they had. But it ended in chafing sores, so I just stopped wearing it. But by then, I was six visits deep in with Feelgood and just rode out the agitation until I slept from exhaustion. By the third week, I was back to running with the halal team and realized I wasn't jonesing for rinds. Coffee's another matter."

"I've heard it's harder to dump than heroin." Nash rolled her finger in the air. "Feelgood mentioned you're teaching?"

"More like mentoring. Mostly on the shooting range. Everyone wants tips from the Olympic loser."

Nash studied the flat tone of delivery. "We all watched you shoot. More importantly, I watched you shoot…"

Muna slumped. "Yeah, not my best days. Something had set me off the day before, and I just couldn't get my head back in the game. The best I can work out is that it just wasn't the same as shooting the alley."

"What happened the day before?" Nash spooned some more stir-fry onto the small wad of rice in her bowl.

"I can't say for sure. There was a commotion during lunch—screaming echoing through the dormitory halls. Oddly enough, not a soul seemed to care. Even the security stood idle, oblivious to the chaos. I heard whispers later that it happened in the German dorms. My nerves were frayed by then, and I needed thick glasses to focus. I considered zoning out to some Zen tapes, but my mind was too cluttered to recall if I'd packed any."

"You have Zen tapes? What kind?"

"No. And that's the thing—I was so distracted I wasn't thinking straight. Besides, is there such a thing? My Zen is shooting and pounding the keyboards. They wouldn't let us log extra practice, and their idea of fast internet limped like a broken leg for a boot disk. By the time it came time to shoot, I'd watched the two from Türkiye. Everyone talks about the guy, but it's the chick. Man, talk about a cold-hearted computer. She's a machine."

Nash carefully laid down her chopsticks and leaned forward. She spiked her elbows on the table and rested her cheek on her balled, clasped hands. Her frown was soft. "Let me guess, even when you got home, your mind kept questioning if you had the tapes, and even if you ever had them."

Muna stuck her chopsticks into the bowl of food and then stared at the meaning. Collecting the two sticks into her right fingers, she laid them across the bowl and collapsed back into the booth. Her voice was little more than a breath. "Yeah. Even past Christmas. I was in a music store on Geary Street. I asked the woman behind the counter if they had Zen tapes. It took her a few seconds to figure out what I was talking about. And then she asked me if I meant disks." Muna looked up at Nash's concerned face. "That's when I realized, for all the geek I was, I don't even have a CD player anymore. Everything is thumb drive or cloud."

"Did the realization stop the questioning?"

Muna reached over to the curve in the booth. Her hand found the now lying down fur. Her hand stroked the ear through her fingers and thumb. "About whether I had the tapes? Yeah. But then the questions about my sanity began. Why did the screaming upset me? What was up with the obsessive memory loop? I must have dumped out my ruck and sorted it a dozen times."

Nash winced, hard. "Ew. Don't remind me…"

Muna giggled sardonically. "So, you know the little pocket that's just right of the center pocket, but not on the side?" Nash thought and then nodded minutely. "What do you keep in there?"

Nash closed her eyes and then slowly squinted. The head shake was slight. "It's small. Knife? Maybe?" She opened her eyes. "A wad of car keys would fit, but I only have three keys on my car fob." She felt what was coming, and she stifled her giggle. "What did you find?"

"Remember the first long drive with the guys down to Orange County?"

"When we met Deep Six."

Muna dipped her head. "I didn't know when you crazies were going to eat again, so I stashed two protein bars in mine. They turned up during the fifth sorting. I kept overlooking the pocket."

Nash took up her chopsticks and pecked at the stir-fry. "Those protein bars have a nuclear half-life of eight point seven million years." She shoved the wad of food into her mouth and smiled at her geek joke.

Muna's face screwed up in grotesque revulsion as her head vibrated. "No. No, they don't. I hadn't noticed the mold until the third bite." She held up her hand. "Not to worry. I had Mike analyze it. No botulism, bacillus, or dengue spores. Just good old healthy penicillin. Mike threw it in the hazmat bucket so Oz wouldn't snack on it."

The giggling felt like old times. Powder sat up and leaned over against Muna's shoulder.

Muna kissed the top of the fuzzy head. "Yeah, I've missed you too."

Nash laid the chopsticks across her bowl and pushed it forward a couple of inches. Sipping her hot tea, she studied the two kids. "So, when did you decide to come back here?" She pointed at Muna. "And you must admit, it was rather dramatic taking an Uber to the train station. Then I tracked you by train down to Los Angeles and over to Las Vegas before catching a military hop from Nellis to here."

Muna rolled her head on Powder's to smirk at Nash. "Look at you, Miss Detective and all. But you missed the half day at Disneyland. I wanted to find out what I had missed the last time I was there with a broken jaw. A Monte Cristo sandwich isn't the same after the blender."

Nash deadpanned the junior agent.

Muna giggled. "Seriously. Extremely messed up. After breaking down in front of Mike and Oz, I was in high school freshman mode. If I'd thought about the credit card trail, I would have found a cab with cash instead of calling Uber to the bus station."

"Maggie's people only found you at the train station in San Jose, and then three days later in Las Vegas. Flashing your credentials at Nellis air base set off bells, but then, they're used to screwball shit coming from Washington, D.C. So they let it pass until my inquiry. But I wouldn't have thought of military hops except I caught one with Trouble and Cotton from Oklahoma City to Albuquerque. They said hello."

Muna snorted. "Did you fly the entire way with the door open?"

"No, ass. It would have messed up the little bladder's hairdo. Speaking of which."

Muna pulled at her hair. "I was looking for a taxi away from the train station in Vegas. I saw some girls, one with this cut. They said they knew a place that would do the cut for free and take the extra for Locks of Love. It was a ride better than a taxi. Now I need to remember to send out Christmas cards."

"Twenty-eight years of religion bites the dust at the slash of fashion to blend in with another black girl?"

Muna's eyebrows rose as her eyes widened. "No. She was white. Just the same wavy curls. It was a strange bonding, but after the haircutter had made the cut and washed it out, she realized we really were a matched set. Her hair was finer, but still the same— wash it, rub it dry, and walk away. I don't know if I'll cut it again, but it's been a relief with this heat. I'd forgotten how sticky it is here in summer."

"This is only spring." Nash pulled some of her braid around and looked at it. Looking up, she smiled. "Just kidding. But let's get back to the day with Mike and Oz." Nash held her finger out— pointing. "And I deeply apologize for not calling you in the night. I'll fill you in later, but continue."

Muna lay back against the booth. "Now there was a shit show. It somehow felt like all the mean girls had jumped me in the bathroom. I'd been dragging my sullen ass around the building and not realizing it was shitting on everyone else. Oz realized what needed to happen, so they sort of got me in autopsy and tried to do a delicate intervention. The poor guys didn't realize they were popping a balloon instead of nudging me down the path. I probably traumatized them for life."

"I think they're tougher than you think. But they have been worried. I went out and filed paperwork for a few days."

"That's when you got my research on those three guys?"

Nash raised an eyebrow. "You're the desert viper?"

Muna frowned. "The what?"

"Asp. The snake who bit Cleopatra and killed her. Well, the English spelling is A-S-P, but the Arabic has the extra *A* between the *S* and the *P*."

Muna choked a giggle. "No, ass. It was As Soon As Possible. But it was all I could find. Squidgy in Paris said Saudi Arabia was playing games about background checks on mercenaries. Probably because they were using so many in Syria and Gaza. But Deep Six had already cut me off, leaving me only with my direct Interpol contacts. Did the information help?" Her eyes popped wide. "Wait. You weren't in San Francisco then. You were here. How did you get the files?"

Nash laughed. "I was wondering when you'd figure that one out. When I was out there, I had popped your locked drawer, but the keyboard and mouse didn't work the dark side. But Mike wouldn't have touched them anyway. So I just had him touch-screen the packet while we Face Timed, and I kept taking screenshots."

Muna smiled a full picket fence of ivory. "Fire. Totally going major gangster." Her hand rose with the thumb and forefinger crossed to make the small heart shape popular with kids.

Nash noticed Powder pumping her front feet. "Yeah. We're going." As she stood, she looked at Muna. "You have classes tomorrow?"

"Morning, then geek lunch with the halal girls. One is turning twenty-five. It's kind of a big deal age with us—quarter century hits hard when you're not married. Why?"

"And the weekend?" Nash glanced down at the phone in her hand.

Muna cleared her throat with a choked laugh. "I might be bribed..."

"Lamb or goat?"

"Lele's choice."

Nash chuckled. "Lamb, it is." She turned her phone to show Muna the text about biryani for Friday night dinner.

DINNER AND . . .

LELE STOOD in the kitchen while the other three caught up. The enormous book was from her limited library of books she had gathered over the years while touring as an itinerant nurse. As the biryani worked its magic in the oven to impact the air and stimulate hunger, she studied and listened—the true magic of being a nurse.

The slight smile picked at her right cheek as she listened to Mina's talent for asking soft questions, which revealed deeper truths. But this wasn't a grown public servant elected to look out for the public's trust. This was family. More importantly, this was part of the family working to find their way back from crisis. Not a crisis of health, which was Lele's wheelhouse, but of mental health and the nature of their work.

"But how's your jaw now? Does it still ache?"

Muna rubbed the side of her face. "When it's cold. Like the middle of summer when San Francisco turns into a deep freeze." Her eyes snapped open wide. "Oh. Wrong case."

Nash groaned.

Mina rested her hand on top of Muna's. "And the nightmares…"

Muna shook her head tensely. "Not exactly. I think the nightmares were more about the explosion. That's why I didn't make the connection at first. I don't swim, but the dreams weren't exactly clear-cut. I felt like I was falling backward into a pool or a body of water. And then I was drowning and couldn't breathe. But there wasn't any pistol-whipping involved." She shrugged her face. "Maybe that'll come later—once I sift all the chaos."

Lele turned at the stove.

Mina noticed the movement and looked over. "Thoughts?"

"The inability to breathe. They put you in a coma because your right lung filled with blood. And then, after the surgery to find the bleeder—from a chunk of shrapnel they had missed the first time— your lung collapsed. So… maybe you're processing the trauma of all that. It happens. Even in a coma…" She pointed at Muna and then Nash. "We still have thoughts or dreams. Our bodies remember them, even if we don't consciously remember what we were experiencing."

Mina leaned back with her arm hanging over the back of her chair. "Is this nurse Lele from practicum? Or from the fifty pounds of words you have there?"

Lele smirked and turned back to her book. "I hide the gray well." Her fingers feathered through her blonde hair and flipped out the back in a single finger. The table rewarded her sass with a round of chuckling.

Turning back around, she crossed her stomach with her arms. Her right hand hung out with the index finger up. Her eyes were loosely closed, a sign Mina was getting used to of the nurse remembering something.

Her finger continued to bounce as she opened her eyes. "You kind of glazed over the breaking down in front of Mike and Oz."

Muna sank shyly into herself. "Yeah?"

Lele pointed. "Only child, right?"

"Right."

"First in your class in high school."

"Your point?"

Lele's palm flashed a stop. "Same for college. Valedictorian?"

"No. MIT is a tough school. I was up against a lot of Asian kids. Not Valedictorian, but Summa Cum Laude. And the point is…?"

"Phi Beta Kappa?"

The edge was creeping into Muna's voice. "Of course."

"Top of your class at Quantico."

Nash groused. "There are no class rankings at the Q. You made it or you were gone. What's your point?"

Lele stepped to the table and rested her hands on the back of her chair. "There's an isolation at the top of the heap, and not having to compete with anyone close. Me? I didn't know how it felt. For me, staying in and out of honor society was a quarterly struggle. I pushed hard my senior year and graduated Cum Laude. But nothing special beyond that. In nursing school, I got my hat and stethoscope."

She pointed at Mina. "She had no choice. Summa Cum Laude and valedictorian or suffer dishonor to the family. It's the burden many Asian kids face." She pointed at Nash. "She couldn't be valedictorian because she's a woman and an Indian. So the sheriff was the golden child. Her college was about getting into officers' training, not about being the top. But I'm guessing there might be a Summa wrestler in that marine. But her only competition was herself and being an Indian. Then she became the slime on the shore in SEAL training. But you… you had to be a grown-assed woman before you faced the pain of defeat. But only because you weren't paying attention in Colorado. If kids in college got shot by a little gun, they would expect some leeway or a lot of coddling. But you were blown up before, and then you got pistol-whipped. But still dragged your ass out there, shot the shitty nasty guy, and then dropped kill shots through a one-inch slot on the fly with that big-assed cannon of yours. And if that wasn't enough, you dragged yourself over to the edge of the cliff and hit the bullseye again. With your guts and jaw dragging in the dirt."

Muna blinked. "Are you saying I should learn to pull myself up by my own bootstraps and stop whining like a little spoiled girl?"

The head shook softly. "Just the opposite. You figured out what sidelined you in Paris. But when Nash called Orange County in the middle of the night, you didn't see it as an extension of your team; you felt it as a personal stab in the gut or back. I'm not the end-all be-all for Mina. We have a team. She gets to talk to any of them. Two surgeons, seven nurses, four techs, two radiologists, and if those aren't enough, she gets to whine at me. It's a team. Nash met Ming somewhere before, but it was you who recruited the whole team. Nash can call them, but I'm willing to bet it's you they come running to help." She turned back toward the kitchen. "I'm just saying. Own who you are and your greatness."

Muna sat quietly, blinking at the nurse's back.

Nash picked at the plate of cut carrot strips and chose one. "So how much of working through the shit has been about doctor Feelgood, and how much from just backing off the intensity of being everything to everybody? I'm assuming the work in San Francisco couldn't have been conducive to better mental health. I mean, the boys seem to lean somewhat hard on you... When I went out, the file piles on Mike's desk stood over a foot deep."

Muna squinted one eye. "Oz tends to leave them in the break room, or on the big table where he hopes Chips or Baby would sort them. Usually, Baby waited until she filled a banker's box full and then brought them to me."

Nash, open-mouthed, bit down on the crisp carrot. She smiled at the bright snap. "Any idea why they sent crates up to move Chips and Baby's computers and stuff, and then just left them in the middle of the room? I mean, who was doing the moving?"

"Andy would know. I was gone by then. What kind of crates?"

"Big heavy-duty wooden ones. Like you would use for moving a motorcycle or car engines."

Muna rolled her head back and forth and then laughed. "Gamers."

"Gamers?"

Lele looked up and turned. "Okay, this I want to hear the explanation for. Why gamers… I mean, I get the boys. They're all game heads or whatever they call themselves. In Paris, I could hear them gaming almost all night after being around the Olympics all day. I think it was Slug and Petey who were below us. But moving Chips?"

Muna leaned back in the chair and turned it around so Lele could get the full effect. "It's high noon, and you've called me out for a showdown in the middle of the street. You brought your pair of Colt 45s. They're pretty. They have them pearly handles, and the metal gleams like you were up all night polishing the silver. All week long, I've been hitching…" She turned to Nash. "Hitching? Is that the right term for pulling your holster up?"

Nash laughed. "How would I know? Do I look like a gunslinger? It's your story. You spent just as much time in Hollywood as I did. Just play your hand… partner."

Mina snickered.

Muna stood. "So I've been hitching up my gun belt…" She glanced back at Nash. Nash held her palms out. "With only a weak little Navy thirty-two. But suddenly, I step out into the noonday sun and I'm carrying a machine gun off a tank."

Leaning back, she pantomimes holding something the size of a large log. Grabbing the imaginary bullet belt, she winds it around in the air and over her shoulder. With the grip in hand, her thumb was ready on the trigger. "In the bottom of your soul, you know it'll only take one slide of my thumb on the trigger. It will slush the street clean of anything in the barrage of bullets way. Now, do you stand there in the scorching sun, sweating? Or do you negotiate?"

Lele bent over, laughing at the small black woman holding something her size and threatening mayhem. "Hell no. I want to see what happens the second your thumb lets go the hounds of hell and how far back it kicks your scrawny ass down the street." She points at Nash and then touches her nose. "Am I right?"

Nash and Mina mirror the nurse silently, chuckling at the small woman. "You ain't wrong. I'm thinking something jet propelled even the coyote couldn't handle against the roadrunner."

Mina stood. "I need to pee. And then I'm hungry. Either serve what I've been dying for this last hour, or call for some pizza."

Muna laughed at the reactions and how funny it sounded when it wasn't in an animated game on the computer. "Okay, but you get my analogy. They are gamers. And Chips is every bit as over the top as Slug. If you pull out a fifty-caliber pistol, I pull my eighty-caliber with the water-cooled sound and recoil suppressor. You pull out your Hellcat, I bring the rocket car. Nothing makes sense because you can have anything when it's a drawing. I don't know where those wooden crates came from, but now I want to see."

Nash frowned. "For what?"

Muna laughed and then twisted her head into a grotesque clown face as she grabbed her side hair and pulled them up into two pom-poms. "First, to figure out what I can send back to them. And second, I want to be a fly on the wall to watch the reaction when the crates get delivered to their front door." Her smirk pulled into a full-tooth smile. "And I'll bet you want to be that delivery driver?"

Nash's deadpan face studied the junior agent. Her left wrist floated into her view as it turned. Leaning forward, she pulled her phone out of her back pocket. Thumbing through her contacts, she poked the name and then thumbed the blue digits.

Her chuff was small as she shook her head. "Mike, we're Face timing." She poked at the speaker symbol.

"Oh. Nash. We were just talking about you. Well, Oz was wondering when you were due back out here."

Nash winked at Muna and rolled her eyes. "Not for a while, Mike. These cutbacks are getting brutal, and the courts aren't making them stop. But listen, I need you to turn the camera around and go over to those crates for the computers."

The man's face darkened as his hand and finger covered the screen. "Um…"

Nash's screen became the floor, moving by. She turned it so

Muna could see. "How are they constructed, Mike? Nails or screws?"

"They seem well-made. The screws are brass. Does that make a difference?"

Muna nodded.

Nash chuckled. "Yes, Mike. Brass means they're designed for reuse," Nash chuckled. "Let me see both sides of each one, please."

Mina stopped as she was coming out of the bedroom. She mouthed at Muna. *"Did Nash just use the please word?"*

Muna covered her mouth as she nodded with enormous eyes.

"Okay, Mike. Be a dear and show me the two crates over in the corner."

The screen changed to the darker corner around the remote dredging computer and Baby's station. Muna pointed at the first crate and wrinkled her face. She whispered, "They aren't empty."

Nash frowned and mouthed. "Are you sure?"

Mike's voice was tiny. "What?"

Nash jumped and smiled. "I said they don't look empty, Mike. Can you feel around that cardboard lining and see if there is something in there?"

"Just a minute. Hey, Oz, it's Nash. She needs to know what is in these crates."

"They're empty. They're for all of Chips' computers to ship down to Southern California. I think."

Nash's phone was suddenly looking at the spackled ceiling from the 1940s.

"Look at this here. There is something in there."

Oz grumped. "Just a minute. Let me go find the flashlight in the breakroom."

Nash opened her mouth to tell Mike to use the light on the phone. Muna waved her hands and shook her head as she smiled. She mouthed the words *all the time*.

"Got it. Batteries are almost dead. But it should work long

enough. Did Muna order us more batteries before she left? What's in there?"

Mike adjusted his phone in a dizzying sweep. "Nash? Can you see what's in there?"

Nash looked at Muna, nodding. "Yeah, Mike. It's perfect."

Muna held her hands out to indicate the largest box.

"See if you can make a hole and peek into the big crate." She glared at Mina. "Please."

Lele snickered as she set down a large bowl of steaming biryani.

Nash recognized the sound of Oz's pocketknife snicking open. "Here. Let me cut the corner."

The phone's screen showed the older man's hands being less delicate than his surgery. The cardboard corner fell away, and Oz stuck the small flashlight into the opening while Mike pointed the camera to look in.

Muna squinted and then tapped the side of her head. Her smile was pure Muna-evil.

"Yeah. That's perfect Mike. Look, I gotta go. Someone just walked in. I'll talk to you two later." She thumbed the phone off as Mina and Lele sat.

Nash looked at Muna. "What do you think?"

Muna kissed the top of Powder's head and then sat in her own place. Taking her first bite, her eyes drifted closed. "Nope. I can't tell the difference between my mother's biryani and yours, Lele."

"High praise. I'll take it." She snuck a peek at a smiling Mina. "We've been... um... practicing."

Mina's shoulders shook softly. "A lot."

Nash raised a single eyebrow and then looked back at Muna. "What's in the crates?"

Muna held out her palm. "You were there. I can't believe you thought the boxes were empties?"

"Mike and Oz said they were empties to pack up the play stations. Who was I to question them? So what are they?"

"Baby's new workstation."

Mina giggled. "They weren't moving out."

Muna rolled her head left to right and back. "Nope... Moving in."

Nash growled. "Eight-hundred-caliber machine gun..."

Muna dabbed the napkin to her lips. "With laser sights and photon torpedoes."

Nash glanced over at her wife. She recognized the happy warrior look on her face. She had heard of several eviscerated congressional personnel who had learned to never be in gun range of such a face. "What are you cooking in that vicious, scheming mind of yours?"

"How much do you think it would cost to ship those crates back to Orange County?"

Nash smirked at Muna. "It would be funner to load them with old junk televisions and stuff, and drop them from a Pave Hawk from say, thirty or forty feet up?"

GET BACK TO WORK

"From what I see, you could use any old sixty-five-inch plasma or a couple of forty-inch screens. Bars burn through those all the time. But they still won't shatter right. You'll need something breakable, like glass."

Nash growled. "But I don't want broken glass all over the place. People walk barefoot around there."

The chuckle was deep and evil. "In that case, you called the right person. We make fake stuff all the time. And a large, shattering monitor, sounding like the world just came crashing down, will be a snap. For keeping the area clean of broken glass, we can keep it all in a puncture-proof bag. Afterwards, just throw the bag in a dumpster. Send me the inside dimensions on all the crates, and I'll get Wes stirring the pot. Who knows? Maybe Wicky or Celeste might want in on this. I heard you met Lurch from the Teamsters."

Nash looked at Muna. "Lurch? Yeah, all seven feet of him. He was at the presentation. His father helped build the western town set. Why? Do you think he'd help, Christopher?"

Christopher snickered. The phone enhanced the evil sound. "He's a Teamster. If you need a bumbling idiot dumping your fragile computers off the back of a truck, nothing beats Baby Huey. It might cost you a couple of cool T-shirts or pizza, but he'd be worth it. There's a medieval tournament in Angeles, um, that's Westwood to you. I'm sure he won't miss a fight in his own backyard. So I'll see if he's up for the game."

"Thanks, Christopher. We'll unpack all this stuff and scrounge what we can, then ship it or bring it down."

"Sounds like a plan. We'll talk soon." The phone snicked to dead.

"Christopher is in."

Mike straightened from unscrewing the crate. "I will assume this is a major asset to have in this endeavor?"

Muna laughed behind the smaller crates. "He's far more than a major asset. He creates special effects for movies. If we wanted these to blow up on contact, I'm sure he could rig them to do so and then rain bubble gum. I still want to sneak into his warehouse and geek out for a day or twenty."

Nash chuckled and nodded. "Remember the giant at the stuntman screening?"

"Lurch? How could I forget a guy like that? Why?"

The tip of Nash's tongue wet the lower lip of her smile. "Apparently, he wasn't a stuntman like we thought. He's with the Teamsters. Christopher is going to talk to him this weekend. If anyone can push this crate off the back end of a truck, he's the guy."

Muna giggled. "More like pick it up and throw it."

"Either works for me."

Muna stood and surveyed the six large crates. "Do you think this would all fit in one of the SUVs?"

Oz strolled in with a sandwich in his hand and mouth. Chewing and swallowing while his left hand waved a finger at the back wall. "There's the armored, stretched, assault Suburban thing the LA office left here last November. I'm fairly sure Andy would pay you to make it go away. They swore they would send a rookie back up to fetch it—but you know how those people are."

Nash stood slowly. "What's the seating configuration?"

Oz opened his mouth to take another bite, but rolled his eyes instead. "Do I look like a used car salesman? Heck, I don't even want to play one on TV. Go ask Andy."

Nash strolled toward what she thought of as her West Coast desk. Powder danced beside her. Nash looked down at the dance. "Okay, girl. We'll go down and talk to Uncle Andy while you do your duty."

As they approached the large black man, he smiled and held out a key fob. "Slot two, next to my van. Make the pig go away, and I'll throw a luau when you get back."

Nash opened the heavy back doors to the stretched vehicle. A half-seat lay on its back between her and the front seats. She turned toward the man standing on the edge of the loading dock. "Hey, Andy. Where do you want the dead body?"

He pointed to the left. "Pitch it in the dumpster. The city collection is getting used to people throwing out everything, along with the baby and the bathwater. Whatever it was in November, it isn't redeemable half a year later. Are there any tactical bags?"

Nash opened the driver's door and leaned back. "Nope. I'm guessing they knew what was in them when they took the silver bird south." She grabbed the small paper sack standing between the driver's and passenger's seats. *Trash.* Throwing it over the van, she heard the satisfying sound of paper hitting the tin of the dumpster.

Climbing in, she stepped on the brake and pushed the start button. The engine ground slowly and then fired. She checked all the gauges. Leaving it running, she flicked the turn indicator for left turns and slid out. Walking around the vehicle, she checked for damage and the lights. Reaching the driver's door, she turned on the headlights and pushed the turn lever to the right.

At the back, she bent to shade the right taillight. *Nothing.*

She opened the passenger door and checked the junk drawer. Only once before had the contents genuinely surprised her. While meeting his mistress, a fellow instructor suffered a heart attack, having left his gun and badge in his car's unlocked glove box.

Nash returned it to him at the hospital, in front of his wife. He had agreed with his wife. It was time for early retirement and a move.

She cleared the candy wrappers, gum, and parking ticket. Only closing the door on the owner's manual and the instruction manual about the Level Two armor.

Returning to the driver's seat, she turned the vehicle off. Glancing back at the spare seat, she left it for later if it didn't fit.

Andy lowered his skull coffee mug. "Well?"

"What kind of luau?"

"How about an everybody's birthday party? Catered in. Bring a friend."

Nash snickered and poked the man's chest. "That means Oz's wife, your wife, and…" She frowned. "Is Peter or Lester dating?"

He chuffed. "Can you talk the girls into coming back? The little one is fun."

Nash laughed. "Have you seen Muna's hair?"

He shook his head. "The tattle tale said three rooms on the dorm level got used last night. That was my only sign you were back. Is she with you?"

Nash nodded. "Yeah, Mike stayed as well. I'll get her to come down. About the pig in the yard…"

"I heard the battery. I'll get it charged up. How are the tires?"

"Good for another five or ten thousand. But the right taillight is out. Completely."

"I'll get the motor pool to replace all the lights. Charge the batteries and change the oil. It's been sitting for too long."

"Thanks, Andy."

"When are you going to need it?"

Nash bent to stroke Powder's head. "We need to run the errands tomorrow, but we can use one of ours. So, the next day with an early start?"

"On it. And send Mighty Mouse down here. Uncle Andy needs a hug."

THE RESTAURANT WAS THE PATH OF LEAST RESISTANCE. When the little bladder started pumping her feet, they also knew they wouldn't make it to Sylmar by one o'clock for the burrito truck.

Muna had warned Nash as they walked across the parking lot. "If the food isn't halal, I don't want to hear about it. We're in trucker territory, and this is the step above finding warm roadkill and snarling and snapping as we eat it on the side of the road."

The waitress, Judy, had surprised them when Nash asked if the chicken sandwich was kosher.

"My mother-in-law eats the chicken, and she has a double kitchen. The chicken is as kosher as a baby after its bris. But hold the mayo if it really matters to you."

Nash pointed at Powder. "It only matters to her. But hold the mayo all around. And she takes her food in a bowl. I can cut it up."

Five minutes later, the cook brought out the food. Two plates for the adults, and a bowl with chopped vegetables and chicken without the skin on any of them. "I have six spoiled rescues at home. No skin, no condiments, and an extra chicken breast in there. These working dogs need to keep up their strength." He barely paused for a thank you and was back at work.

Muna bit into her sandwich and moaned softly. "Mm... fresh tomatoes and lettuce. I missed so much of the West Coast. You don't realize it until you try to find a red tomato at Quantico. One of the halal girls held up a picture of a handful of red cherry tomatoes on her phone. She said they only existed where AI could redraw the colors." She rolled her eyes. "I told her the first time she has a fresh salad in California, it's going to destroy her concept of what the internet tells her."

Nash swallowed and dabbed her mouth with the napkin. "So, which helped the most? Feelgood or the halal girls?"

Muna hung her head and then looked out of the side of her eyes.

"Am I a bad person if I say it was getting released to shoot again? Or retaking the hand-to-hand combat courses?" They both snickered. "Interesting question. But probably just talking with Feelgood. No judgments, no, but we also have work to do, or it being about work when it's at the dinner table. But hanging out with the halal girls provided grounding, but also a point from my old perspective I could look back at from where I've grown to. I don't think any of them have aspirations of being field agents. But they also don't have any thoughts about being shot at. Or in fights. I didn't see any of them taking the combat course."

Nash held up her hand and pulled out her phone. Muna watched with a frown. Nash found the contact, pushed the number, and then thumbed the speaker.

The grumpy growl was anything but welcoming. "Federal Bureau of—"

Nash jumped in. "I'm calling about the Schmuck Schnelling funeral. Was it at six or in the deepest evil bowels of midnight?"

"Right after we cut fresh screw threads into the fumbling jar head. I heard you got arrested for dancing naked in Hollywood."

"All a lie to fool the rubes back east. Listen, Max, we're having a meeting here with some junior agents-to-be. In your seventy-seven years as a field agent, how many times have you been in a firefight?"

The man coughed to clear his throat. Nash winked at Muna. "Only one serious one. But a few exchanges with lead—but nothing I would classify as a firefight."

Nash raised one eyebrow. "Can you talk about the serious one?"

"Sure. The court ordered suppression clause ran out once the divorce was final. What do you want to know?"

Nash and Muna both chuckled. "Are you still sleeping with her?"

"Sure. It's always spicier with someone who isn't your wife. But we can't conceive of living anywhere else. Or with anyone else. Is that all you needed?"

Nash glanced at Muna and nudged out her chin.

"We haven't met, yet, Max, but this is Muna. I've been at Quantico this last month and hanging out with some girls who wear hijabs. So their worldview, and how they view their world going forward, is somewhat skewed. I'm not sure they plan fieldwork, but they don't even have a concept of being shot at."

Nash added, "Or worse."

"Ah. The penny just dropped. Muna. As in the computer squint in San Francisco. And the Colorado agent who couldn't stay out of the way of bombs, bullets, and, if I remember right, a pistol-whipping? That Muna?"

Muna growled. "Yeah. That's the one."

"So, did you shower with them in the gang showers?"

"No."

"Then sit them down and get naked enough to show them every scar. Explain the truth and how the old scars and broken bones affect you on chilly mornings. Wait. Does it ever get cold in the Sunshine State?"

Muna glanced at Nash. "You were right. He has a doctorate in being an ass."

The deep growl didn't hide the sound coming from a smile. "I resemble said remark. But seriously, don't hold back. Explain everything, especially about you being still alive, and still voluntarily a field agent. That part matters. The scars are just little trinkets of chachka on the shelf getting dusted or polished in the shower. But they remind you about taking the bullet for a lot of civilians. And you're willing to do it all again."

Muna growled. "Well, maybe without the bombs or pistol-whipping. Drinking a succulent brisket through a straw is simply wrong. And don't even get me started about a nice, sweet kugel."

"Preach it, girl. If that's all, I have some agents to go flog."

Nash picked up the phone. "Thanks, Max. Stay safe."

30

DROP AND COVER

MUNA SUPPRESSED her urge to touch. The battered armor was torched, scarred, and fake. But it was the real deal if you had read the graphic novel, watched the animated cartoon, played the game, and binged the series. The green plates were darker than she would have thought, but the suit of armor was still Kai-125—the badass woman warrior.

"Muna?"

She turned slowly. "Hmm? Yes?"

Nash held her right hand on her hip. "You need to listen to this. You can play with the space suit later."

"Armor. But what am I listening to?"

Christopher reached over and tipped the crate off the table. The structure landed flat on its side, but inside it sounded like a giant bull crashing through a large plate-glass window and into a china shop.

Muna jumped back with shock on her face. "How...? What is in there...?" She looked in horror at the tall man, smiling in satisfaction.

Christopher chuckled. "It gets worse." He rested his hand on one that was almost a twin of the largest crate they had brought down. "We had your dimensions and the video you took in San Francisco. Del is a magician at falling apart. The screws in this unit are a brittle plastic." He pointed across the warehouse at Del standing on another table next to an identical crate.

Del smiled and rotated the crate up onto a corner to let it fall. The crate rotated some in the air and hit a corner. A loud crash of breaking glass and splintering wood revealed the crate's contents: broken computer screens.

Christopher explained. "Oh yeah. We dipped the screws into Nitrogen Tri-iodine. Very unstable once it's dry. The least jar, and the corners... well, you can see. The minor explosions get lost in the rest of the crash. What do you think? Will it do the job?"

Muna looked back from examining the heap of trash. "I think it will get their attention."

Nash and Powder stopped at the edge of the heap. "But you have five crates. If you kick them off one at a time..." She glanced back at Christopher. Crossing his arms, he smirked at Del.

Del hopped off the table. "If we show you all the guts and bolts, the sausage doesn't taste as good. But trust us. Once we have an audience, the show will be spectacular. They might be the gamers we've heard of, but they are gaming to replicate what we did on screen before they thought of it."

The two men fist-bumped and came away with thumbs up.

Nash remembered the gold statue of Oscar in the office. She would never doubt its authenticity again.

THE QUIET ORANGE COUNTY STREET WAS JUST GETTING busy. A small girl with the fluffy pom-poms bouncing on the top of her head slowed as she turned into the large driveway. The pink T-shirt with the company logo spread across the small back as she stopped at the door and bent over to catch her breath. Her hands pushed against the black leggings-encased knees. A slow count to ten, and the right arm reached out to open the door. The door latch buzzed, and she pushed.

Upstairs, munching on a piece of toast, she slipped into the chair in the corner. Her right hand strummed across the keyboard, and the monitor lit up. She studied the three screens. The left screen had cross sections of the river and marina that were mapped on the middle screen. The top cross sections showed the current depths, and the bottom showed the depths needed after the dredging.

She turned to the screen on the right. Quarters divided the large screen. One quarter held a mug shot of a dead man. The hamburger mark of three horizontal lines suggested there was a file or multiple files under the photo. She recognized the name of the now-known terrorist mercenary working out of Syria.

Two of the other quarters also held mug shots of dead men. From the dotted red lines mapping out his face, she knew the facial recognition programs were still running. Leaning forward, she looked at the small blue labels. The current searches were using African and Asian search databases, probably focusing on the Middle East. They had been running for seventeen days, nineteen hours, and twenty-three minutes. It always amazed her that there were so many faces to sort through once you stopped looking at Americans or white people.

The fourth quarter was blank. She clicked on the quarter. The hamburger appeared in the upper right corner. She opened the menu and sorted through to the security protocols. She clicked through and found the seven cameras she wanted. In the one camera, she watched as the oversized truck eased into the front driveway. The aged sign was easily readable. Global Electronics Transport, Inc., out of Sylmar, California. She looked at the time block. *Right on time.*

Baby turned into the large computer room and stopped. She studied the person in the corner seat. Looking down at her own pink shirt and black leggings, her face froze in a frown. Quietly, she walked to the corner. Grabbing another chair, she slid close. Her voice was conspiratorially hushed. "What do you think you're doing?"

The woman side-eyed her. "If you ever want to date Eight Ball again, you'll shut up and go find something else to do. Like, go have another bowl of Froot Loops with Chips. But you had better hurry. She's about to get extremely busy." Muna pointed at the security camera feed with the truck.

Baby stood and turned. "I need to pee."

Muna watched the feed. Two men walked to the back of the truck, where a liftgate would match up to the front door of the building. The shorter man grabbed the clipboard and walked to the door of the building while the larger man opened the back of the truck.

The front door buzzed. Muna could hear Ming in her office and the echo on the feed. "Yes?"

Christopher leaned toward the door. "Global Transport, ma'am. We all gots a delivery for... wait a minute... I had it rat here. Ah yes. A Chip Robinson with Dap Sex." He scratched at his longish curls and turned to look at his partner leaning on the back of the truck.

"What is the delivery?"

Christopher fumbled the multi-page manifest. "Says here... um... seven crates of computer parts. It be just about all we ever move anymore. Is Mr. Chip Robinson here? He needs to sign for this stuff."

Ming switched to the overhead general paging. "Chips, there's a delivery at the front door for you."

The voice echoed up from the cafeteria area. "I ordered nothing, and Slug said it's not his."

Ming thought for a moment. "Jazz, can we please have an armed response to the front drive? Slug, bring the boys." Switching back to the front door intercom, she stalled the guy in the blue jumpsuit.

The sound of soft-soled feet running filled the cafeteria and the second floor. The stairs thundered as the herd of boys descended to the main floor. Muna waited until the computer room was empty of the girls, and she felt Ming walk past.

She clicked on the security monitor's hamburger and sent the display to every computer screen, and then spun in the chair. Her tennis shoes stopped her spin. Bunny's face was more of a surprise than anger.

Muna held her finger to her lips, shushing. She pointed at the screens. "They're all recording. Trust me. You might want to be at the front door for this."

Bunny squinted her left eye. "This better be good, or I'll personally slap the handcuffs on you."

Muna beamed her large fence of white teeth. "Oscar-winning performance."

As they raced down the stairs, Bunny glanced at Muna's pompoms. "What did you do to your beautiful long hair?"

"It probably made more than a few wigs for people who needed it more than me."

They raced out of the front door and slowed down as they stood behind all the Deep Six colleagues. Chips and Ming lead the group. Jazz stood back to one side.

Ming looked over at the manifest in Chips' hands as the woman flipped through each page. "Where's it from?"

Chips turned to the last page as the giant of a man gently slid the large crate out of the back of the truck. "Oh shit. It's the computers from the FBI office in San Francisco."

Jazz's arm shot out at the man now wavering with the large crate on his shoulder. "Careful with that. It's costly and delicate equipment."

Christopher hollered from in the back of the truck. "Hold up, Lurch. You're hung up on the tie-down strap."

The strap snapped tight as the man stumbled backward. Two steps and the next crate slid out—pulled by the strap. And then the next crate, and the next... Lurch stumbled one more step as the large crate rotated over his back and headed for the driveway. Trying to catch himself, Lurch grabbed the strap as he fell backward—pulling the rest of the crates with him.

The first crate hit its corner. Rigged screws exploded as the glass shattered. The rest of the crates hit various places around the first heap of trash. More glass shattered as hands raced to cover mouths and gasps. Utter destruction on a video game was one thing, but to watch tens of thousands of dollars of custom-built computers fifteen feet from your own shoes is an out-of-body experience.

Christopher stood at the end of the truck, staring at Lurch, who had danced clear of all the mayhem. Stifling a giggle, Christopher's mouth pursed in a tight mew. The voice was of a tiny child instead of his six-foot-six or Lurch's seven feet. "Ut oh."

Chips and Ming gasped at the gigantic heap of lumber, cardboard, glass, and computers—still blinking.

Nash rolled around the back of the truck, holding her phone. "As much as I'd love to relish the looks on your faces, I need a computer and some help. Muna?"

Muna stepped around the crowd. "Yeah. They've only found the guy I found two weeks ago. But they're still looking. What have you got?"

"Guymon, Oklahoma. Nytah Woods just texted me. Her granddaughter might be in Guymon."

Ming closed her mouth as she looked at Muna as if she were a twin to her youngest employee. Her hand and finger rose to point. "I let you in the building."

Baby stepped forward and slung her arm over her twin's shoulders. "I've been in the building since last Wednesday."

"No. You were out running..."

Muna shook her head. "When have you ever known Baby to run?" She turned to where Chips was pushing around pieces of the junk heap. "Give it up, Chips. Baby's new workstation is still in San Francisco and almost fully assembled. A sweet rig, too."

She looked at Christopher and Lurch leaning against the back of the truck. Their smiles were self-satisfied and full of mirth. "As promised. It was the best... Ever."

They bowed. "We aim to please."

Slug stopped next to Muna. "What is all this? And what was glass? I haven't seen glass since the days of cathode ray tubes."

"Um?"

They all looked at Nash. "I'd love to shoot the shit with you all, but we need to go find this Guymon, Oklahoma."

Ming held up her phone. "Siri, where is Guy man, Oklahoma?"

Jazz walked around the mess and stood next to Nash. "Nice entrance. Now, how is the city spelled?"

Nash rolled her phone over, and Jazz typed it into her maps. Pinching the screen, they looked at the westernmost point of the panhandle. "Looks like a... ew, tiny airport. It might be better to get to Amarillo and then drive. Who is this granddaughter?"

Nash looked up at the green mohawk with red tips. "Indian girl. Not eighteen yet. Possibly kidnapped, or just a runaway. But she's been missing for over a month." She punched the number on her phone.

"Travel this is... Oh, good morning, agent. Where can I ship you off to now?"

"I'm in Orange County, Rick. How about getting us three to Amarillo, Texas?"

"It would be easier to get you to Kathmandu via Latvia and Gambia."

"Is it possible? And how fast?"

The man's fingers rattled his keyboard. "LAX in two hours to Dallas. While you're flying, I'll try to find you a small airplane to Amarillo."

Nash rolled her eyes closed as she looked at Jazz. "If it's a small plane, they might land at our actual destination, which is Guymon, Oklahoma."

Rick snickered. "There's no such place as a gay man in Oklahoma."

"Careful, big guy, you have two butch lesbians here. Don't make me talk to your husband."

"So, I'm assuming this guy's place is north of Amarillo...?"

"Yeah. Time is of the essence here."

Jazz rested her finger on Nash's arm. "I might have a better idea. Ask him how long the runway is at Amarillo."

Nash frowned. "Hey, Rick, can you find the length of the runway in Amarillo?"

"Sure. It's the seventh-longest runway in the United States. Don't ask me why size matters, but it's thirteen thousand five hundred. It would be tight, but you could drop a 747 on it. Why?"

Nash watched Jazz making a phone call. Jazz nodded that she'd heard.

"Thanks, Rick. I think we're handling it all here."

"Glad to help. Safe travels." Her phone snicked and was dead.

Jazz looked at the sky. "Hey, Clay, I need to get three federal agents to Amarillo ASAP." She listened and pointed at the heap in the driveway.

Nash smiled and pointed at Christopher and Lurch as they pulled large bags out of the back of the truck. "It's all part of the service."

Jazz nodded. "Warm it up. We'll have them down there in thirty minutes." She thumbed the phone and slipped it into her back pocket. "I assume you have your uniforms with you."

Muna walked around the corner of the truck and handed Nash her rucksack. "I can change on the plane." She turned to the men, shoving the broken crates into the silver bags. "Thanks, guys. You're the best. And good luck with the fighting Saturday."

They waved.

Muna turned and bobbed her head back and forth to wave her pom-poms. "We're good to go."

Jazz eyed the hair and looked over at Baby. "This is going to take some time to get used to."

31

DRIVE FOR COVER

"Thank you." Muna sipped the mixed fruit juice the flight attendant offered her. "Oh, that is good."

The woman bowed slightly. "Kids these days only think of the juice they can taste... or think they taste. If I had the beets, I could whip you up a strawberry milkshake with no berries. Beets for color, carrots for sweetness and texture, apple for taste, banana for texture, and pineapple for the tang strawberries have. Add protein powder, and you have the energy drink I got through high school with. I'll write it down for you. I have a feeling you three are on the go all the time."

Muna pointed at Nash and snapped her fingers and thumb closed. "She's not wrong. But I have a whole different understanding of shakes than you do."

Nash held her coffee up. "I'm good."

"I'll have some dim sum crab puffs steamed in about five minutes." She checked Powder and continued to the back galley.

Nash leaned over and peeked at Muna's laptop. Her voice was soft. "When did crab puffs become halal?"

Muna snickered. "I saw the container when I used the bathroom. It's crab spelled with a K. It's made from Polak, which is a whitefish and spelled with a K at the end, which is where they get the K for Krab. The package also had the little K on it. It stands for Kosher, but also works for halal."

Nash pointed at the small square in the corner of her screen.

Muna clicked on it. The screen filled with the quartered screen at Baby's station. Muna shrunk it and continued with her live search. "While I was in Baby's nasty girl's room, I installed a siphon. Anything coming up on what we are interested in will automatically siphon a copy onto my nasty mobile feed." She glanced at Nash. "Did Nytah have any more details on the girl?"

Nash pulled up her phone and looked at the text. "Yeah. It's not her granddaughter, but another missing girl. Mack Tyler at the Interstate Motor Lodge. She's in room four. Near the office. And probably scared out of her mind."

Muna studied Nash's face for a few heartbeats. "I'm guessing Mackenzie."

Nash chuffed softly. "Or named after daddy's work truck…"

Muna pointed at the screen. "East end of town."

They looked up as the flight attendant approached.

"The pilot says putting down at Guymon is a no-go. They have a portion of the runway torn up. Either construction or tornado repair. But he called ahead, and the local office in Amarillo says they'll have something called a unit at the general aviation office. It's still a two-hour drive, but it's the best we can do."

Nash held out her hand. "Don't apologize. This probably saved us a couple of days' travel. The best I could have done was LAX to Dallas. And still a long drive."

"Do you have any idea when you might need a lift out?"

Nash looked at Muna, shrugging. Nash pointed at Powder sleeping, or pretending to, on the large chair. "She's the boss. And she doesn't really share her plans. But my guess is we'll be stealing the unit and taking it to the Oklahoma City area."

The blonde winced. "Ouch. That's a lot of driving. Aren't you based out of Orange County?"

Muna and Nash snickered as Powder rolled over to show them her back. "I'm in DC, Muna's in San Francisco..." Nash rolled her eyes sideways. "And the princess decides where she's working by the weather, the treats, and how much bedtime she can log with her other mommy. But no. We're based out of both ends of the world, but our territory is quite literally the world."

She looked at Muna.

Muna shrugged. "Barbados, Paris, Geneva, East Covina, you know, the glory spots."

The flight attendant smirked. "You almost had me getting jealous... until you go to my old stomping grounds. I grew up in Azusa. It's next to Covina on the other side."

Muna glanced at Nash. "Well, if it makes you feel better, we never actually made it to Covina. But we did get to a place called the City of Industry. And kept it from turning into the crater of industry."

The woman frowned in confusion.

Nash rolled her eyes. "We defused a huge bomb that some very nasty terrorist had planned on taking out a major section of the city."

The woman looked at Nash's long braid, and Muna's hair—still in twisty pom-poms. "Which one of you is the bomb expert?"

Nash and Muna pointed at the body in the tactical vest. Powder groaned at the attention.

THE MAN AT THE OFFICE PAUSED IN THE BACK-OFFICE doorway as Nash and Muna flashed their credentials. He backed up one step and grabbed a key fob. "The guy from the FBI said to please bring it back drivable. Oh. And something about not taking it to Colorado. He mumbled something about scrap metal."

Nash growled. "How was he dressed?"

The older man barked a short laugh. "Like a desk weenie on his first important job." He kept Nash's stare. "Oh, hell no. You can smell a mechanic a mile away—even if he wasn't wearing a blue jumpsuit. But he stressed the drivable bit."

Nash looked at Muna. "Yeah, drivable. We have no problem with it. He just won't like where he'll have to retrieve it from."

The man smiled with rubber lips and held up his palms. "Not my problem. I just pass along the key and message. My work is done here."

Muna nodded. "And damn fine work it was, too." She looked down at the fob. "Oh, great. Another pig."

The three walked out to the black suburban. Nash opened the back as Muna continued to the driver's side door. Climbing in, her only comment was, "At least they left it stock."

Nash hesitated, putting the rucksacks in the back. "Roll down all the windows and run the air-conditioning. Let's air this latrine out for a minute or two."

Muna started the engine and rolled down all the windows. "Whoa. I thought they were supposed to turn them back in after a hundred thousand miles." She set the turn indicator to the left and slid out.

Nash stepped back to see the back light. "How bad?"

Muna walked past, looking at all the metal and the lights. "One eighty-six and change." She nodded as she got to the front. Nash changed the selector to right turns.

Muna continued counterclockwise, as Nash continued clockwise. "What did this pig do? The metal is all original and even looks like some wax was applied not that long ago."

Nash closed the back doors. "My guess is it was the motor pool, queen. Only taken to the prom, and logged some long runs to who knows where. There's a well-used tow hitch receiver on the back here."

They climbed in, and Powder took command of the center console. Muna clicked her belt and adjusted the mirrors and radio. "What's your guess? Trailer or boat? And what is that smell?"

"If they used it for camping, it only saw the pleasant side of KOA. So I'm guessing a power boat with no slip. There's a large lake near Tulsa. But if it pulled a trailer, I'm going with FBI meet and greets at small-town parades and county fairs."

"And the smell?"

Nash rolled her eyes. "Powder farted, or years of private use with some serious kids' athletic teams and unclean, sweaty uniforms. Or we just go with the decomposition of a dead body or three." Powder turned her head and gave her a hard look. "What? Your farts smell."

Muna pushed the start button. The after-market GPS on the dashboard glowed into life. Muna chuckled. "What do you bet they never cleared their trips?"

"No bets. Let's see if the guy fished or camped."

Muna scrolled through the trips. "Lake, river, lake, lake, lake, whoa, how far up the Mississippi can you get away with? Dude, stop before you hit Canada." She scrolled to the end. "Yup. Lake fishing or the Big Muddy."

Nash snickered. "That's the smell. Rotting fish from too far away. Get home late and forget to clear the back out. By the next day, the smell had etched itself into the steel. If we leave this in Oklahoma, we'd be doing them a favor."

Muna selected drive and nosed the SUV out of the parking lot. As they turned onto the highway, Muna glanced at her watch and then at Nash. "I don't know about you, but all those little dim sums did was remind me we never got a decent meal."

Nash glanced in the side mirror. "Which is code for you missed out on having Chef pamper you?"

"I get hungry these days."

"Are you still on the pork rind wagon?"

"Yeah. I just can't think of a good enough reason to start up again."

Nash glanced over and studied the smaller woman. "Are you sleeping better now?"

The pom-poms bounced with the wobbly head. "Yes, and no. The therapy helped. Hanging with the halal girls even more. I think it was the grounding of just being me again."

"And the martial arts and range time?"

Muna's right fist shot out, fishing for a bump.

Nash bumped the fist. "Amen, sister. A-fucking-men." Nash glanced at her orange-faced dive watch. "Might as well find something to eat. We won't get there before twilight anyway."

"Wait until the morning light?"

Nash thought about contacting in strange situations. Every situation had its own pros and cons. Supposedly, the girl was there alone. But the question always arising was: who had booked the rooms next door?

LATER, THEY FOUND OUT. THE MAN IN ROOM FIVE SAT outside his door. His use of a two-liter bottle for an ashtray showed signs of him being on watch for a few days. The white wife beater shirt and work pants showed stains and wear. Even with the wild, uncombed comb-over, the giveaway was the lack of slippers. The boots were as professional as Nash's spit-polished black service boots.

Nash and Muna watched with binoculars and a spotting scope from across the street. Muna growled over the steering wheel. "Do you think his breath smells as bad as this rig?"

Nash dialed in the spotter's scope for a tighter view. "I think his health, in general, is as squared away as his boots. It's hard to see, but he's got speed zippers on the laces. He is either a fireman or some kind of paramilitary. Either way, if she's in room four, she's bait."

Muna rested her wrists over the steering wheel and looked at Nash. "How do you want to play this?"

Nash leaned back gently into the seat. "We can get to the girl later—if she's there. But I want to neutralize him first. The other question itching the back of my neck..."

Muna dipped her head. "Is it a one-man stakeout?"

Nash didn't look, but held out her left fist. Powder sniffed at it as Muna's fist connected. "I'll take the first watch. I'll wake you at midnight."

Muna handed the binoculars to Nash. With a turn, she positioned herself with half her shoulder and back against the door and half against the seat. Her head rocked back softly to the window, and her breathing slowed.

Nash continued to glass the motor lodge windows and doors.

The man in the stained wife beater shirt lowered the cigarette. Using his middle fingers to grab the mouth of the bottle, he dropped his cigarette into the damp mass of past cigarettes. His eyes never moved from watching the street.

Nash smirked. *No stranger to long surveillance.* She moved the binoculars to watch the curtain in the room where the building made an elbow. The window looked down the front of the building. There was no car in front, but she was positive the position of the curtain had changed a few times. This would be the room to watch over the visible watcher.

Drawing the phone from her pocket, she looked up the new contact and began the text.

How soon?

01:40 or 02:00

Putting the phone away, she glanced over at Muna. The lower lip vibrated softly from the breathing as she slept. *Just like a Marine.* The snoring from the back seat was also soft. Nash pulled the binoculars back up and watched the curtains.

32
WAKEE, WAKEE

MUNA STRETCHED AND YAWNED. Powder looked over from the center console. Muna smiled. "Hello, princess. Did you have a good nap, too?"

"She's been wondering why I've been letting you sleep so long."

Muna stared at the luminescent ticks on her watch face. "What happened to midnight?"

"The guy in the t-shirt came back out and sat for an hour. The guy in unit seven stood in his doorway. They talked. If the girl is in number four, she's staying in. The curtain glows like the television is on. But I haven't seen the curtains move."

Muna reached for the water bottle, which was still in the cup holder. "Thoughts?"

"What kind of little girl outfit did you stash in your rucksack?"

"The Baby uniform and my Hello Kitty night shirt," Muna replied with a smirk.

Nash's head ground around, her eyes narrowing with suspicion. "Can you holster a gun in those leggings?"

Muna let out a short, amused laugh. "No way. If I could, half the girls at Deep Six would line up for concealed weapon permits. I'd need a belt for a safe holster. Might as well slip into my leathers.

Are we doing the old Girl Scout cookie sales routine in the dead of night? Which door are we hitting?"

"Seven," Nash decided, her voice low and steady. "I want to quietly take them out first. I figure they're the brains of the operation. We get the drop on him. See if he's willing to chat. If not, it's gag and zip-ties, then on to door five."

Muna squirmed past Powder and dove into the back seat. Nash glanced back and watched the ninja shadow ooze over the second seat and then the third.

Nash studied the windows. None of the curtains had moved. "Body armor."

"Already on."

Nash snorted softly. "No. Pass me mine."

The ninja pushed on her shoulder. Nash grabbed the familiar shape. As the two black legs slid forward, Nash peeled off her shirt. Pulling the mass of the Velcro, she opened her armor. Raising it to her face, she sniffed. "Hmm. Maybe it wasn't just the mommy car." Pulling it over her head, she drew out her braid and pushed the Velcro back closed. She studied the white shirt and then looked down at her black armor. Her mouth twisted sideways as she looked over at Muna. The Kitty was sleeping on a black t-shirt. *Blackout it is.* She tossed the shirt at the back seat.

"That's what I figured. Why give them a target?"

They both pulled their weapons, dropped the clip, checked the load, and reinserted the clip. Both had two clips on each side of their body armor. Mostly for when they shot on a range, but also, you never know.

Nash pointed at the elbow in the building. "Pull us around the back. We can use the sallyport to avoid the other rooms. Pull your hair into the pom-poms and do the little girl thing when he answers. He didn't look very tall, so a nine mill in the nose will get his attention. Walk him back into the room and onto the bed. We'll be right behind you. Zip-ties?"

Muna opened the Velcro-sealed tops of two narrow pockets running from chest to side. "Check and check."

Nash opened hers. "Check and check."

Muna turned the light switch from automatic to off and pushed the start button. The large vehicle was a dark shadow crossing the street and driving around the back of the motel.

The knock on the door was a single knuckle: two taps, a pause, and a single tap. Muna didn't need to keep her ear to the door. She watched Powder. The ears perked up in an arch, and her nose touched the door. Muna put on her best rendition of Baby's face.

The door cracked for a heartbeat and then swung open. A man stood in his jungle camouflage boxers and white t-shirt. The deadwood beige hair stood in a wonky faux-hawk. "Who the fuck are you?"

Muna's face changed from the wide-eyed little girl to the mature agent who had no time for anything that could progress to a pistol-whipping, or worse. She stepped through the doorway. Her nine-millimeter stuffed his left nostril until it hurt. "I'm the tooth fairy." She walked him backward until his legs hit the bed, and he sat. She kept pushing the pistol into his nose as she kneeled into him with her one knee in his crotch. "I'm going to grant you two seconds before you lose your teeth. Who do you work for?"

"I don't know."

She backhanded the pistol across his nose. He howled.

"Your jaw and teeth are next."

His eyes ticked to the left and grew larger. The lesbian mafia had arrived. "Honest. We don't know. We've never seen the guy. He's just a voice on the phone. Money shows up in the mail."

Nash silently closed the door and squatted behind Muna. They could hear the zip-ties binding his ankles.

"Who is in room five?"

"Nobody."

Muna struck the front teeth with the heel of the grip and immediately covered his mouth with her hand—muffling the scream. Her deep voice was more of a growl. "We don't want to wake the neighbors."

Nash stood at the side of the bed where she held out the man's Glock 29 and a cell phone. "Roll him over."

Muna eased onto the knee beside his thigh. "One false move, and I might have to make some loud noises. Roll."

The man knew what was coming and rolled over. Hesitantly, he moved his hands to his sides. Nash leaned over and zipped his wrists together. Putting a zip-tie on each arm above the elbow, she zipped a third between to connect them. Pulling, she cinched his arms to his back. She pushed the man over onto his back.

Muna returned her knee to the man's crotch. "Now, my friend here is more of a knife kind of girl. She can make you bleed for days. In fact, she's an expert at bleeding for days. She's also an expert at skinning a body alive. Nothing has entertained me like that in at least a year. So, I'm going to ask you again. Who is the man in the filthy wife beater who smokes too much?"

"Hank."

"Does Hank have a last name?"

The man's eyes turned hard. "Fuck you."

Nash stood with the man's wallet. "Cleland Stonewall Cotton. Hum, McAlester, Oklahoma." Nash looked down at him. "You should have stayed in Choctaw Territory, Stonewall. Or do they just call you Stoney?"

"Fuck you, Indian."

Muna shifted her weight to the outside knee and mule-kneed the man's crotch. As his eyes rolled up, she put her hand over his mouth in case he threw up. She gave him a slow count of five.

Nash leaned over and, in the dim light, showed Muna the photo in his wallet. The woman was blonde, as was the maybe teenage twin girls. Nash triggered her commando knife, and as the knife clicked out, Muna giggled.

"Oh. Twinkies. And blond to boot. We haven't fucked up twins before."

Nash leaned in. "You see, Cleland, you are just the appetizer. And when we're finished with Hankie, we'll be ready for more of a meal. And as you called it, you know we Indians just love a good scalping."

Muna kneed him again and covered his mouth. "She leaned in. Now, let's start again. Who do you work for?"

The man watched Nash fish through his wallet with her knife. "Honest. We've never seen the guy. He just calls."

"What does he sound like?"

"Like a foreigner. German, maybe. He pronounces work like verk."

"What do you call him?"

"Our boss once called him Roman. I don't know if it was the guy's name or where he was from."

Muna's eyes narrowed, and she leaned forward. "Your boss?"

The man shuddered his head. "Not so much a boss and another guy we work with."

"Kidnapping young girls. And what...?"

"We just get the girls. They want to be movie stars or some kind of shit. We just take them where we're told."

Nash leaned in close. Her voice was glacial ice. "Roman? Or Romanov? Sergei, maybe...?"

The man's eyes widened as his face blanched.

Nash's head bobbed gently as she stood. "Sergei fucking Romanov. I should have known."

Muna nudged his crotch to get his attention. "Great, Cleland. Now we're getting somewhere. Let's get back to your former partner, Hankie. Last name." She held her hand ready with a backhand with the butt of the pistol.

"Johnson."

"Great. And the girl in room four? Full name. I'm getting bored and need to go pee."

He thought about staying quiet or saying something else, but

Muna flinched with the pistol. "She goes by the name Mack. That's all we know. We never know their last names."

Muna patted his chest. "Good boy. Now we're going to get to the next level. This is the part where you save your darling little girls. Your boss." She wobbled her head. "Or the guy you work with. Your choice."

"Winter. Tom Winter."

Muna patted him on the chest again. "And where do we find him? Does he have the other girls?"

The man's jaw clenched as his face darkened.

Muna slowly wagged her head. "Oh, Stoney, you were doing so good." She eased her weight onto her left leg and looked at Nash. "Cut him. Maybe start with his nose, and then maybe we can mail his ears back to mommy."

He squirmed. "No, wait."

Muna pushed on the man's chest as if dismounting. "That's not how it works, Stoney. You had it easy with me. Now we're up to the semi-finals. So, it's Viper's time up to bat. You didn't want to play with me. So I get to pee while you get to bleed."

Muna rolled off him as Nash dropped onto his hips like a cowgirl. "Now where were we? Oh yeah. I get to turn your nose into a chicken fillet." Her hand flexed, and the blade shot out of the handle.

"Okay. Okay." The man sagged in on himself under Nash's weight. "Yeah. He has five other girls at his camping lodge. We brought the Mack girl over here as bait—to see if anyone was looking for us. She called one of the other mothers. Honest. That's all I know. I'm just following orders."

"Where's his camping lodge?" She held up his phone. Turning it on, she faced the phone toward his face to unlock it. She could feel his body relax further at the realization he had no more resistance.

"It's under Winter Camp. It's a training camp for the militia."

Nash moved the phone to one side to study the man. "Well, well, Stoney, you keep coming up with surprises. Which militia?"

"First Oklahoma, but others use it to train as well. Winter has a heavy weapons permit, so we can use full auto in the shooting valley. He even has an RPG and a mortar. Some of the boys like to blow up old cop cars and shit."

Nash found the Winter listings. "What's this 'Winter Tires'?"

"It's his business. We all buy our tires from him."

She smiled at the listings, which also contained the addresses she would need. Shifting back to Settings, she changed the lock code for the phone back to 1111 and turned off the facial recognition. Scanning the apps, she found a few more she recognized as being attached to other known nefarious groups.

The knock was soft. "Stone?"

33

WELCOME TO THE PARTY

Muna spun out of the bathroom without flushing and stepped to the door. Her whisper was a soft growl. "I've got this."

Nash leaned close to the man's face. "When she cracks the door, you invite him in. Nothing else or I'll ventilate your head." As she climbed off him, she slipped the knife back in her pocket and drew her pistol. The tip of the barrel barely fit in his ear. The soft click of the safety switching off sounded like a sonic boom in his ear.

Nash nodded in the dim light. Muna opened the door and let it swing open a few inches.

Nash nudged the man's ear.

"Come on in Hank."

The man pushed the door open. As he stepped into the dim room, his eyes grew large as he spotted the three large letters on Nash's chest.

He reached to pull the pistol out of his pocket.

Muna's pistol nudged the back of his head.

Powder's teeth paused close to the man parts at his crotch.

"Did you really think she was stupid enough to come in here without backup?" Muna cross-reached to tap the man's hand. "Raise your hands and my dog leaves your balls intact."

Hank let go of the grip of his pistol and slowly raised his hands. Muna drew the pistol out and glanced at the battered Colt 45. She fingered the release, and the clip dropped. "Jeez. Does your grandpa know you're out flashing his hundred-year-old service weapon around? If you ever shot it, you'd have a forty percent chance of the barrel blowing up in your face."

The man whirled around on his heel. His right hand slapped hard at her hand and the pistol. The Beretta spun out into the air and dropped to the floor. His right hand swung back as he stepped in close to Muna.

The pom-poms rolled forward toward her forehead as her head jerked back—out of the swinging hand's way. Her left hand, swinging the heavy, antiquated pistol, crunched into his crotch as the four cow-dog teeth sank into his buttocks. The man groaned a pained howl and collapsed to the floor.

Muna planted her boot on his shoulder and pushed him over onto his face. Picking up and holstering her pistol, she flipped the neutered forty-five onto the bed. Dropping her right knee onto the injured cheek, she reached for the left ankle. Pulling it back, she slapped a long zip-tie just above where his sock should have been. She zipped it close, but left room to feed in another tie. With the new loop, she tightened the first on the ankle.

"Hey. That's too tight."

She glowered at the back of his head. "Shut up."

"I have my rights, you know."

"Tell that to the guards in Guantanamo."

"I'm an American citizen and patriot."

Nash growled. "Engaged in domestic terrorism, kidnapping, human trafficking, along with aiding and abetting international terrorists. Now do like the woman said and shut up."

Leaning forward, Muna grabbed his right wrist. Having already fed the zip-tie through another loop, Muna hauled the now-bound wrist back and brought back the other. She zipped and tightened the loops around the man's wrists, securing him.

Putting most of her weight on her knee, she leaned forward. "Next time a lady tells you to behave, I'd suggest you listen and do as you're told." She looked up and smiled at Nash, who was dialing her phone.

"Yeah. Come on ahead quietly. We still haven't breached room four yet." She thumbed the phone and slipped it into her pocket.

Nash tapped the nose of her pistol on the cheek of the first man. "Okay, Cleland, it's time for you to shine and earn your early release like we talked about."

The man understood how she had just screwed him with his friend and therefore anyone he ever worked with. His glare was hot and dark.

"What should I expect in room four?" She gently stroked the pistol along his cheek. "Is she alive or dead? Is there a booby trap, or is she tied down to the bed?"

"Fuck you, bitch. Go find out for yourself."

Nash smiled. "Well, so much for cooperation from the paid informant on the inside." She looked over at Muna sitting on the other man's butt. "Jeez, Cream Puff. I guess you pushed him a little too far. Maybe we should let Jaws have her way with his crotch and find out if it's still tender?"

The man howled. "She's chained to the bed so she can use the bathroom. I swear. But keep the dog away from me."

They turned at the soft knock at the doorway. The man dressed in a tactical vest and black camouflage jumpsuit stepped in, smiling at the scene. "Did someone call for an anti-terrorist assault team? Or to just have the trash taken out?"

Nash tipped her chin out and up. "Come on in. The party's over. We'll go recover the girl in four. I think some friendly female faces would work better than the SWAT routine."

A tall blonde stepped in behind the other Homeland agent and filled the doorway. "Hey, it's our best pickup line in the bars after midnight."

Muna stood and looked up at the small giant. "Yeah, but do they still respect you in the morning?"

The first guy snorted and jerked his thumb back at his partner. "He's still married to her eleven years later."

Nash holstered her weapon and pointed at the door. "Okay. We'll leave you two to swap old fantasy tales while we ladies see about a young girl."

"Are you leaving the dog?"

Muna burped a laugh. "Who are you kidding? She's the top of the incident command structure here." She reached up and patted the larger man on the armored chest. "Just don't get into trouble here. We'll be back in a few." She squeezed one of the flash-bang grenades and rolled her eyes large. "Ooh, you've been working out."

The man flushed.

The first man tipped his head at Nash. "I know Felix is some kind of goofball, but is she always like that?"

Nash shrugged. "Kids. What do you want? How long have you known Felix?"

"We've done some Homeland online classes together. I've seen the wild hair... Why?"

Nash chuckled. "You do know he's only twenty-one and dating a multi-millionaire who flies him off to Paris occasionally in her private jet, right?"

He shook his head. "I knew he was a nerd gear head... but? She must be a nerd, as well." Suddenly, he frowned. "Wait. We took those classes during the pandemic. That would have made him...?"

Nash smirked. "Underaged. And yes, his girlfriend is the biggest nerd you can find." She pointed out the door. "My team calls."

Muna lightly tapped her knuckle on the door. "Mack? It's the FBI. Can you open the door for us?"

The muffled response was full of sleep. "Huh? What?"

Nash tried the doorknob. "Sweetie, it's the FBI. We're here to take you home. Can you open the door for us, please?" She scrunched her face in a grimace at Muna. "Viper?"

Muna chuckled silently. "Cream Puff?"

Nash looked down at Powder. "But I love Jaws."

They listened to confusing noises of movement and then heavy scraping. Light slapping noises around the doorknob sounded more like fingertips. "Just a minute."

The sound of furniture moving was short.

The knob turned and Muna pushed softly.

Naked and sprawling on the cold floor, the girl's vulnerability was stark. A handcuff bit into her raw, bleeding ankle, a testament to her struggle. Its chain snaked across the room, looped over the bed, and anchored somewhere on the bathroom side of the bed. The bed itself was awkwardly dragged halfway into the cramped room, an unwilling participant in this grim setup. The drag marks carved into the cheap vinyl flooring were a testament to the will of the girl.

Nash growled. "Which man has the key to the handcuffs?"

The girl's mouth opened and froze. Muna squatted. "The guy in the filthy wife beater, or the guy who doesn't smoke?"

Mack closed her mouth and sagged. "The smoker. I don't think I'll ever get the smell out of my mind."

Muna patted the girl's shoulder. "Trust us. We'll make this right... Well, better." She looked up at Nash. "Go kick him in the balls until he tells you exactly which pocket they're in."

The girl looked up. "It's his front left pocket."

Nash smirked and ground her head back and forth. "See. I don't think you could ever know. I guess we must do what the boss says." Nash smiled at the girl's wan smile. She turned and left. Powder stayed and licked at the bloody ankle.

"That feels good. But..." She looked at Muna. "Is it safe? I mean... he won't bite me or anything... right?"

"She. Her name is Powder. She just knows what to do to help. It's one of her superpowers." Muna pointed at Powder. "Nash and I are just the scouts. Powder is the entire Fifth Cavalry. You're more protected now than ever in your life before. She's put her life on the line for my partner and me several times."

The girl curled toward her ankle and the dog. "Hi, Powder. How ya doing?"

Muna pulled her phone out of her pocket. "I guess it's going to take some time to get the keys." She smiled and held out her phone. "How about calling home to let them know you're okay?"

The girl didn't move. "I'm… I don't think…"

Muna's head moved up a tick and then down. "Trouble at home?"

"Kind of. We had a fight…"

"And that was the last time you were home."

The shoulder and head sagged. "I was sofa surfing for the last few weeks. I was with Kristina when we heard about the party."

"Party?"

"It was just beer. But it was some older guys. There was a cabin…" She peeked at Muna. "I know. Every slasher movie starts with a party at a cabin in the woods. But it didn't seem like that. We were just early. Or something."

"Did a party ever happen?"

"I don't know. I don't remember. We only drank about half a red cup of beer, and then I felt like I might be sick. I remember trying to find the bathroom…" Her eyes jumped about Muna's face—looking for answers.

"And that's the last thing you remember?"

Her lower lip pushed out. "Then we woke up in a bedroom, but there were just mattresses on the floor. There was a bathroom, but with bars on the window. They fed us, but only twice a day. I don't think the men were staying there. We heard a truck come and go."

Muna frowned. "How did you know it was a truck?"

"It reminded me of my dad's work truck. And I could smell the diesel. There was a sus guy with greasy, stringy hair that looked like he had never washed it. His hands smelled like diesel and rubber. Like he handled a lot of tires."

"What color hair?"

"Brown. But almost black." She ran her finger across her cheek. "He has an old scar across his cheek. I think his name is Willie or Will. Maybe it's Wills." Mack glanced up.

Nash rattled the keys. "It always amazes me how stubborn some men insist on being. I must have asked him at least a dozen times." She kneeled and unlocked the handcuff. "It looks like the nurse was here." She scratched around Powder's ears and looked at Mack. "How about we get you back to Oklahoma City?"

"Can we get some food? They only feed me in the morning."

Nash glanced at Muna with a smirk. "What would you like, Mack?"

The girl sagged as her eyes grew large. "Pancakes. With strawberries. I haven't had pancakes since I left home."

Muna smiled. "You want eggs and bacon with that?"

The eyes got larger as the smile sealed the deal.

3 4

GATHER ROUND

Nash stretched her legs along the edge of the shade. The backyard tables were empty except for the remains of lunch. She watched Muna, on hands and knees, try to convince Powder to act like a dog on the grass. Nash chuckled as Powder gently rolled over and snuffled at the three puppies watching the strange woman.

"What's funny?"

Nash snorted softly at her phone. "Muna. She's trying to teach Powder and three six-week-old reservation dogs how to act like a white man puppy."

Uncle's voice rumbled like large rocks tumbling down a small waterfall. "Ain't gonna happen. That girl never did chase a stick. She was working before she weaned. So what kind of compound?"

Nash looked at the printout Muna worked up. "We have a little over a thousand acres. There's a low valley running on one side. As best as we can figure, that is where they play with the big guns. The one guy admitted to an RPG and some machine guns. I won't rule out AK-47s and AR-15s with a minimum of bump stocks. But if they're playing with the bigger stuff, they probably smithed them into full autos. Things are getting nasty out here, also out in the open. We have a helicopter with dual mini guns in New Mexico that shot up a jeep and three Arabs. I don't know if they're connected or if it was just about the two and a half million in dead presidents."

The whistle was low. "That's a lot of jerky."

"I don't think they were buying jerky."

Uncle burped a chuckle. "I wasn't talking about your case. Junior just walked in and dropped two heavy garbage bags of jerky."

"Where did he get it?"

"I don't know. Didn't say a word, just walked back out."

Nash watched Muna roll around on the grass with the puppies as she sipped from her mug. "Well, you don't just find jerky on the side of the road."

"Nope. That road stuff usually still has the skin on it." Nash heard the squeak of Uncle's favorite chair. "Holy crap. Where did you guys get all of this?"

Nash could hear the higher squeak of Homeland's youthful voice. "Alex took the other half over to the VFW building to share with the tribe."

"But...?"

Nash strained to hear what was going on in California.

Uncle put his phone back to his ear as he laughed. "Junior popped the supply truck for a new grow just north of here. I guess we have some new guns and half a ton of jerky, rice, and beans. I guess it's going to make winter a little happier around the valley. So, Homeland is here. Do you want to talk to him?"

"Sure."

"Hey, Nash. How's it hanging?"

Nash laughed. "Felix, you're not old enough to know that slang. How's Tree?"

"We're back on the good to fly list. I heard about your out-gaming the super gamers. She wants to come up and try camping next month."

Nash almost choked on her coffee. "What motel?"

He snickered. "There are some nice ones in Reno. There's even one or two who stop room service by midnight, so kind of roughing it… I think. Uncle's note says you have Homeland questions…?"

"We're in Oklahoma. We have a militia compound we need to take down with the least number of collateral casualties. They have some young girls. They're human trafficking."

"Automatic weapons?"

"Probably mostly. They have a range they are legally allowed to shoot big stuff on."

His hum suggested his brain was already putting out smoke signals. "So what's the Homeland angle?"

"We believe Sergei Romanov is involved."

"There should be a contingency there in Oklahoma. Or just use FBI and some ATF."

Nash growled in her coffee mug. The echoes deepened closer to angered bear than Nash.

Felix laughed. "Okay. I'll bite. Which part didn't you like? The FBI or ATF?"

"You were there when we took down the drug lab in Harkin…" She stopped. Thinking.

The voice was small. "Nope. I wasn't eighteen yet."

"Well, I know you'll remember Colorado, even if I don't."

The silence was calm. His voice took on a more mature presence. "You don't trust those you don't know. I get it. But we can't get there with the buggy and her kids before the weekend. Even if we all share the driving of the bus."

"What if you fly? Does the Barrett fit in Alex's drug-runner airplane?"

"Sure. But even if we bring the sheriff, that only makes six against how many?"

Nash rested her phone on her leg and then pulled it back up. "Let me consult with the magic woman." She looked at the aggressive puppy grabbing at Muna's right pom-pom. "Hey, Muna?"

"Help. I'm being attacked by vicious beasts here."

Nash groaned at the new Muna. "Work calls. Did you see any sign of the compound being on reservation land?"

Nytah stepped into the open sliding glass door. "Is it in Oklahoma?"

Nash looked at her as Muna rolled over. "Yeah...?"

The woman bounced her eyebrows and ticked her head. "Then it's on tribal land. The case of McGirt v. Oklahoma went to the Supreme Court, and they gave three million acres back to the Creek Nation. It essentially makes almost all of the state Indian territory. But more importantly, the northland this side of Tulsa."

Muna stood, and the tiny terrorist turned on its siblings. "What are you thinking?"

Nash glanced at Nytah. "A small army of law enforcement, we're guaranteed, lacks militia compatriots, who they might warn we are coming."

The woman in the door snorted. "That would be anybody of color. Red, brown, yellow, or green. How many do you need?"

Nash's mouth pulled back on the right. "How many tribal police or sheriffs can you muster?"

"If I work some magic with some Oklahoma National Guard, I think a couple of hundred. Kidnapping girls and selling them for sex don't sit well with many people. When do you need them?"

Nash raised her phone. "Today's Monday. So ahead of people going to shoot up their weekend. So Thursday evening or Friday at first light. I'm sure the two boys are screaming civil rights over at the tribal jail. Even with the chief's resolve, they get a lawyer soon."

Felix sounded through the phone. "We're packing now. We'll bring drones as well."

"Good thinking. Reach out before you take off."

The kid laughed. "We don't have to fly with our phones in airplane mode. That's a commercial thing."

Nash growled playfully. "Go pack, kid."

Nytah stepped onto the patio and pulled her cellphone from her bib overalls. "Let's see how many hornet nests we can stir up."

Nash peeked into her mug and stood. "I'm going to need more coffee for this. Muna, loop in the deputy director. Or at least call Donna."

MUNA LEANED TOWARD HER LAPTOP. THE SHADE OF THE back patio became useless in the last hour of the day. The side-lighting made her cock the laptop on the table. "Oh, we might not need a tank or whatever those big things are."

"MRAP? Why? What do you have?"

Muna turned the laptop around for Nash to see. Her fingernail tapped on the two words.

Nash picked up her phone and searched through contacts. She pushed the number and spiked her elbows on the table.

The phone rang once. "Tell me you have something more fun than a fire, LT."

"Pequeño, how fast can you be in Oklahoma City?"

The firefighter hummed. "Just me, or a team?"

"We'll be taking down a militia compound that's on tribal territory, but also National Forest. A charge of fire trucks lends an element of surprise that the sortie of MRAPs doesn't."

"Don't tease me, LT. I'm sitting here with thirty law enforcement firefighters. And the emphasis is on the fighters. I think only one or two didn't knock sand out of their butt cracks."

Nash frowned at Muna and Nytah. "I thought your team was only about eight or ten?"

"My Hot Shots also came. We just wrapped up an annual team training, which included weapons familiarization and practicums. What parts do you want?"

Nash's eyes became slits as her smirk pulled back up to evil. Her right thumb rose for Muna. "Operational silence. The compound is trafficking young girls. One of them is Scissors' granddaughter. We can't use local talent; they might be connected. Where you at?"

The man chuckled. "I can't wait to hear more about how Scissors is involved. What's for breakfast?"

Nash looked at Nytah. "He wants to know what's for breakfast. He's got about thirty friends."

The woman laughed. "White boys, Indian, or Latino?"

The laugh was friendly from Nash's phone. "I heard that. We're omnivores except Poncho. He won't eat roadkill. But pancakes will work for him."

Nash laughed. "We've got you, Pequeño. The head cook is Scissor's widow." She nudged her chin at the Indian woman. "He says cook's choice."

"I'll get the girls over, and we can whip up pancakes, eggs, machaca, fried bread, and tortillas. If they can't find something to eat, the Micky D's is just down the state."

Nash nodded. "What time?"

The woman hung her hands in her bib overalls. "Seven or eight too early? It's nice out here at that time of the morning. We can start the grills when the sun comes up."

"Does eight work for you?"

The man chuckled. "Yeah, we can sleep in late and mosey on down. Even with the heavy trucks, you're only three hours from Wichita. You mentioned militia. What's the sit-rep, LT?"

"I'm thinking Thursday dinner or Friday before sunrise. In either case, the camp will lack weekend warriors eager for a fire-fight. They've got a license for automatic weapons and heavies. So we can expect RPGs to field guns. But I'm hoping it won't come to that."

"Roger. We'll pack appropriately and see you just before eight. Have a good night, LT."

Nash turned her phone down on the table.

Muna smirked over her laptop. "Now that puts a unique spin on things."

Nash grimaced. "Where do we bivouac thirty armed forest rangers?"

Nytah turned away as she blushed. The silent laughing shook her shoulders.

Nash narrowed her eyes and then rolled one eye at Muna. "Wise Indian says the old woman has a dirty mind."

The woman turned back. She pursed her lips tightly as her eyes sparkled. She licked her lips. "I'm just thinking if they be housebroken, we can spread them around with the women. Most of us live in three-bedroom houses. So an extra guest or two is nothing."

Nash pointed at the backyard lawn. "You could probably fit twenty of them right there. These guys are smoke jumpers. So they're used to sleeping on fire-burned ground. The grass stained all over Muna's back would be like a featherbed."

Muna looked over her shoulder. "I have grass stains? Where?"

Nytah laughed and waved her hand down. "Not to worry. I've bleached out worse. And on a white shirt—a piece of cake." She turned back to Nash. "So with the crew from Tulsa and the Creek guys…"

Muna pointed at her. "You promised three women in the Creek group."

She laughed and held up her palms. "The sorority is coming. And Becky hinted at a few more female law enforcement officers who have jurisdiction. So we have plenty of representation."

Nash shook her somber face. "With a rescue like this, it's not about looking good. It's all about having plenty of friendly faces when we get the girls out."

Muna rolled out her finger into the air. "Studies have shown that when guys rescue females of any age from other guys, it's not a rescue. The females don't feel safe until they are with other women. It's why some more prolific pedophiles have had females working with them to groom the children."

Nytah rocked her head. "Like the guy with an island."

"Like the guy with an island."

35

LISTEN UP

NASH LOOKED out on the backyard, now jammed with more tan, olive-drab, forest-green, and forest camouflage than the morning breakfast had gathered. Tulsa reservation police, in their para-military uniforms, had arrived just before breakfast service ended. A younger officer had intimate knowledge of the now militia training camp that had been a Boy Scout summer camp. With Muna's help on the computer, they made a large map drawn with crayons on butcher paper, filling two tables shoved side-by-side.

An older National Guard commander, and a member of the Cherokee Nation from south of Tulsa, arrived for lunch. He poked his gnarled middle finger at the buildings drawn with red crayons. "You should have used a gold crayon for this building here. It be an iceberg."

Nash narrowed her eyes and cocked her head sideways.

He chuckled. "Yeah, my wife tries to use the same side-eye crap on me all the time."

"Does it work?"

"The look and four dollars will get you dangerous coffee at the Waffle House. My nephew helped build this building. There're four times as much under the building as you'll see on top. They poured a lot of money into a seemingly simple office." He looked up at Nash. "You're the top of the command structure named Running Bear?"

"Nash." She pointed at Muna. "Agent Muna al-Faragi is my second in command, but anything she says goes. Especially if you have knowledge, we can use going in."

The man dipped his head at Muna. "I'll call the nephew right after I fill the hole in my gut with the chili I'm smelling."

Muna held out her hand. "Eat. I'm here all day."

As the day dragged on, the backyard turned into clusters of groups who hadn't seen each other for a while, or meeting new people to know. Muna and Nash both commented on phones being passed around for new contact numbers.

"Did they ever call you back?" Nash took a moment and sat next to Muna.

"I sent a text to Felix two hours ago. But unless Alex installed a mobile hotspot on his plane, they're skipping from cell tower to cell tower about every minute or so. So it probably won't catch up with them until they land for fuel or something."

"Felix said they were packing and leaving last night. Even in a slow chopper, I'd think they would be close by now."

Muna reached out and rested her hand on Nash's shoulder. "They are four grown-assed men. They can take care of themselves."

Nash gave her a slitted side-eye and noticed Muna vibrate a nod to toss her twin pom-poms back and forth. "You can't grow your braid back fast enough. You being almost Baby's twin is extremely unnerving."

Muna chuckled. "Yeah, I was thinking about letting Nytah give them a little trim before they grow out too much."

Nash lowered her left hand to the nose that was pushing at her knee. "Yeah, we're going." As she stood, she looked down at Muna, wobbling her head more. "Ass."

Muna snickered and then looked up at the three women studying the map. "Can you add anything to the map?"

The one looked up. "What satellite are you using?"

Muna sensed another nerd. "I'm burning Google Earth Pro. It's the best I can tap into with this laptop. Why?"

The slender woman stepped down the table and put her hand out. "I'm Madge, just like the badge. I'm the geek for the Cherokee Nation Tribal Police. But I'm a Major in the National Guard attached to Space Force. Let me see if I can access something better for you."

"Muna. FBI. We go by squints."

The woman chuckled and nodded. "Because we squint into the screens. Yeah, I keep asking for bigger monitors."

"What are you running?"

"Triple twenty-sevens. Interlaced 1080p. So last decade. You?"

Muna snorted. "Come over to the dark side. We have cookies and hot pork rinds. But my wall is a double stack of triples. OLED forties. But I think someone might force me to go one-twenty curved wall to pair up to my new water-cooled server farm."

Madge slapped her chest. "Sign me the hell up." Her eyes narrowed. "What spice on the pig bellies?"

"Beyond Scoville." Muna's left hand rose from under her chair and held out the bag.

The hand was hesitant and then pulled out a skin. The nibble was tepid. But the smile spread, advertising the mark of a convert. "Where do you get these?"

"Large truck stops until you're ordering obscene quantities. Then you let the big blue smile deliver."

Informal groups had powwowed around the large yard until Nytah and her squad formally called dinner. The teams lined up fast, as everyone had been smelling the cooking for over an hour.

A small drone slowly lowered in front of Nash, with her fork of food already in her mouth. Gently, so as not to spill the chili down her shirt, she pulled the fork back out. "Muna? Did you ever get hold of Felix or any of the boys?"

At the other end of the table, Muna was studying another, smaller drone, hovering, unnervingly silent. "I think he's getting back to us right now."

The backyard, filled with a hundred people, was eerily silent as they all sat watching the two drones hovering above the main table. Someone *eeped* as a drone quietly eased out from under their table and rose to eight feet.

"We've got two more over here." More rose from other places among the tables.

"Is that a snake?"

"Where?"

"There. In the grass."

Nash growled. "Felix. Get your ass out here right now."

The drone bobbed up and down three times as dozens more of the smaller drones oozed from the crowd and ascended to the eight feet of the originals.

The first large drone crackled with static. "Please welcome your Overwatch team. The Deep Six raiders and posse."

Muna shook her head at Nash. "I get to strangle at least one of them. You don't get all the fun."

Everyone's eyes jerked to the side of the house as the small gang strolled into the backyard. Felix and Tree led with their arms around each other's waists. Chips and Baby skipped in as Slug and Petey brought up the rear of the nerds with their remote controls strapped to harnesses.

The old men followed.

Nash glanced over at Muna. "Uh oh. Bradey looks like he needs to find a hot tub. He must have been in the back seat of the plane."

Alex and Uncle waved at Nash and turned to come over as Felix clapped his hands and made a shooing motion, and the drones left en masse.

"The kids wouldn't let us warn you."

Nash growled as she winked at Uncle. "That's okay. I haven't spanked anybody for at least a year. What took you so long?"

Alex pulled up a chair. "We landed last night. But the RVs weren't ready until ten this morning. So we did training on the drones all day. Besides, our watch drone showed you were busy, anyway."

"RV? Watch drone?"

Alex squinted and pointed at the neighbor's rooftop. "We flew Gollum in last night. He's the little bump on the right end of the ridgeline. He's a 47-SD. Visual only, but takes in all this backyard."

Nash rolled her head toward him. "Alex, where did all those other drones go?"

"Felix either has the snake in his back pocket, or it's still wandering around here somewhere. But the others went back to the bus. Stack. Stuck, or whatever the kid's name is, will stick them all on their chargers. Sweet Thing is driving them when they're in swarm mode. She's an amazing talent there. Deep Six rented two barracks buses and a business office bus. We're in the office, and they will control the Overwatch drones from there. As well as communications. If that suits the head of the command structure."

Nash watched the kids making new friends in the yard. "They're all over talented. It gives us hope. Uh oh." She cocked her head toward Muna at the other end of the table. "Red alert, Muna. Your twin spotted your pom-poms."

The squeal of the incoming rocket started twenty feet away from the target. Muna braced.

Baby rushed over. "I thought it was you, but wasn't sure. We're twinkies, now." Her hug crushed Muna's neck. "And we can even share clothes and stuff."

Muna eased the young woman back a bit. "Let's just stick with... um... the look-alike thing. The badge and guns stay in my possession."

Baby mock-grumped and crossed her arms. "Can I still play with Eight Ball's little brother?"

Muna glanced over at Nash. "Sure. If you put him all back together, you can date him. But stay out of my spacesuit."

Baby spun and dropped to sit on Muna's knee. She rested her arm along Muna's shoulders. Leaning close, she dropped her voice for only them to hear. "I know this much touching makes you uncomfortable, but you have no idea how much we all missed you three. Deep Six was like being back on the streets, and everyone was cold and hungry. The least little thing could have people snapping at one another. Nobody would even game. It was so weird." Her eyes snapped wide. "Oh, and the large crate the big guy dropped off the truck…?"

Muna frowned. "Yeah?"

"Tree and Ming paid those guys to bring it up and set it in the middle of the conference table. Kind of like a big-ass trophy. It's total riz."

Muna hesitated and then rested her hand on Baby's. "We'll have plenty of time later to go over things. But, for now, who's going to be running the Overwatch?"

"Chips. It's her juice. She does it for the gamers, so this will be a stroll through the park."

"How about you go quietly and tell her we need to talk with her? Thanks."

Baby stood as she pulled her pinched thumb and finger across her lips.

Chips wandered over, spooning a load of children-colored tiny doughnuts from a large bowl into her mouth. The mouthful of cereal didn't affect her speech. "Ready to talk, Overwatch?" Froot Loops?"

"Um…" She swung and pointed at Nytah. "That one. She has grandkids. But it's not the same without the load of fruit Mike keeps in the fridge."

Muna waved her hand at the large pots of home-cooked stews and meat. "All this and you weasel a stinking bowl of cereal?"

Chips dropped the spoon back in the bowl. "Which side of the Rio Grande are we on?"

"East."

"What's the farthest East that you can get survivable Mexican food?"

Muna snorted. "Truck stop?"

"Where?"

"Texas?"

The blonde shoveled another spoonful into her mouth as her head ground side to side.

Nash burped a laugh. "Pueblo. Chunkies on the southbound, headed for Shiprock."

Chips touched her nose with the handle of the spoon and swallowed. "And I'm not resorting to Pop-Tarts and jerky for this mission."

Nash pointed at the women still serving. "It's Nytah's granddaughter we're here for."

Chips set her bowl on the large crayon map. Turning, she called out, "Team Slug. Time to huddle up." Turning back, she spread her hands on the map. "We'll need highlighters and markers."

36

NINE MINUTES AFTER MIDNIGHT

THE HUMIDITY HUNG in the stagnant night air. Moonset was forty-one minutes away. The young man child, sitting in the work bus, scanned his six screens in a sweep. Nothing had changed except that the gate guard was back out of the shelter to smoke another cigarette. *Those cancer sticks are going to kill you if the prison time doesn't.*

Stuck glanced down the bus at Sweet Thing, working the other drones. The new flexible, roll-out monitors Team Slug was creating lined up along the worktables. "How's the refresh rate, Sweet Thing?"

She frowned and then shook her head to look at him. "It wouldn't sell to gamers, but they're okay with the drones. Nothing looks glitchy, but they are not the same as my OLEDs."

His eyes moved back to his monitors. The thirties had become compact enough to pack six in a case along with their stands. His science fair project of a thinner, lighter monitor shell had caught Slug's eye. The job offer and a chance to exit high school early came a week later.

The white-hot dot at the front gate followed the same trajectory as the previous twelve or fifteen cigarettes had. Stuck made a silent bet the butts all lay on the road within a foot of each other.

The second screen was a static view of the five main buildings in the center of the camp. The box they had designated as the office showed cold. *Their air-conditioning bill must be enormous.* The three-bunk buildings showed warm. A push-in on the drone's scan, earlier, showed inferred heat sources of a dozen people sleeping in each building. But shortly after ten, there were five bodies in the office. None had left, but they no longer showed on the scan. Gaming terms would say they had *gone to ground.* Or, realistically, were in a basement or exited via a tunnel.

Stuck glanced over at the door opening. He recognized Baby, but then, the hair was wrong. The woman held her hand out. "Hi. We haven't met yet. I'm Muna."

Sweet Thing glanced over. "Hey, Muna. Glad you're back, but grow your hair back."

Muna chuckled as she shook the young man's hand. "Why? So you can tell me apart from my twin? We were thinking about dying our hair pink and green."

Sweet Thing rolled her eyes as she scanned one of her screens. "Do that, and Frank will have his coyotes bury you where no one will ever find your bones." Her hand rose and waved Muna over. "Check out the new screens the wunderkind have wrought."

Muna squeezed the kid's shoulder as she passed. "Welcome aboard the fun bus."

Sweet Thing, without looking, grabbed the upper corner and bent the large monitor toward her. Muna stooped and looked inside the rolled screen. "And it still displays? What kind of magic is this?"

Sweet Thing pushed the corner back. "Chips and Slug saw a display in Amsterdam when they were there for the dredging conference. The display wrapped around a pillar; however, it was an LED display. They asked the guy at the booth if they sold them and then bought six. The guy rolled up the displays in a six-foot tube and then asked if they would fly with them. So he rolled them the other way, and they were only a four-foot tube. The LEDs were only static, but the boys reverse-engineered to make them active."

Muna chuckled as she leaned over and sniffed the screen. "Something smells like a new business for Deep Six." She stepped back and looked at the screens. "What have we got?"

Sweet Thing yawned and sipped on her coffee. "This over here is the valley where they do the boom-boom things. We haven't detected any human bodies over there. Mostly it's small stuff like raccoons or possums. Bats like crazy, but that calmed down after the moon went down."

Her arms moved to the other side. "I'm watching the north side. If they run from the main camp, my guess is this ridge along here. Maybe throw some of the tribal police along this road. If they check in when they deploy, we can guide them to the best location and then target them when the rabbits bounce."

Muna frowned at the young teenager. "Who are you, and what did you do with my Sweet Thing?"

Sweet Thing swung her chair around as she sipped on her large thermos mug. "Hey. Two years ago, when we ran Overwatch on the drug war in the OC, we learned a lot. And a bunch of us girls learned to grow a pair real fast. I know I'm not alone, but I replayed a lot of the tapes. Ready to grow up or not, life doesn't care. It's just coming. So we either get ready, or we go home. And you know us girls and boys of Deep Six—we don't back down. We come to play and win. And who knows? There are some girls down there"—she pointed at the screen—"who need our best help. So we are in it to win it."

"How many people?"

Sweet Thing leaned her chair back. "That's your cue, Stuck." She glanced up at Muna. "He's driving the IR over the main camp. I snuck in some side view earlier, but..." She pointed at the kid.

Muna stepped over and looked at the screens. "What have you got, Stuck?"

He tapped the three buildings glowing green. "These are the

barracks. We've got a dozen persons in each, so there are thirty-six." He held up his index finger. "But..." He tapped on one box, noticeably darker than the surrounding forest and grounds. "This is the office. It's dark because it's cool or cold. Probably the premium air-conditioning for the mondo honchos." He glanced back to make sure he hadn't lost the older woman.

Muna narrowed her eyes. "I'm with ya, squirt. I'm not pushing a walker... yet. Was there anyone in the office?"

"The heat signature was warmer. We think there were five people. But they aren't showing in the Flair currently, so we're thinking a basement." He peeked back. "We never saw them exit the building."

Muna thought about an old case. "Or an underground tunnel to somewhere we're not watching. We've seen it before."

The kid grimaced. "I've been thinking about just that." He tapped the office's dark square. "Call me crazy, but if they're air-conditioning this, and you need to push fresh air into a tunnel, I would expect to see an anomaly at the ground temperature."

He turned his chair to face Muna and formed shapes with his hands. "A tunnel has no mass to keep thermal mass like the ground does. Usually, the ground at ten feet deep is around fifty-four degrees Fahrenheit. And for a tunnel, if you're going to drive over it, you'll want about eight or ten feet of structured dirt. So that hollow is going to show a cooler shadow." He waved his finger around the office building. "And I don't see that happening."

Muna turned and looked at Sweet Thing. "How is he at the dredging?"

The girl snorted. "He picked up all the concepts as Slug and Tree spun them out." She squinted at the young man. "Tree took you down under... what? The third week?"

"Second. But I already had a passport. New Zealand was awesome. But it's the remediation work they're doing on the north shore of Australia. There's the best stuff. They're casting three-meter jacks out of old concrete and unrecyclable glass. They foam the concrete with captured carbon to lock it up, and then they throw the jacks in the ocean and make the bones of a new shoreline. The cutter dredge pushed out the sand and mud, and it finished building the new shoreline. They are reclaiming one to three kilometers of ground they had lost in a tsunami a bunch of years ago."

Muna smiled and looked at Sweet Thing.

The girl grimaced and pushed out both hands and palms up. "See. Dredge geek. He doesn't fit in with Team Slug, and he's not a research nerd like us girls. He's a dredge geek. His mind works in solid concepts."

Muna rubbed her chin as she studied the kid. "So, where do you fit in?"

"I think I'm going to be working with Chips for a while." He tapped on the backside of his screens. "These are my shells. I reduced the thickness by thirty-seven percent, and we're down to half the weight. These six screens, mini tower, and all their hardware fit in a carry-on with room for a change of clothes. Dredges are a wet environment, even in the office or the dredge crane. No matter where, the computer is within twenty feet of a body of water. So we either seal them or make them run in the wet." He smiled. "I love a challenge."

Muna rocked. "How old are you?"

He pointed at Sweet Thing. "I just turned seventeen—same as her."

Muna turned to frown at Sweet Thing. "And Baby is…?"

"Fifty-nine going on seventy thousand. But she'll only cop to sixteen. It was so funny seeing you with the pom-poms. You really could pass for twins."

Muna smoothed her hand over the French Curl. "It's growing back. But all that hair went to a good cause… and I needed the change." She pointed toward the back of the bus. "I think my bed is…"

Sweet Thing nodded. "Bathroom and the upper rack. I'm waking up Nash and Powder at three..."

Muna raised her hand. "Same."

At the door to the sleeping pod, Muna stopped and leaned against the one wall. Her knuckle rested against the other. "Hey, Stuck?"

The kid looked over. "Yeah?"

"What kind of name is Stuck?"

Sweet Thing snickered. "It really is a nickname..." She turned to smirk at Muna, "...for once."

The kid blushed. "Stuart Tillerman Charles Kostopoulos. My parents named me after my two grandfathers. And the nickname stuck."

37
WHERE'S THE FIRE?

WHEN THE AIR seems to lose its solid darkness and there is breath between the branches, there is a stirring in a forest. Birds ruffle their feathers as they blink away the dark. Small animals with fur either retreat from the night's hunting, or begin their search for breakfast. Insects loosen exoskeletal legs as they move from their nights freeze; a protection from being spotted by predators with movement tracing foci.

Some larger animals step cautiously between the trees to remain hidden. And others stroll absently from their protection to suck on a burning ember at the end of a cigarette.

The guard frowned at the flashing red lights approaching. As he turned to go fetch his rifle, his nose bumped into metal—the end of a pistol barrel.

Muna smirked. "Yeah, you won't be needing the rifle. How about slowly turning around and clasping your hands?"

The man shuddered a small fart and did what he was told.

Nash wound the three-foot-long zip-tie around his wrists, through his belt loop and belt, and back to his arms. Pulling it all tight, she walked him back to the weighted pole blocking the road. She pushed on the counterweight. As the pole stood straight up, she sat him down with his back to the weight. The new zip-tie kept his arms tied to the weight as Muna pulled the red ball gag into the man's mouth.

As Muna leaned over to buckle the gag on the man's head, she chuckled. "Relax. And be glad you're not the guy we have the pink bra and panties for to go with his black leather harness."

The man's eyes swelled with fear.

"Nope. You get to keep your pants on as long as you stay quiet. But first, where are they keeping the girls?"

The man mumbled.

Nash rolled her head and eyes as she waved the Forest Service trucks through the gate. "Silly me. You can't talk. Okay, let's start over. Are the girls in any of the barracks?"

He shook his head.

"The commissary?"

He shook his head.

"In the office?"

He shook his head.

Nash frowned.

Muna draped her hand on Nash's shoulder. "Let me try."

Nash turned her head. "No kicking him in the nuts... unless he lies."

Muna lowered her head to the man's face. "Are they in the basement under the office?"

His face turned dark, and he didn't move.

Muna smiled. "You see... I guess you weren't familiar with the rules of the game. I ask a question, and you either nod or shake your head. So let's try this again. Are the girls being held in the basement or basements buried under the office?"

His face darkened, and his eyes narrowed further.

Muna cocked her head to look at Nash. "Do I have to accept it as a confirmation, or is it a lie by not playing along?"

Nash shrugged. "Well, we either let you kick him, or let Jaws work on his crotch."

Muna winced. "But the last guy lost his right nut and most of his cock. He was halfway to becoming trans something."

Nash shrugged. "Leave him. We're burning daylight."

Muna spun and left her right heel in his crotch. Leaning back, she got close to the moaning man's head. "If you're not here when we get back, the dog gets her way with you until she's well fed and satisfied. You understand?"

He nodded and groaned.

The twelve large firetrucks had parked with their headlights lighting up the barracks and office. Rangers, deputies, tribal police, and the National Guard silently apprehended and tied up those in the barracks. Silently walking them into the parking lot in their underwear, they made them sit on the ground—zip-tied, and ball gagged.

Nash leaned toward Muna. "Great call on the sex toy store. I bet they never thought they would sell out of those ball gag rigs."

"By the guy's reaction, I'll bet they only sold a few a year."

Nash, Muna, and Powder watched as they accounted for the last of the militia. The Forest Ranger with the white helmet walked over. His voice was soft. "Only thing left is the office building."

Nash dipped her head. "Do we have the guy who knows the workings of the building?"

The ranger turned. "Neal?"

The older man walked over. He held out his phone. "I've got Davey on the phone. We can face time if nothing is obvious."

Nash tapped the com unit in her left ear. "Chips?"

"Overwatch, go."

"Any heat in the office?"

"Nothing on the overhead. Give me a minute with the side views."

They felt, more than heard, the small swarm of drones pass overhead.

Nash frowned at Muna. "Where did those come from?"

Muna shrugged. "They probably hitched a ride on the back of

the trucks. There's a nice soft bed on some of them with the hoses. That way, they don't slide around."

Nash and Muna's com units buzzed.

"Overwatch, this is Long Shot. I've got a couple of armed bogies showing up on my Starlight, but they don't show on the infrared. It looks like they came out of a ground passage near the north wall of the office."

A double click answered.

A shotgun shattered the gray of the morning, followed by the sound of a sound-suppressed rifle.

"Big Dog, Long Shot. Target is acquired."

Nash looked at Muna. "I hate this part." She touched the earbud switch. "Can you disable?"

The voice still sounded like a testosterone-raging, over-eager pre-teen. "I can go for the shoulder, but they're moving around a lot."

"You have green light. But please, no skip shots."

A lot of swearing and another series of shots immediately followed the deep roar of the .50 caliber Barrett.

One more roar of the Barrett, and the other rifle was silenced.

"Clean up on aisle six, please."

Nash turned to Muna. "Bang Town protocols. Powder has the lead." She turned to the ranger. "Lieutenant, Neal, you're with us."

The door was locked. Nash thought about kicking the door, but knew better. Boots did nothing to steel doors set in steel doorjambs —but break ankles. She turned to Muna. "Can you pick a lock?"

Muna pushed her lower lip out. "Sure." She pointed at the other end of the front porch. "Stand over there."

Muna held her finger on the door where the deadbolt was located. "Long Shot?"

"Got it."

Muna stepped away. "Someone also locked the doorknob."

"Done."

The Barrett roared, and the doorknob disappeared. One more roar.

"Hold one. Let me be a gentleman."

The Barrett barked again, and the door swung open.

Nash leaned close to Powder. "See if there are any booby traps."

Powder paused at the door and then entered. A few minutes later, she stood in the doorway and looked at Nash. Turning, she went back inside.

Neal followed as he held his phone out. The voice of his son was clear. "Okay, wait a minute. Is there a hall to the left?"

Neal turned so the man could see. "Alright. That door on the left should be the bathroom. The first one on the right is an office, maybe?"

Nash and Powder looked in. "Office."

"Then there should be two more offices at the end of the hall. One on each side."

Powder glanced in both and sat at the wall in the middle. The wall was built-in bookshelves, sparsely filled. Nash chuckled. "Yeah, girl. We've seen this act before. Where does he put his hand?"

The voice on the phone chuckled. "Exactly what I was going to tell you. There's a reason the hallway is five feet wide. But I don't know how to open the secret door."

Powder stood on her hind legs. Her left paw braced on one shelf as she touched her nose to the three books held by two bookends made of twin Colt .45s welded to thin metal plates, so the barrels faced up. Nash had seen similar bookends in the military. The pistols were never real.

Nash pulled the three books. They pivoted forward on a hinge, and she felt the trigger wire pull a latch. The bookshelf swung free.

She only let it swing open about a foot. "Tom Winters? FBI. Come up with your hands up."

Silence.

Chips' voice crackled in Nash's and Muna's ears. "Big Dog,

Team Yah Hey says the trap door is open. He's asking about dropping a flash-bang."

Nash looked at Muna. Muna shrugged. "Then we'll know if they're down there."

Nash pushed the secret door open enough to see the light at the end of the stairway. "Bombs away, Overwatch."

The flash and concussion flared and echoed up the stairs. Only muffled yells. Empty.

"Okay, let them know we're going down. They can come in through the tunnel."

The double click was sharp.

The room was what could pass as a man cave, furnished in cheap, semi-overstuffed leather furniture. A large screen TV faced two couches. A lack of fresh air enhanced the years of male DNA.

Nash snorted. "Screw together Gotz-at-Ikea." Muna nodded. The hidden door cum bookshelf stood open with markings from the flash-bang. The three tribal police stood frowning in the doorway. Nash looked at the older man. "Neal?"

The man was scanning the basement with his phone. "Where now, Davey?"

"See the bathroom? My guess is the oversized shower doesn't work."

Nash waved her finger. "Where do they touch, girl?"

Powder entered the walk-in shower and stood on her hind legs. Her nose touched the hot water faucet.

Nash smirked at Muna. "Rock, paper, scissors?"

"Naw. Just pull or push and turn. It's not like they need a secret code anymore."

Nash stepped in and pushed. The knob didn't move. Grabbing the knob, she pulled. The trigger was only half an inch of movement. She turned the handle clockwise. The back wall opened about two inches.

Nash peeked through the crack at the stairs leading down. She reached out toward the three cops. "Two flash bangs, please."

She pulled the pin on one and lobbed it down the stairs. Pulling the pin on the other, she waited with her head turned and eyes closed. With the concussion ringing in the stairwell, she threw the second down. The results were what she wanted. Moaning joined the screaming.

Nash shouldered the false wall and thundered down the stairs. At the doorway, she stopped, peeked around, and then strolled into the large room. Four men lay on the floor, holding their heads. They had dropped their weapons on the floor except for the one holding his pistol to his head like it was an icepack.

Muna pulled the pistol and sneered. "Cheap Chinese Glock knockoff." She handed the weapon to the tribal officer, collecting the other handguns in an evidence bag. Pulling the extra-long zipties from the back of her tactical vest, she handed a couple to the other cops. "Figure-eight on the wrists, then through the center belt loop, and back for another figure-eight. Then cinch it all tight. They can scratch their butts, but not their nuts."

Nash glanced over with a smirk. "So Larson is still teaching at the Q?"

"Nah. He was just there to sit in on one of my lectures. Hanson showed me the trick. With so much skin contact and winding, they don't have marks they can whine about, but they also can't get loose. Someone must cut them off. Let's check the girls. The boys can finish here."

They looked at the two closed doors. "What do you think?"

Muna bounced one eyebrow and stepped back. Grabbing the blonde by the hair, she pulled. "Get up." She walked him to the door with her pistol behind his ear. "If someone is in there. You get shot before I shoot them." She reached for the doorknob.

The man nodded.

Muna opened the door with her left hand and pushed hard. The man tried to lean forward to get out of the line of sight, but Muna dropped behind him as her knee kicked the back of his right knee. He buckled as the man in the room shot.

Muna held her weapon close to the blonde's ear as she put three rounds into the man across the room. Two in center mass and one through his pistol hand as it swung out with the kinetic energy.

The blond fell forward into the room as the other man fell to meet him. Muna stepped on the blonde's back and kicked the other man's pistol into the corner. "They never learn." She rolled the blonde over. She holstered her pistol as she pointed out the bleeding to Nash. "Dinner says it shattered his clavicle."

"Lung?"

Muna snorted. "Oh, the lung is toast. But he'll live. You think this other coward hiding in the rat hole is Winter?"

"Yeah. Looks like his ads. The leaders always sacrifice their sycophants as cannon fodder."

An officer stepped into the doorway. "The girls were in the other room. You want to talk them down. They look like they're close to hysterical."

Muna nodded. "Yeah. This slasher movie wasn't what they signed up for. Come on, Powder. Let's go meet some nice girls."

Nash nodded as she tapped her earbud. "Chips? Chips?" *Crap. Buried too deep.* "I need to go up to get reception." She looked at the cops lining the others up against the wall. "I'll be right back."

"Chips?"

"Overwatch. Go."

"Did we have any EMTs or paramedics in the group?"

"Four or five of the rangers. I'll send them your way. What do we have?"

"Two down, and probably some sedatives if they have some."

"Will do."

38

HOME BUT NO ANSWERS

COOTER'S FADED blue hair lay scattered on the chest of her grandmother as they lay on the large chaise lounge under the shade of the patio. The girl hadn't left Nytah's side other than to use the bathroom—where she set a record for a teen alone in any bathroom. The other girls had been taken to their respective families. No parent threatened them with corporal punishment in front of several SUVs of law enforcement officers. The families were just happy they were home safe and sound.

Nash let Muna ask the questions. Maybe it was the size, or maybe it was the closer age, but she had connected with the girl. The voices were soft as they talked.

Nash wished she could sit closer, or maybe it was the ringing still in her ears from the flash bangs. But she was only catching about every third word, and they made little sense. But Muna would fill her in later. It looked like she was taking notes on her pad, but Nash had watched the routine before. She was recording. And the glasses she was wearing were filming. Nash snorted softly in her mug. She had forgotten about the Clark Kent glasses with the visual and sound feed that Felix and Alex had built.

The nose pushed against her knee. Nash dropped her hand and

pulled softly on the floppy ear. "Yeah. Let's go for a walk." Standing, she softly squeezed Muna's shoulder. The head barely nodded. The camera and cameraperson concentrated on the young girl.

Turning left in the front yard, Nash thought about the time. She found the deputy director's cell number and thumbed it.

"Jeez, Nash. We finished dinner two hours ago. Even the dogs have fallen asleep on the couch. I was afraid something else had happened."

"Something else?"

Tony chuckled. "Where are you?"

"Nytah Wood's house in the southeast end of Oklahoma City. It's near Tinker Air Base. Muna is debriefing the granddaughter, Nita, right now. The grandmother, Nytah, misremembered. The girl is only fifteen years old. Which will push the kidnapping and human trafficking into aggravated status."

"It gets better."

Nash frowned as she watched Powder squat. *Only pee.* "How so?"

"According to the national news... pick a channel, any channel. The media are blowing up over this. Even FOX is reporting it like the genuine media. But evidently, one girl is only thirteen. And the guy in the hospital, losing his hand from a gunshot wound, is also a highly respected lay minister in the area."

"He is also a respected campaign fundraiser and donor, as well."

"Like you were reading their script. You've heard none of this?"

"We escorted the girls to their homes and brought Cooter... er... Nita here. I haven't even called Mina yet."

"Well, unless World War III breaks out, or Putin surrenders, this is going to be on an endless loop for at least another week or two."

Nash kicked at the scrub lawn. *The sweaty air doesn't help the grass fend off the heat.* "Did you get a report on the girl's names and who the thirteen-year-old was?"

"Just a minute. I've got the report in my email. Hold on."

Nash and Powder crossed the street to the small neighborhood park. The nod to entertainment for the kids was the obligatory hand-pushed merry-go-round. Also known by some as the vomit machine. But there were no benches for the elderly or pregnant mothers. Nash sat down on the merry-go-round and waited for Tony. Powder's muzzle felt good on her thigh as she played gently with the ears.

"Okay. They didn't put the last name in. Unless the last name is Mack."

Nash snickered. "Take a guess at what her daddy does."

"Drives trucks?"

"It's as close to my story as I wanted to get. But man, I could have sworn she was more like seventeen or eighteen. She's going to be screwed up and in therapy all her life."

Tony cleared his throat. "Speaking of therapy, how's our agent doing?"

"It's a process. After this… we're going to need some downtime. And a lot of talking. Not therapy, but more like sister-talking. There's a new side to her… and I'm not even sure she's aware of it."

"How so?"

"She kicked two of the subjects in the crotch. Not torture, per se… but it looked a lot like she kind of enjoyed it. Maybe getting revenge for the pistol-whipping. I don't know, but we need to talk about it."

The silence stretched out. "I'm not a five-foot-tall black woman who's had her jaw busted by being pistol-whipped… nor can I play one on TV. So I'll let you sort it out with her. But other than that…?"

"In a lot of ways, it's like these last several months never happened. But there's something there. We just need the time. Away from work."

"Well, on the books, she has a couple of years' worth of personal time coming. But knowing where she lives and works, and what days and hours she answers the phone—take all the time you need or want. I'll sign off on it. If you can, bring back a bottle for me."

Nash's eyebrows jumped up. She hadn't thought about Barbados. "I'll keep you in the loop."

THE KITCHEN TABLE WAS FRIENDLIER THAN TRYING TO find an all-night diner. And probably about five thousand calories lighter. Nytah had taken Cooter to bed with her. It wasn't the first time she had comforted the child over the years. Nash and Muna both guessed that the grandmother and granddaughter would be in touching range of each other for a long time.

Muna sagged the side of her head into her hand with the elbow spiked on the table. "They didn't molest them, but the threats were there." She hit play on the computer.

"They didn't touch our breasts or down there... but it was the way they dragged their finger or hand along our hair or shoulders. Especially the guy they called Hank." Cooter's head rolled along her grandmother's chest. "A real creeper. I don't think I ever saw him wear any clean clothes."

Muna pushed forward to another spot she had bookmarked. "Did they ever mention where they were going to take you girls?"

"No." Her eyes blinked a few times. "Not really. But they hated the guys they were giving us to. The one guy called them Sand Skunks. And I guess they're in New Mexico. They just used letters for where. I think it was something about a barbecue."

Muna looked up, recalling. "Would the letters be ABQ?"

The head nodded on her grandmother's dress. "At first, I thought they were having a barbecue. But then one guy spoke slower, and I could tell it was three letters. Does it mean anything?"

Muna and Nytah chorused. "Albuquerque."

Muna nodded. "It's in the middle of New Mexico."

Muna stopped the computer and looked at Nash. "There's a lot of other stuff she didn't realize she overheard. I'll probably need a few weeks to pull this all apart, but I think your shot-to-shit armored car robbers were the buyers. But now we'll never know."

Nash nodded. "Or who owns an extremely deadly helicopter. But we do have the name of one connection."

Muna's head wobbled on the heel of her hand. "Romanov. You did get those photos from Syria…? Man, it seems like a year ago."

Nash leaned back against her chair. "You've been up almost twenty hours. Go grab the rack. I need to call Mina before she goes to bed, and then I'm on the couch. I measured it this afternoon. You'll fit the bed, but my feet would hang over. I've got the couch. Powder can have the chair."

Muna closed the laptop and gave her a two-finger salute as she dragged herself up out of the chair. "No shooting range in the morning. Let's sleep in."

Nash watched Muna retreat into the semi-dark hall. The night-light filled the floor with a warm, cheery glow.

Opening the sliding glass door, Nash and Powder stepped out into the backyard as the phone buzzed. The temperature was cooler, but no less sticky.

"Busy day."

Nash snorted as she sat on the picnic table bench. "Well, one of us needs to make headlines. Tony told me about the news, playing it all on an endless loop. How are the meds going?" She could hear the exhaustion as Mina lay back against her stack of pillows.

"I had the last round of chemo yesterday. So today I got an infusion of platelets and red blood cells. I'll get whites in a couple of days, along with any vitamins they think will help."

"Would some vitamin D help?"

"Don't tease me."

Nash rubbed the soft ear on her leg. "Aside from traveling to shoot, Muna went home one weekend last year. But she missed her birthday the year before. That was why her parents came to San Francisco."

"She's burning the candle in the middle as well."

"You're the expert."

"Yes, Mrs. Kettle. So what's your thinking?"

"Forced time away from work. Burner phone protocol. And let Lele have control of all laptops."

Mina rolled over. "I'll talk to my teams tomorrow. What about Tony?"

"He's already signed off on it. Whatever it takes. And if we need it, we can get the lieutenant to find us a shooting range to blow off steam with our service pieces."

"So, when are you coming home?"

"We have a few days in San Francisco to prepare for separation, and then I'll be home. Put Lele on notice, and work out the logistics with your oncology team. You're the priority here. At worst, I drag the little girl and Muna up to the Pocono mountains and go hunt snipes or something."

"I call bullshit. The Poconos don't know shit about fine scotch or beaches."

Nash could hear the battery level bounce off the bottom. "Or sheep. Speaking of which, start counting. I love you tons and miss you. Your daughter sends a nose push."

"Nuzzle her for me. Goodnight."

ALSO BY BAER CHARLTON

The Very Littlest Dragon: NEW Editions
(All-new full-color ebook, a paperback with
coloring pages, and a full-color Collector's Edition hardback)

Stoneheart — Pulitzer Nominee 2015
Angel Flights
What About Marsha?
Pirate's Patch
Flat Surf

I Drink Coffee and Make Shit Up
One Writer's Journey Without Signposts

JOLIE "ROCKET" ROBERTS SERIES
Dry Bridge of Vengeance – Book One
Dry Ridge of Redemption – Book Two

THORNY WALLACE SERIES
Death in the Valley – Book One
Light to Light – Book Two

SOUTHSIDE HOOKER SERIES
Death on a Dime – Book One
Night Vision – Book Two
Unbidden Garden – Book Three
Boomtown – Book Four
One Day Under the Grass – Book Five
Southside Hooker Series: Books 1–5 Box Set

(Collector's Edition hardback & ebook available)

ABOUT THE AUTHOR

Bestselling author Baer Charlton graduated from UC Irvine with a degree in Social Anthropology, monkeyed around for a while, and then proceeded onward with a life of global travel, multi-disciplinary adventure, and meeting the memorable array of characters he would come to describe in his writing. He has ridden things with gears, engines, and sails, and made things with wood, leather, and metal. He has been stitched back together more times than the average hockey team; his long-suffering wife and an assortment of cats and dogs have nursed him back to health after each surgery.

Baer knows a lot about many things in this world. History flows through his veins and pours out of him at the slightest provocation. Do not ask him what you may think is a simple question unless you have the time to hear a fascinating story.

You can find more at
www.mordantmedia.com